A Hard Rain

by

Philip Soletsky

A Hard Rain by Philip Soletsky

Cover Artwork: Rachel Carpenter Artworks

ISBN-10: 1500194360

ISBN-13: 9781500194369

To the Hollis Writer's Block.

You guys rock.

One

The storm hovered, stagnant, just off the coast of New Hampshire, circulating lazily in a counterclockwise fashion, scooping up vast draughts of the Atlantic Ocean and pouring them all across the state. Rivers and ponds overflowed their banks, dirt roads became impassable mires, mudslides had closed at least three sections of highway, and trees unable to find purchase in soil reduced to the density and consistency of quicksand were falling over hourly, often taking phone and power lines with them in their acquiescence to gravity.

It was one goddamned awful mess.

Our small town of Dunboro, New Hampshire was, quite rapidly, turning into one homogenous smear in shades of dark grays and muddy browns. The rain fell, and fell, and fell, from a sky the color of hammered pewter by day and the dark of a dusty coal bin by night. It had been doing so for over ten days now,

1

three inches in the last twenty-four hours, approaching thirteen inches since we had last seen the light of the sun.

I shrugged my shoulders inside my jacket which felt like it weighed about fifty pounds. Designed to protect me in a fire, it was only moderately waterproof, and after two hours in the seemingly endless downpour it had become sodden. I tipped my head forward and watched the mass of water that had accumulated in the brim of my helmet spill off and spatter into the puddles on the ground at my feet. This, I told myself, was the glamorous side of being a volunteer firefighter.

The Dunboro volunteer fire department was overburdened and stretched thin. Several roads, like the one that I was currently guarding, were flooded and impassable, and in total darkness because most of the streetlights in town were out. There were power lines down all over. Basements were filling up, and we were helping out with portable gas-powered pumps wherever we could spare a man. If there was a bright spot to be found in all of this, it was that the damp had permeated everything, and there was no longer anything in town capable of catching fire.

The glare of headlights filled the road ahead of me and I turned on the heavy-duty flashlight that I was carrying on a strap over one shoulder and waved it back and forth across the approaching car, signaling the driver to stop.

When he pulled over and rolled down the window I leaned in to talk to the dark haired man behind the wheel. "The road's out up ahead." I informed him.

"Out? I just came through here this morning," he protested.

"There's been a lot of rain since this morning," I replied,

2

just as I had for the last dozen motorists trying to get through here. "There's at least four feet of water across the road ahead. Where are you trying to get to?"

"Four corners."

I noticed the vehicle was a dark green Dodge Durango with a lot of ground clearance, but nowhere near enough for the road ahead. I hoped he wasn't going to give me an argument, the cheap bravado of oversized SUV drivers who are sure that they can muscle through anything. Thankfully, it turned out that he wasn't; he accepted my directions without a squabble.

I stepped aside and the driver did a three-point turn majestically in about seven points, the car clearly larger than he was capable of maneuvering, and went on his way. I returned to standing in the middle of the road drowning an inch at a time.

It seemed to me that I had taken showers that were drier.

Checking my watch I was surprised to find that it was only early evening. I felt certain that I had been standing there for hours and as dark as it was it must be considerably later. I searched the sky for any hint of light, any thinning of the clouds, and saw nothing.

A wave of exhaustion suddenly washed over me and I leaned forward, my hands on my knees. The strap on my shoulder slipped and the sway of the heavy flashlight almost tipped me onto my face. Leaning over opened a gap in my jacket collar at the back of my neck, and rainwater from my helmet brim rushed right in. Nice.

These sudden periods of weakness, I thought of them as personal power failures, I carried with me as a reminder of my recent brush with death. I had been trapped in a basement fire and rescued after my respirator tank had run out of air. The injuries I had suffered, the perplexing and conflicting symptoms I displayed, had baffled the physicians, though I did seem to be improving slowly.

With immense dedication to my physical therapy I had gotten rid of the cane that I had needed during my convalescence four weeks ago. The day that I had stopped using it I had run it through the band saw in my workshop cutting it into a dozen short canelets. I admit that it had been childish on my part to do so, but it had felt so damned good to be done with it.

If I had still had it with me I would have been leaning on it.

I probably wasn't in quite good enough shape to be standing out here for six hours at a pop. The doctors had not yet cleared me to perform normal firefighting duties, but John Pederson, the chief of the department, and I had talked about it and he had consented to my request to let me stand a few shifts on road detail. Rattling around at home had been starting to drive me nuts. John hadn't really been in a position to refuse help from anyone, with the department fielding endless calls for assistance. His own two sons, ages fourteen and sixteen, were standing guard on other flooded roads elsewhere in town. When all hell broke loose, child labor laws got a little lax. If I got into trouble, I could always use the radio on my belt to call for relief, except that the repeater on top of Follett Hill had failed two days ago and much of the town, including the spot where I now stood, was smack dab in the middle of a communications hole.

I got really dizzy for a moment and was forced to kneel down suddenly in the roadway, my right hand flat on the blacktop. The flashlight hit the ground next to me, its tough plastic case absorbing the impact without damage. I took deep and even breaths, trying to avoid hyperventilating, my mouth set in a firm line, willing myself to grind through it. If water was still running down my back I couldn't feel it. My skin felt clammy and a little bit tingly as if most of my body was asleep.

At a gleam of light off the roadway I looked up and saw another pair of headlights approaching. I forced myself back to my feet, the dizziness swelling like a soft warm balloon in my head and either I swayed on my feet or the town experienced a minor earthquake. I fumbled with the flashlight, turned it on, and waved it in the general direction of the approaching car.

It kept coming.

A shot of adrenaline to my bloodstream slapped a little more spine into my back. I waved the flashlight more energetically, adding my other arm into the action as well.

And still the car came. I had no way of knowing if the driver even saw me.

I moved to the side of the road and stood behind a stout oak, waving the flashlight and peeking at the approaching car around the tree trunk.

The car, a dark Porsche, sped by, accelerating as it headed down the road towards where the pavement vanished into the murk. It threw up an enormous wave when it hit, its momentum damping quickly, coming to a stop half submerged, right to the level of the windows.

I sloshed over to the car, muck filling my boots, and found a woman sitting in the driver seat chest deep in water and crying. For just a moment, less than a fraction of a second, in the reflection of my flashlight she looked just like Sharon Bishop.

That was impossible of course, but it took longer than I would have expected to force the image from my mind. The woman in the car had blonde hair, either dirty blonde or just plain dirty, plastered to her head. Her light colored top had become mostly see-thru and she wore no bra, her nipples pink and erect. Yet even as disheveled as she was, she was achingly beautiful, with a perfectly symmetrical oval face and an alluring tilt to her eyes. She would turn the head of every man within fifty feet. Just like Sharon.

The dashboard indicators were still lit, though the car had stalled, so I reached past her and turned off the ignition. "Miss. Are you alright? Are you hurt?"

She ignored me, sobbing louder, pounding her hands against the wheel. She got two weak hoots out of the horn, and then nothing. The electrical system must have shorted out.

I unlocked the door and pulled it open, hauling against the minor suction as the water level inside and outside the car reached equilibrium. I reached across her and unbuckled the seatbelt. "You're alright. Let me help you out of there. It's just a car. It can be fixed."

She stopped sobbing like someone had flipped her off switch and glared at me with wet, angry eyes that underneath glowed with a searing light of crazed terror. "Do you think I care about the fucking car? All I had to do was get out of town. Now he's going to find me and kill me for sure!"

"What?"

She slapped at my hands when I tried to help her up and clawed her way past me out of the car.

Another pair of headlights illuminated us, another car coming down the road. The last thing I needed was for that car to plow into this one in the dark.

I turned away from her and started waving the flashlight at the approaching driver, holding my other hand up. There was a splashing sound behind me and I glanced back over my shoulder to see her thrashing through the thigh-deep water, moving away from me along where the road would have been had it not been flooded. "Miss, I – stop!"

I checked the other car, which was gliding to a halt where the pavement ended, then looked back at her again. She was going at a pretty good clip, putting distance between us, just a smudge of gray, ghostly in the headlights against the darkness that surrounded her.

The car honked at me and the window whirred down. The driver, a woman, leaned out, shielding her eyes from the rain with the flat of her hand. "What's going on? Do you need any help?"

"Hey!" I called out, but the fleeing woman was gone from my sight.

The night and the rain had swallowed her whole.

Two

I stood in the thigh deep water next to the flooded car staring into the darkness with the rain flashing silver in the beam of my flashlight, tendrils of panic beginning to weave their way through my nerves.

Now he's going to find me and kill me for sure.

Who was trying to kill her? Why? What could I do about it? The panic made me desperate, and I gave my radio a try, though I knew it was a futile effort.

The driver of the other car was just realizing what I already knew, that we were in a communications dead zone. "Why doesn't my phone work?" she asked me.

I briefly entertained the possibility of sending the driver to the fire department with a message, but the car had Vermont plates and it was unlikely that she had any idea of where the station was. In the dark, with many roads blocked by water and trees, it would be difficult to give her directions to get there. The best I felt I could do at the moment was get her on her way, which I did. I knew that there were several fire department trucks driving around surveying the roads and hoped that one would come by shortly.

Looking where I had last seen the woman, I could see no sign of her at all. The road was an indistinct dark wash of water vaguely defined by the trees on both sides. I tried to figure out how far she would have to go to get past the flood. How far would I have to go to get into the next area of radio coverage? I was frustrated to realize that didn't know the answer to either. I did know that the water might go chest deep on her or even a little deeper before she passed the worst of it.

She may have decided not to stay on the road; she may have left it to try and find somewhere that wasn't flooded. She could have wandered into the pond or stumbled over some submerged debris in the dark. If I followed her I could suffer the same fate, even worse if I suffered another power failure.

I might be better off going to the fire department and gathering search teams, though with personnel spread thin it would take so long as to be almost pointless. In fifteen or twenty minutes she could be half a mile from here in any direction. We were neither equipped nor manpowered to mount a search operation in this type of weather at night.

And what of the traffic I had been directing at this spot? Someone could slam into the Porsche in the dark, and my first obligation was to the job that I was assigned.

Though I couldn't see how I could stand here behaving as though nothing had happened either.

As near as I could tell all of my alternatives sucked and the tendril of panic inside me wound a little bit tighter.

As luck would have it, just then I spotted our forestry vehicle coming towards me. But, since you can never have enough good luck, Roger Fiske was driving it.

He rolled down the window as he pulled up, taking in the scene of the Porsche waterlogged to the window line, "Nice fuckup, Fallon. Watching a road too much for you? Goddamn, when I look at you and realize what the fire department has come to."

"Ordinarily, Rog, I'd love to hang out all day and have you tell me about what an embarrassment I am, ghosts of firefighters past rolling over in their graves, blah, blah, blah, but the driver of that car ran off, and I'd like to get back to the department to report to John."

"Fucking Fallon," he said as he pulled the radio handset from its hook on the dash. He should have known as well as I did that the repeater failure left this area dark, but I let him try anyway. He might get lucky – the car radio had more transmitting power than my hand unit – and it wasn't like he was going to listen to me anyway. After a couple of tries to raise dispatch, he threw it in the general direction of the dashboard angrily, where it bounced off and landed somewhere on the floorboards on the passenger side. "First you, now the radio."

I tried to open his door but it was locked, so I reached through the window and unlocked it, and then opened it. "Out."

"What?"

"You're going to watch the road for a while, and I'm going to take the truck to go tell John."

"Yeah, right," he laughed gruffly, "over my dead body."

I was soaked to the skin, a little nauseous from nearly passing out and the adrenaline letdown and whatever, and I'd completely had enough of his bullshit, "Don't fucking tempt me, Rog. I'm warning you."

He looked like he was going to let it come to blows for a moment, but then must have realized that I could probably take him, even as much like walking death as I suspected I looked at that moment, and that I was willing to let it go that way; it was his call.

He got out, "You put a dent in this truck, and you'll never hear the end of it."

I'd probably never hear the end of this in any case.

I gave him the flashlight and radio, got in, and slammed the door. I rolled up the window and cranked the heat up to full blast as I turned the truck around and headed towards the station house.

I realized as I drove that I was gripping the wheel way too tight until I concentrated on taking a few deep breaths and unclenching my fists. Goddamn Fiske.

Three

The rest of the block was without power but the fire department emergency generator was humming along just fine. The fire station house looked almost like a mirage, golden light spilling from the windows and a long rectangle shining through an open bay door. I pulled the forestry truck alongside and entered through the side door.

I found John Pederson in the meeting room looking over a long map of the town that was unrolled on the conference table, its four corners weighted down with three coffee mugs and a pry bar. With him was Max Deaks, the assistant Chief. John was tall and lean, an ex-marine and a veteran of nearly forty years of firefighting. Max was more round than tall, Oliver Hardy to John's Stan Laurel. He had been a Dunboro firefighter for over forty years, and two of them had been friends going back farther than that.

"When was the last time someone checked the dam?" John asked.

"Couple of hours ago, Robert and Bruce Jonet went by there."

John frowned a little bit, "They're just kids. I want you to get over there and look at it with your own eyes. You know that land."

"OK, I'll check it out."

They were talking about Baxter's Dam which had been assembled by farmers, none of them with degrees in dam building, a hundred or so years ago. It had seen little maintenance since then, and under the additional load caused by the recent and ongoing rainfall, it didn't look good.

As a favor to John, earlier in the week I had blown the dust off my PhD, shimmied into a wetsuit, and taken my best crack at performing some measurements and calculating the probability of a breach. The irregularity of the stone blocks that made up the dam, my inability to accurately calculate the volume of water in Birch Pond from survey maps, and the generally unpredictable nature of just how much more rain was in our collective futures, were all working against me. Nonetheless, the outlook was poor even if my numbers were way off. There was a seventy five percent chance that the dam would fail spectacularly within the next thirty days if the pressures remained the same. If the pressure increased due to an increase in water in Birch Pond that timeline only got worse, and more rain was forecast.

I recommended we get sandbags to firm up the dam. John had put in a request to the state, which at the moment had something of a major run on sand, bags, and the manpower to fill and stack them. Other towns farther north had already had some homes destroyed and at least one major roadway had completely washed out, effectively bisecting the town of Antrim into two isolated entities. The National Guard was up there doing sandbag detail to keep things from getting worse. Our request was noted, but on the list of places requesting sandbags we were presently ninth.

"Better ninth than never," John had told me grimly.

If the dam collapsed there were dozens of houses downstream that were in danger, eight of which I was certain would be completely or at least mostly destroyed. John had had those eight homes evacuated. He had needed a court order to force some of the homeowners out, and they were not happy about it.

"What truck do you want me to take?" Max asked. "Mine is already out with Winston."

"The forestry is just outside." I chimed in.

They both looked up, noticing me for the first time. Max looked at John who nodded. Max picked up his helmet off the table, and threw me a quick two-fingered salute and a "Fallon" as he went out the side door.

"Aren't you supposed to be at Baxter's Crossing?"

"I was," I responded, then proceeded to tell him the story about the woman in the Porsche.

"How long ago was that?"

"Fifteen minutes."

"Shit, she could be anywhere by now. Was she hurt?"

"I don't think so. Just wet and terrified for her life."

"You told the cops yet?"

"I radioed it in as soon as I got into repeater range while I was on my way over here."

"Who'd you leave over at Baxter's?"

"Fiske. He was driving the forestry."

John winced. "Had to be Roger, didn't it?"

My sentiments exactly.

Having never been in a fire department with anyone other than John as Chief, yet having heard stories from other departments, I felt that he was a good one. That said, his sort of hands-off approach to this conflict, which initially I had thought was a good idea, wasn't a solution. My problems with Fiske had begun last year in the aftermath of the murders, and had done nothing but deteriorate further since then.

I appreciated John's position. Fiske had almost as many years on the department as he did and many friends among the crew. Any attempt to discipline him could result in a mutiny with a dozen or more of his veterans walking out, something John needed to avoid as the Chief of a small, understaffed volunteer department.

On the other hand, it was bad for department morale not to say embarrassing as hell to have his firefighters cursing and taking pokes at each other while on fire calls, which hadn't happened yet but was only a matter of time. I had offered, in the name of department harmony, to resign. He had so far declined that offer.

John looked grim. "I hate to say it, but there's nothing we can do about her now. We'll keep in touch with the cops and if anyone reports seeing her we'll roll on it. Agreed?"

I wanted to disagree. I wanted to get a fresh flashlight and scour the roads myself if that was what it took, but that was a bad idea rooted in Sharon and the past, and I fought to put it aside. "What do you want me to do now?"

"I want you to go home."

I started to object, but he put up his hand stopping me. "Admit it, Jack, you look like hell. You gave me a couple of hours today, but you're nowhere near one hundred percent. Go home, recharge your batteries, and come back when you're sure you can. It doesn't help me to work you until you drop somewhere and become a problem yourself."

"OK."

"Besides," he added with a sly grin, "Valerie called. Her temperature is right and she wants you at home."

It was no secret around the department that Valerie and I were trying to have a child and that we were having a little trouble conceiving. At first we had been sort of discrete about it but somehow – maybe simply from the frequency, urgency and periodicity of her calls someone had figured it out, or maybe she had told one of the other firefighter's wives – word had gotten around the department. To say that it was the topic of many jokes in the station house would be something of an understatement.

"OK, I'll go."

On my way out the door he called to me, "Good luck, son, we're all counting on you."

Four

Ordinarily the trip from the fire station to my house took just ten minutes, and for a fire call I had done it in a shade less than four, but I had to go the long way around, up and over the top of Follett Hill, to bypass flooded roadways. While I was up there I pulled over into the Ernest P. Heflan Scenic Overlook, a pretty grandiose name for a single wooden bench in a clearing with three parking spaces marked by a small wooden sign.

I had once tried to find out who Ernest P. Heflan was, but no one seemed to know. A couple of firefighters claimed the sign has been put up years ago at the then unnamed scenic overlook as a drunken prank, and no one had ever challenged its legitimacy. The state had even repainted and repaired the sign a few times. I had my doubts that it was true, but like most small town tall tales it was a pretty good story. Still, it was surprising that the name Ernest P. Heflan returned no hits whatsoever from Google.

I stepped out of my truck into the rain, pulled the collar of my coat up around my neck, and moved to the edge of the clearing. The clouds were so low that I had a momentary instinct to duck, but they had thinned slightly and the gloomy light turned the view down the length of the valley into a moonscape, all shades of gray.

Birch Pond at the north end was high, crazy high. It had already flooded some low orchard to the east, trees poking out of the water in an orderly grid pattern, the apple barn at one side practically floating. In comparison Baxter's dam at the southern end looked tiny, like something a kid might throw together to stop a creek in the back yard. From this perspective I couldn't imagine why it hadn't failed already.

I could track with my eye the line the water would take if the dam blew, the houses in its path, the point where it would rush the banks of the Nissitissit River in Brookline and join that swollen river on its way down into Massachusetts. I made a mental note to estimate what damage the extra flow in that river might cause to the south and warn the authorities accordingly, then figured that the State people must be keeping track of such things. Certainly I wasn't the only guy looking into all of this, was I?

I turned one hundred eighty degrees around and looked up at the cell tower across the road and a little farther up the hill. The tower was still standing, and the security lights around the generator housing were on, so I couldn't understand why the department radio repeater wasn't relaying signals to the dispatch center. Maybe water had gotten into the wiring. Could we come up here and rewire the transmitter lines, bring ourselves back into the 21st century? Technically the Phone Company owned the tower and we were just piggy backing on the structure. They would probably be unhappy with us climbing around on it, but if we were neat about it, they need never know. I made another mental note to mention the idea to John the next time I saw him.

Standing there in the rain, shivering, my hair plastered to my head, I fully recognized that all this ruminating and planning was just stalling on my part, a lame ass delaying tactic to avoid going home to Valerie. Had our marriage really fallen so badly apart?

I got back in my truck and completed the drive home, parking the car in the middle of the horseshoe driveway near the front door. I killed the engine and sat behind the wheel psyching myself up, disturbing really because I had little idea what I was psyching myself up for.

When she heard me come inside, Valerie called "I'm upstairs."

I climbed the steps with all the enthusiasm of a man mounting the steps to the gallows.

Valerie and I had some serious problems that we weren't talking about.

Last year when I had been injured, almost killed in truth, while trying to catch a killer, Valerie had changed. Our relationship had changed. When she had almost lost me, the quick-to-laugh, strong woman with the supermodel good looks had undergone a sea change. The exterior was the same woman I fell in love with every time I laid eyes on her, but inside was a timid creature, clinging to me, constantly worried about where I was and what I was doing. I felt myself smothered by her attention, well-meaning though it was, and her lack of independence was driving me away.

That wasn't going to get any better when I told her about

the woman in the Porsche and that I wanted to look into what had happened to her.

The other big change that had occurred was that Valerie wanted a child. Now. Sooner than now if possible. And while we had talked in the past about our plans for a family, her sudden desire to have one contrasted badly with my feelings that, in a time of questions about my health, if anything we should be pushing plans for a family farther off.

Presently Mother Nature, for reasons I did not know, seemed to be siding with me, but as essentially healthy people I felt certain that it was only a matter of time before a child entered the picture. Was that smart? And what would I do if we continued to try and fail and Valerie suggested some type of fertility treatment?

Our dog Tonk met me at the door to our bedroom. I reached down and ruffled his ears. He looked up at me and yawned, smacking his big flappy bulldog lips together, and then lay down and put his head between his paws. Though the door was open he innately knew when he wasn't welcome in the bedroom. Neither one of us wanted our baby, at least I had always thought of him as our baby, to watch. It's always distracting when he yawns, and even worse when he snores.

I peeled off my wet shirt as I went into the bedroom and tossed it through the bathroom door into the shower where it landed with a splat. Valerie was on the bed, lying on top of the covers, wearing a sapphire blue satin camisole top and nothing else, her blonde hair fanning the pillow around her head, her blue-green eyes half-lidded. She patted the bed next to her. "You look cold. Let me warm you up."

She was as beautiful to me as she had always been, but it was a parody of sexual foreplay, a rote script we had both run through so many times all the pages were dog-eared. As a couple we had enjoyed a wonderfully recreational and fulfilling sexual relationship, and I found now that I was chafing, both literally and figuratively, under the schedule and rigor of her fertility regimen.

My resolve withered, along with some other things I might need soon.

I didn't want to force a confrontation because I didn't know where it would go, and I didn't know where I wanted it to go, and I didn't know what the hell I was doing. So I went to her, half my mind on her, half my mind on what we weren't talking about, half my mind with Sharon and the distant past, and half my mind on the woman in the Porsche. 200% overload. And the fact that we weren't talking about any of these things, and that we were planning to add a child to the mix, made me think that I should get my head examined.

Five

In our new mode as a couple who didn't talk about things, the next morning I told Valerie that I was headed back to the fire department, but not about my plan to drop by the police department first to check on the driver of the Porsche. While technically I had not lied to her, I nonetheless felt badly about the omission.

As I entered the Dunboro Police Department the first thing I saw was the Sheriff, Bobby Dawkins, standing behind his desk with his back to me, a phone held to each ear.

Bobby was about my age, but perhaps half again my size in every dimension. He had become sheriff of Dunboro after his uncle had retired. When running for office he had used his uncle's campaign posters and had the same name, and it's entirely possible that many of the voters hadn't realized that they were not in fact voting for his uncle. That possible small deception aside, he had turned out to be a pretty good sheriff.

Now his usually crisp uniform shirt was bunched and wrinkled across his enormous shoulders and had become partially untucked from his pants on one side. I wondered how long he had been wearing it and how long it had been since he'd seen his bed. The wastepaper basket next to his desk was filled to overflowing with Styrofoam coffee cups. A matrix of empty cups, two rows by four columns, occupied one corner of his desk. He was pacing slightly in short strides, as much as the twin phone cords allowed.

A large map of Dunboro, made up of dozens of Xeroxed pages all taped together, hung on the corkboard that covered the wall behind him. Several roads across the town were marked in highlighted colors of blue, yellow, and pink. Past his right shoulder I could see Baxter's Crossing, where I had been stationed, marked in blue, so blue probably meant that the road was flooded out. What the other two colors signified I didn't know.

The phone to his right ear was pulled slightly away from his head, and he was speaking into the phone on the left. "Did the tree damage your house at all?" A pause. "Yes, your potting shed, you mentioned that, Mrs. Farmer, but did it hit the house?"

Sensing me behind him, he turned suddenly, almost strangling himself in the process. It took several moments for him to get untangled and get the phone on the left back to his ear. "Your what? Did you say your cat?"

He held up a finger of his right hand telling me to hold on for just a second, "Mrs. Farmer, I can't, what's that?" He listened, "I understand that, but I –" He listened again. "Yes. Yes, Mrs. Farmer. OK. As soon as we can." He hung up the left hand phone. "Unbelievable," he muttered to himself.

"Sally," He called to the department's elderly secretary, who was typing at a computer at her desk across the office, "Get Pitman on the radio. See if he can make his way over to Emmy Farmer's place. She says a tree fell on her potting shed and she thinks her cat is inside. On the way, have him drive past Stickley, I'm worried about that culvert washing out and taking the road with it."

"OK, Bobby," she said. She got up from her desk and shuffled through a door at the end of the room that led to the dispatch center.

"Jack, good to see you up and around," he transferred the phone to his left and held out his right to shake, his meaty hand engulfing mine whole. "You look like crap."

"Thanks, you too."

"Yeah, well," he sighed, "No rest for the weary. If this rain keeps up we're going to have to relocate the whole town to higher ground."

"Do you want to finish your other phone call? I can wait."

He looked at the phone in his hand as if he had forgotten that he held it. "I'm on hold with the State Police barracks in Concord, hoping to get a couple of Staties in here, trying to get some relief for the department. I'm sure I'm not the only town yelling for help. Their plan is probably to leave me on hold until I hang up."

"When was the last time you slept?"

He rubbed his eyes with a thumb and forefinger. "Oh, I don't know. What day is it? Seriously, I'm fine. The rain brings its own set of problems, but no one seems to want to commit a crime and get wet in the process, so regular calls are way down."

"Speaking of problems, did you get a chance to look up the owner of that car?"

"You think she was serious? Someone was going to kill her? It's been twelve hours, Jack. If she was really in trouble a loved one would have called wondering where she was or, God forbid, a body would have turned up. She was probably drunk. Drunk and overreacting."

What he said made sense, and after a long night of replaying what she had said in my mind a hundred times – *Now he's going to find me and kill me for sure* – I was no longer certain what to believe, but with Sharon in my past I wasn't going to ignore a plea for help, not again. If it turned out that she had been drunk, that would be fine. The alternative was unthinkable.

"You might be right. I just want to check up on her, see that she's OK."

"Well, then I'm not sure this will help you. It's not her car."

"Whose car is it?"

"You won't believe -" he suddenly spoke into the phone, "Yes, I'm still here." A pause. "That's right, Dunboro. I need some relief here. I've got two officers working double shifts." He held up his finger to me again.

"Who?" I mouthed silently.

He pulled a pad towards him and scribbled on it with a pen he pulled from a redwood cup on his desk. "I know. Yes, I know. I'm not looking for a reassignment. Just a shift or two to get my officers back on their feet."

He dropped the pen onto the blotter and spun the pad around so I could read it.

"I realize everyone is having problems, but my department is falling behind the curve here. We're running on empty and we're going to start making mistakes."

It took a second for the name he'd written on the paper to sink in. I should have realized, given that the car was a Porsche, and how many of those do you see in a town like Dunboro? Still, it was a surprise. "No shit," I breathed.

He cupped a hand over the mouthpiece of the phone. "None whatsoever.

Six

Probably the closest thing Dunboro, New Hampshire has to a celebrity is Garrison West.

His parents, planning to celebrate their 20th wedding anniversary in Hawaii, were onboard United Airlines flight 175 nonstop from Logan Airport in Boston to Los Angeles when it was hijacked and flown into the South Tower of the World Trade Center. Seated in 22A and B, his parents attempted several calls to their son's school using the Airfone. Garrison, home from school sick and sleeping in, missed them.

While the nation was held enthralled by the images of the burning towers on their televisions, Steven Nadeau, a college dropout taking a continuing education class in journalism at the Nashua Adult Learning Center, had an idea. He called a high school buddy who was a ticket agent for United and got a copy of the manifest for flight 175. Armed with that, a phone book, and a road Atlas he drove to homes in southern New Hampshire and northern Massachusetts, hoping to find someone who had a loved one on the plane, looking to get the first interview capturing the raw pure emotional moment of watching your husband or wife, son or daughter, aunt or uncle dying on television.

He was stymied, however, by the fact that it was a Tuesday morning, and most everyone was at work or out on errands, and inconveniently not at home to allow him to conduct what he was certain would be a Pulitzer Prize winning interview.

He was on the phone complaining about that very fact to his girlfriend, when he drove his faded and rust-pocked Toyota Corolla to the fourteenth residence he had visited that morning. He passed between the brick pillars marking the end of the West driveway and ascended to the top of the hill where the home perched with panoramic views of Milford, Brookline, Mason, Wilton, and, on clear days, Purgatory Hill in Mont Vernon. Slamming the door of his car, waking Garrison inside the house, he stalked to the front door prepared to stab the doorbell several times and move on to home number fifteen.

As he was going up the long brick walk from the parking area to the front door, phone clamped to his ear, he noticed that the outdoor landscape lights looked like miniature Japanese lanterns, each powered by a solar cell on top no larger than an Oreo cookie, which he described to his girlfriend. He asked her if she could think of a way to get information about where people worked from the data on the manifest. She couldn't, she replied, and maybe he should leave those people alone, that they had enough problems, and is it even legal for him to have the manifest in the first place?

"Baby," he whined, "This is how reporters do things.

Aren't you going to help me?"

His finger was poised at the doorbell button, just about to press it, when Garrison opened the door. Barefoot, dressed in loose, faded jeans that hung on his thin frame, and a wrinkled white T-shirt with the logo of a snowboarding company on it, Garrison looked up at Steven in sleepy Nyquil-fueled confusion. Using an instinct that would, together with his questionable ethics, serve him well as a reporter, Steven rotated the cell phone away from his ear and snapped three quick images of the then small for his age seventeen-year-old Garrison. As he was not looking at the cell phone screen, the first photo missed the subject completely, catching a pretty good angle of the chandelier in the West front hallway. The second cut Garrison's face in half. But the third picture was the money shot.

Ten minutes later Steven had his interview and Garrison had learned that he was an orphan.

The interview, so amateurish as to be almost incomprehensible, was never used anywhere, but the picture of Garrison appeared on the cover of Newsweek. In it, Garrison's sleepy countenance was a blank slate upon which the viewer could project almost any emotion: numbness, forlorn abandonment, sorrow, shock. Thrust into the national spotlight, without his permission he became a poster boy for any number of nine eleven related causes, once even appearing on posters on both opposing sides of a single issue at a protest rally.

He received the very first payout in 2002 from the nine-eleven victims fund; some one point three million dollars was paid directly to the then just-turned-eighteen Garrison. His parents themselves had also left him a fair amount of money between life insurance and savings, though no one was certain exactly how much.

Garrison parlayed his exposure into some snowboarding contracts and did the talk show circuit, even meeting Oprah, but eventually his fifteen minutes of fame passed.

Afterwards things started to go downhill.

Though previously an honor student, Garrison's grades slid badly and he just barely squeaked his way out of high school. He remained living in the home he had shared with his parents, and it gained something of a reputation for being party central for all of southern New Hampshire. His notoriety became limited primarily to the Dunboro PD, who was often called to the house for noise complaints. Garrison seemed clean and sober, but several times his guests had been charged with drunken disorderly and DUI, and although he couldn't prove it Bobby was certain that some drug use was happening on top of the hill as well.

And now Garrison's Porsche was in three feet of water, the driver having fled after claiming someone was going to kill her. Just what did all that mean?

I didn't know, but it had my spider sense tingling.

Seven

The driveway up to the West house was surprisingly long and crowded closely by trees on both sides, and I found myself wondering how it was kept clear during the winter. It took no less than three switchbacks as it worked its way up the hill. A small stream, swollen to a minor torrent by the rain, ran alongside, passing through corrugated steel pipes underneath the roadway at the switchbacks. At the top the dense tree line opened suddenly, magnificently, into a vista that encompassed all of southern New Hampshire. It was so high up that the lowered storm clouds seemed to press heavily down upon the house at the center of the clearing.

I guess I'd have to call the style of the house California modern; odd angles and pieces of the home came together to form a jagged roofline of numerous peaks, gables and valleys, pierced along its length by no less than four stone chimneys. The clapboard siding was stained dark brown. The asphalt of the driveway ended in a parking area covered in some rust-colored crushed stone. A barn-like structure stood at one end with five garage doors in the nearest face, all closed. I parked my truck next to the brick walkway leading to the house.

As isolated as it was, I wondered just how much noise was necessary to warrant a noise complaint from the neighbors. Perhaps he was bothering the passengers of low-flying aircraft.

After I shut off the engine I sat with the rain rattling on the windshield, roof, and hood.

Did I really want to get involved in all of this again? My last try at amateur sleuthing had nearly killed me, a reminder of which I carried every time my strength failed and in the twisted and puckered line of scar tissue on the side of my neck. This was Bobby's job, as Valerie had told me perhaps four thousand times as I dragged myself through physical therapy, literally almost kicking and screaming.

Then I reminded myself that I wasn't really sleuthing anything. No crime had been committed, except perhaps a charge of reckless driving. The car had not even been reported stolen. It was unlikely that Garrison would answer the door covered in blood and carrying a butcher's knife. More likely, the woman, whoever she was, was somewhere drying off and sobering up.

I got out of the truck and dashed up the walkway past a number of what had probably been very attractive flowerbeds before the rain had mashed them flat, to the overhang by the front door.

I planned to ring the bell, find out if the woman was OK, and leave.

At least I got the ringing of the bell part right.

As he answered the door, my second look at Garrison West, if you counted the Newsweek cover as my first, showed a gangly teenage boy who had grown into a handsome young man. He was not covered in blood. He was still barefoot, still wearing a pair of baggy faded jeans, and still in a T-shirt with the logo of a snowboard company on the front. Except for the fact that this shirt was blue, it could have been the same one from the Newsweek photo. His face was full, with a thin nose, soft brown eyes, and a mouth that was pouty, almost feminine in its fullness. He had a neat diamond of trimmed beard centered on his chin, the rest of his face shaven. His hair was long and thick, hanging almost to his shoulders, and brown, clean, and well-brushed with a sort of overall body wave. Someone from my generation would have called the style the Jacqueline Smith.

He leaned against the partially open door, "Yeah?"

I probably should have thought out my opening a little more carefully, as standing there at that moment I couldn't exactly figure out how to begin. Part of my problem was that I had been expecting him to be expecting me, or at least someone from the police department about his car. He wasn't acting like a guy missing a Porsche. Was it possible that he didn't know it was gone?

"I'm here about your car."

"Which one?"

"The Porsche."

"Which one?"

I thought for a moment that his record had skipped, and then realized that he must have more than one Porsche. I'm not a big car guy, and didn't recognize the model of the car. Instead

I went with, "The black one."

He shrugged. Indifference? Dismissal? Confirmation? He walked away from the door leaving it open, which I took to be an invitation to enter. I followed him inside, closing the door behind me.

The front hall was devoid of furniture. The place could have really used a coat rack, or an umbrella stand, or a bench. Something. It had nothing. The bare walls to the left and right of the front door cried out for a picture, some piece of art. The left even had a picture hook mounted on the wall, but whatever had been there had left no clues, no shadowing on the paint to indicate its size or shape.

The hallway continued straight into the depths of the house and also branched off to the left, down two short steps, into a large open living room. Garrison headed for the living room, and I followed.

The room was huge, maybe sixty feet long and forty wide, and over two stories high, reaching up to a peaked roof of pine truss work. A wall of windows looked out on the parking area, my truck, and the barn. The wall opposite the windows had a stone fireplace. It was a big one, about eight feet across, but looked small in the large room. As a mantelpiece it had an enormous slab of redwood ten inches thick.

I counted six couches, three loveseats, and two recliners, all mismatched, except that they were all in black leather and all generally pointed in the direction of what had to be the largest rear projection television ever available on the market. It was nearly ten feet high and half again as wide, and could have replaced the Jumbotron at a football game. It was off at the moment, and the vast expanse of lifeless gray glass was a little unnerving. Who even needed a TV that big? You would be able to see Paris Hilton's pores. There was a jumble of videogame systems, sound components, and various CDs and DVDs scattered on the floor in front of it.

One wall of the living room had been converted into a climbing wall, with dozens of multicolored handholds bolted to it and a safety winch system mounted up on the trusses in the ceiling. That must be a lot of fun at parties. I suspected that he had added that after his parents had, well, you know.

Enough sightseeing.

"My name is Jack. I'm with the fire department. Your car is over on Baxter's Crossing near Birch Pond."

I waited. He said nothing.

"It's in about three feet of water."

Nothing.

"It's going to have to be towed somewhere."

More nothing. I was talking out loud, wasn't I? And not just thinking these thoughts in my head?

The lack of response was starting to get to me. This is why Valerie and I didn't have kids; I just don't have patience for this kind of crap. Maybe I should bring her up here to meet him and see if it would hit the snooze button on her biological clock. Then I reminded myself that though I was still associating Garrison with the teenager on the cover of Newsweek, he must be closer to twenty-one.

"Did you know it was missing?"

He shrugged again, and then walked to the fireplace where he retrieved a garage door opener from the selection piled on the mantel piece. He went to the windows and pressed the button, then watched silently as the fourth door from the left trundled up revealing an empty space, the next car over just visible in the darkened garage from this angle.

"Is that where it was?"

"Yeah."

We stood watching the rain fall and the garage.

"Mind if I go take a look?"

A shrug.

I smacked my lips. "OK then." I went out the front door, closing it but making sure first that it wouldn't lock behind me, and ran across the parking area into the open garage door. I had no idea where the light switches were so I waited for my eyes to get accustomed to the dark. There was a bulb that I could see in the garage door mechanism that should have come on when the door opened, but it must have been burned out.

When my eyes finally adjusted I realized that there were a lot of cars in the barn; the empty parking space in front of the open door was the only one in the entire building. Some of the cars towards the back were covered in sheets, but the half dozen or so closest to the doors were uncovered. Three of them were exotic sports cars. I recognized a yellow Ferrari. The two others with it were models I didn't recognize, one red and one an eye-searing color I can only describe as electric metallic purple, looking almost alien in design, like wheeled flying saucers. There was another Porsche, this one dark green but otherwise indistinguishable, at least by me, from the one I had seen yesterday. There was a big black pickup truck, jacked up high with lots of added chrome and light packages like a life-sized

Hot Wheels car. There was a red convertible BMW Z4. This kid had a lot of cars. I also noticed two motorcycles parked against the wall beyond the last car in the row.

The empty spot in front of me was just that, empty. If I had been expecting to find a discarded driver's license, the broken heel from a women's shoe, or a scrap of paper with some mysterious message on it, I was disappointed. There was nothing, not even a spot of oil or a sinister smear of brake fluid to mark where the car had been parked.

I left the garage and jogged back to the house.

Back in the living room Garrison was still standing in front of the windows as if he had not moved while I was in the garage. When I came down the stairs he pressed the button on the remote and watched the door trundle shut.

"Do you know who was driving your car?"

Before answering me, he went back over to the mantel and carefully returned the remote to the stack. "Lauren?"

"Are you asking me, or telling me? There was a woman driving the car, dark blonde hair? Is that Lauren?"

"Lauren?" He said again, though maybe this time he said it a little less like a question.

"OK, Let's say it was Lauren. Lauren what?"

"Wilkes?" Maybe he said it as a question again.

"Did she drive your car often?"

A shrug.

I blew out a breath. "I could use some words here."

"She could drive it when she liked."

Wow, a whole sentence. Subject, verb, direct object – everything. I felt like I should frame it for posterity. He may have had twenty cars out in the garage, but this kid was on a word budget like I couldn't believe. He didn't seem slow, just completely disengaged, like nothing mattered. I wondered if Bobby was right about the drug use and if he was on something. I couldn't see any obvious needle marks on his arms.

"OK, well, she drove your car into the water and she looked upset about something. Do you know where she is right now?"

"Home?"

"And home would be?"

"She's renting a place out on, um, that road past, um, that other road."

Mapquest he's not. I'd only been living here a few years and he's lived here his whole life, but my internal map was more complete than his was, though I am in the fire department and that's a quick way to learn the roads in a town.

"Can you be any more specific?"

"It's near the ball field." He replied.

"The ball field?"

"The ball field."

"Dunboro? Milford? Brookline? Bedford? Wilton?" There were a heck of a lot of ball fields around. Every town had one. Some had two or three.

He sighed, like somehow it was my fault that baseball was

America's pastime. "I can drive you there."

"You can?"

He nodded, halfheartedly as if he was hoping I would turn down the offer.

I decided to disappoint him. "That would be great."

Eight

We took the Beemer.

As I walked around to the passenger side of the car I admired the finish, trailing a finger through the droplets of water clinging to the curve of the fender. Very aerodynamic sexy. Even not being a car guy I could understand the attraction of the sensual functionality of a sports car, a vehicle designed for nimble maneuverability, like a dancer or an athlete in peak condition.

The interior smelled of leather, the seat mounted so low and tipped back it was almost like sinking into a steeply pitched recliner. Back in my college days I'd slept in less comfortable beds. As soon as we were seated with the doors closed we blasted out of the barn, the rain drawn into a vortex in our wake.

As disconnected as he appeared in life, Garrison came alive behind the wheel of the car. He was a very active driver, continually fussing with the radio, the heater, touching and adjusting the mirrors, and shifting gears about twice as often as necessary, as if the car was never quite right for him, performing quite the way he felt it should.

He headed north on Route 13, veering off just before the Milford town line to the west, passing under the power lines and heading down Trembley Road.

The rain continued, the sky one continuous sheet of gray without any lighter patches at all to give some hope that it might break up soon.

The car had extremely low ground clearance, and I wondered if even six or eight inches of water would give it problems, which described the vast majority of roads in Dunboro. Trembley Road however headed generally uphill. He turned off to the right just before Trembley ended in a cul-de-sac onto Garnett, pulling the car to the curb in front of a small but well-kept ranch house painted a pale yellow with black shutters. Twin tracks of cracked concrete with grass growing between them ran alongside the house and ended at a side door. There was no garage, at least not one visible from the road. I didn't see a car.

"This it?"

He nodded.

He was right in that Lauren Wilkes' house was down the road past another road, but we were a good mile or more from the nearest ball field, unless Milford had one closer by that I didn't know of.

"Did she have a car?"

He shrugged.

41

A blind person would have a lot of trouble holding a conversation with Garrison West.

Exasperated I asked, "Is that a yes or a no?"

"I don't know. I don't think so." he answered gruffly, as if asking for a vocal answer from him was a really big imposition.

"Fair enough."

I looked at the house. There were no lights on inside, no bluish cast in the windows from a television set. It didn't look like anyone was at home.

I got out of the car and fast walked through the rain up the concrete walkway to the cover of the overhang by the front door. I didn't see a doorbell so knocked loudly.

I waited.

Nothing.

I knocked again.

More nothing.

I tried the front door and it was locked. I wasn't prepared to break into the house even if I had had legal cause to do so, which of course I didn't.

Nothing seemed amiss when I peeked through the gauzy curtains covering one of the front door sidelights. There was no broken furniture, no spilled blood. I didn't expect to see a big pile of abandoned mail; I had just seen her yesterday.

Garrison reached past me, slid a key into the lock, and unlocked the door.

She drove his car; he had her house key. I wondered again about the nature and depth of their relationship but couldn't think of a way to ask about it that didn't sound inappropriately snoopish. I realize that snoopish is probably not a word, and am willing to go with buttinsky if pressed. In any case, I wasn't sure it mattered if I found her doing yoga while wearing headphones turned up too high for her to hear me knocking. If I found her bludgeoned to death with a frozen leg of lamb in the kitchen, then that would be a whole different story.

Now that he had unlocked the door with a key I felt that I was on better legal ground: he was letting me in, and I just wanted to see if she was all right.

Firefighters could search a house this size for a person in the dark and the smoke in five minutes. Not interested in violating her privacy, I promised myself that I'd be in and out in ninety seconds flat.

He opened the door and we both stepped into the front hall, which is an overly fancy name for a stretch of hallway perhaps ten feet long. An arch to the left opened into the kitchen. Through an arch to the right was a small living room, two tweedy armchairs facing a battered Sony sitting on a mission style oak end table. I had to admit that it wasn't the Grande Theater y Casa del West, but it seemed cozy enough.

I did a quick scan of the kitchen. No bludgeoned body. I didn't check to see if there was lamb in the freezer; it wasn't my place to do that kind of search. There was no table to eat at in the kitchen, so unless she stood at the counter while she ate, she probably dined while sitting in one of the chairs in the living room. A door off the kitchen opened on a small closet that served as a pantry. There were three or four boxes of spaghetti, rigatoni, and penne, a couple of boxes of seasoned couscous, a five pound bag of jasmine rice, and an unopened box of low fat Ritz crackers, but no body. Lauren clearly wasn't a disciple of the Scarsdale diet.

When I moved back into the main hallway Garrison followed at my heels like a puppy.

"When was the last time you saw her?"

"A couple of days ago."

"Did she take the car with her then?"

No answer.

I looked back at him and he must have realized that I had missed his shrug reply, so he did another one for my benefit. Courteous to a fault.

I wondered about him and his utter lack of concern for a missing probable girlfriend and a submerged fifty-thousand-dollar car. I filed that bit of odd behavior away, but realized as I did so that the folder of Garrison's behavior that could be classified as odd might be very thick indeed depending on how low I was willing to set the bar.

I went down to the end of the hallway. There was a small bedroom on the left and a bathroom on the right. There were no ' bodies sprawled out in either one.

On the bathroom sink top was a tube of toothpaste and a toothbrush, as well as a little dish of cotton balls. The tub-shower combo had nothing but a few rust stains, a bar of soap, a bottle of shampoo, and a green washcloth hanging over the towel bar. The washcloth was dry.

In the bedroom the bed was made.

I've never been one of those people who make the bed. What's the point? It's just going to get unmade again about sixteen hours later. Valerie is one of those people who make the bed as was, apparently, Lauren.

And there I go, referring to Lauren in the past tense. I took a breath and moved on.

The nightstand held only a clock and lamp, no paperback, no loose change, no scraps of paper.

The closet was a walk-in number containing the usual jeans and blouses. There were a few items that looked pretty expensive to my eye, but I'm not a great judge of clothes. I didn't see a suitcase or duffle bag of any sort, and there were quite a few empty hangers, but that didn't necessarily prove anything. I had a lot of empty hangers simply because I dry cleaned a lot and never threw the hangers out, but I did own four suitcases of various sizes.

The dresser had a scattering of makeup stuff on the top, the mysterious bottles and tubes and boxes with which women build their faces. There was also a Lucite frame with white matting holding the only picture I had seen in the house thus far. In it a handsome older man with a good tan and neatly combed gray hair, wearing a mustard yellow cardigan over a white dress shirt with narrow dark crosshatching, was next to an attractive older woman with expensively styled blonde hair, probably a dye job if her age was close to his. She was wearing a dark blue blouse with a cameo of some type pinned over her heart. They were both only visible from the waist up and she was a little taller in the picture, as if he was seated in a chair and she was perched on the arm. They were clasping hands, a heavy gold wedding band visible on his finger, a thin loop of diamond baguettes on hers.

It was a professional picture with good composition and

lighting. The dark blue of her blouse complemented the dark crosshatching on his shirt a little bit. There was a little sparkle in their eyes, but no red eye.

"Are those her parents?"

I knew the shrug was coming and mimicked him as he did it.

"Any idea where she might be? Someone she might go to after the accident?"

I went to shrug along with him again but he surprised me by shaking his head instead. I was almost but not quite certain I saw the slimmest edge of a smile on his lips. Was his whole disconnected thing an act? Was he playing with me? I stared at him, but got only his sleepy gaze in return. Maybe I had imagined it.

I felt like spreading my arms wide and proclaiming loudly to the world, perhaps in a British accent, "I, the great Sherlock Holmes, have determined beyond a shadow of a doubt that this woman is not at home," but I resisted. Just barely.

Maybe someone was after her and she had packed the suitcase I didn't find with some stuff that wasn't on the empty hangers in the closet and fled, and that suitcase was in the Porsche right now. I know I didn't see her run off into the rain with it. If so, she had left her toothbrush and toothpaste behind. That was peculiar, but not damning; those items could be replaced later if you forget to grab them while running in fear of your life. I could ask Bobby if he found a suitcase in the car.

Alternatively, she just didn't own that much stuff, a suitcase included, and she hadn't gone anywhere. What would then explain her behavior at the car accident? I didn't know. Maybe she was on something. Maybe, and I was starting to warm up to this theory, she and Garrison were both on something, and she had some sort of paranoid reaction and ran off certain that someone was trying to kill her. It explained her behavior and maybe his as well. What it did not explain was where she was now, and I was a little concerned that in whatever condition she was in she could harm herself or possibly someone else. I couldn't think of anything I could do about that other than warning Bobby of my hypothesis.

In either case, I didn't see any point in standing there any longer, unless that is she was suddenly going to walk through the front door. I waited a moment in the silent house.

She didn't.

We stepped outside and Garrison locked up. I dug one of my business cards out of my wallet. I'd had them printed up just recently and they read, "Jack Fallon, Carpenter/Firefighter/Physicist' along with my phone number. Before you read too closely into that order, I'd like to point out that it is merely alphabetical. It seemed to cover all my present bases nicely, though I was considering if I should add 'junior crimefighter' or something similar to the list.

I handed the card to him. "Would you call me if you hear from her?"

He looked at the card and then gave me what I was rapidly coming to think of as his trademark shrug.

"Can I get a lift back to my truck?"

"Yeah." He pushed the button on his key fob and the car flashed its lights as the doors unlocked. I slide inside, settling into the deep leather of the passenger seat, and we drove away.

Nine

Back at the house Garrison pulled the car into the garage. We stood in the rain outside as the garage doors trundled down, then separated, him towards the house and I back to my truck. I wondered if it would serve any purpose to try and track Lauren by the light of day or if the rain would have obliterated any signs of her trail.

"Hey," a voice called to me.

I turned to see a woman standing under the overhang at the corner of the garage. She wore new blue jeans so tight they were practically intravenous and a black puffy nylon-shelled jacket that billowed around her. Her shoulder-length hair had been bleached white blonde and it looked like it was all split ends, probably from the chemicals though maybe the humidity was to blame as well. Her face was pale, her eyes very large and dark.

By looking at her I wouldn't have cared to try and guess her age to the nearest decade. I figured that she must be about the same age as Garrison but something in her eyes somehow made her look older, a lot older.

"Hey," I answered.

"Have a light?" She held up one hand, a cigarette in the V between her index and middle fingers.

Garrison came steaming back, though he had been almost to the front door. He snatched the cigarette from her hand with a motion like the striking of a cobra. "I told you not to smoke near my house!" He shouted at her. He crumbled the cigarette up and then dropped the pieces on the gravel and ground them further to bits under the toe of his shoe just to prove his point. Without another word he spun and stomped back towards the house.

We both watched him as he entered and slammed the front door.

"Have a light?" She asked again, a fresh cigarette magically tucked into the V between her index and middle fingers. She seemed remarkably unruffled by Garrison shouting at her.

"Sorry, no."

"Thanks," She replied flatly.

I turned to go.

"Are you looking for Lauren?"

That stopped me in my tracks. I turned back.

She ducked her head a little shyly, "I heard you talking to Garrison inside. I was in the kitchen."

"Have you seen her?"

She shook her head, "Not in a couple of days."

I walked over to her and took shelter underneath the overhang. "My name is Jack Fallon and I'm with the fire department." I held out my hand.

"Kristen," she responded and shook my hand with the one holding the cigarette, some deft move positioning it out of the way to keep it from getting crushed, then as an afterthought added "Adams." Her hand was cold, stiff, and boney, lacking a cushion of flesh, like a mannequin's.

"Where was Lauren when you saw her?"

"Here," she gestured with her chin at the house. "Garrison had some people over and we were hanging out, watching movies."

"Lauren drove Garrison's car into the water yesterday over near Birch Pond, said that someone was trying to kill her, and then ran off."

Kristen nodded, though I didn't know if it was as a confirmation of the events or if she was nodding that she already knew about them. "I haven't seen her in a couple of days," was again her response.

We stood in the silence watching the rain while I considered and rejected any number of questions as too confrontational or intrusive. What was she doing in the kitchen? What was her relationship to Garrison? Who did her hair?

I finally settled on, "Did Lauren seem alright the last time you saw her?"

She flicked the filter of the unlit cigarette expertly with her thumb, as though knocking off the ash, examining the end for several seconds. She looked up at me, those large, dark eyes peering deeply into mine, which was somehow a little unnerving, "She was fine. Hanging all over Garrison as usual."

"You don't sound happy about that."

She shrugged quickly, feigning an aloofness she didn't feel, and for a moment, just a fraction of a second, she looked like the young girl she probably was, but then the moment was past.

I tried a different tack. "She and Garrison are serious?"

She held up one hand, the one with the cigarette, and made a seesawing motion. "Garrison doesn't want to be pinned down, but Lauren wanted it to be serious."

"Did that cause problems between them?"

"Not for Garrison. And I think Lauren saw him as a challenge. The effort is part of the game." She made a jerking off motion with the hand holding the cigarette, which was disturbing coming from this woman with the young body and the ancient eyes. I suppose that summarized her opinion of dating, or perhaps of men in general.

"Do you know how long she had been around Dunboro, or where she came from?"

"She's been hanging around here for most of a year, and she told me once that she was from Los Angeles. She said that she was looking to get away from the craziness of the city, that she liked Dunboro for the peace and quiet. "

I made a mental note to try and find out if Los Angeles was her home. Had she gone there?

"Do you know where she is? Who she would go to if she

was in trouble?"

She answered both questions with a single shake of her head.

"Do you know of anyone who would have a reason to hurt her?"

She gave me another shake of her head.

It was possible that Kristen had something important to tell me, but like Garrison she wasn't exactly forthcoming with her answers and I didn't really know the right questions to ask. I was just spinning my wheels here, so I settled for handing her a business card and asking her to call me if she thought of anything or heard from Lauren.

"Do you think something happened to her?" She asked.

"Do you?"

She considered this for a while, and then answered, "I don't know."

"Neither do I."

She looked at the card for a moment and then back up at me, and again I found myself somehow dissected by those dark, infinite eyes. "Then why are you looking for her?"

"Because no one else is."

Ten

Not every strange thing that happens to me ends up as a life or death struggle in a burning building with a ruthless killer. Sometimes they turn out to be just strange, confusing events, and it appeared that Lauren and her disappearance after the car accident were going to fall into that category.

Bobby had the car towed to the police station and gave it a search. He found the key still in the ignition, but the only fingerprint that he managed to lift from it was mine from when I reached past her to shut it off. What he didn't find was an ID, a suitcase, a purse, or any indication of any kind that Lauren had been in the car at all. If she had been carrying a purse the night of the accident I didn't see it, though if it was a small one I could have missed it in the dark. I know she didn't run off hauling a suitcase of any size.

Despite her dire prediction, Lauren didn't turn up anywhere

dead, but she didn't turn up anywhere alive either. She had just vanished.

She didn't own a car that the state knew about, nor even a driver's license, which was unquestionably strange.

Just for the heck of it I tried to find her parents.

Any idea how many Wilkes there are nationwide? Heaps and tons. Even if I restricted myself to just New England, and in the picture from Lauren's bedroom her parents did for some indefinable reason exuded a certain New England-y feel, it was still far more people than I could cold call and ask if they had a missing daughter named Lauren. Los Angeles proved to be even worse.

Forty-eight hours later Bobby filed a scant report using the information provided by me and Garrison, the car was headed for what I suspected would be a very expensive overhaul at the local repair shop, and we all went back to our lives.

There was some tantalizing mystery surrounding Lauren Wilkes, but there didn't seem to be a way for me to get my fingernails underneath the edge and pry the lid off.

In the meantime, other things required my attention.

My unofficial role at the fire department became larger. The rain continued to fall, further endangering Baxter's Dam, without an end in sight. There were a lot of basements to pump, downed trees and power lines to deal with, and flooded streets to close. The culvert at Stickneys's did wash out, taking half of the road with it. Another pink line appeared on Bobby's map. Pink apparently meant that the roadway was damaged. With so much going on the Chief had little choice but to enlist every able-bodied person he could lay his hands on, medical leave be damned. I promised to avoid any heavy lifting.

I didn't know about other firefighters, but the map in my head was becoming increasingly tangled as I had to continually reroute around the ever-changing and deteriorating road conditions. More than once I found myself driving a truck to a call, only to find that the route I had picked was impassible and had to backtrack to locate another way around. We took to writing notes right in the road books in the trucks, the guy in the passenger seat making up the directions and telling them to the driver on the fly. Let me tell you, it's not fun driving twenty tons of firetruck in the pouring rain at forty miles an hour when the guy in the seat next to you shouts, "Turn left... now!"

Valerie passed through an extremely fertile couple of days which we gamely ground our way through. Mechanical and unsatisfying to all involved doesn't begin to describe it. Then her temperature peaked, or spiked, or traversed through a chicane or whatever it did, and the chance had passed. Maybe we had been successful, maybe we had not. Only time would tell.

We took the opportunity to get out of the bedroom and over to the mall just to wander around. It was nice to escape from the house where all the windows showed us was gray and rainy, to the mall where the windows were filled with happy mannequins and piles of shiny new stuff.

We paused at Victoria's Secret, their window display of half a dozen mannequins dressed in diaphanous night shirts and matching thongs in a rainbow of colors. We looked at each other, shook our heads, and moved on.

Valerie spent some time at the window of a shoe store trying to explain to me the difference between two pairs of black pumps that looked absolutely identical to me.

"The one on the left has a bow."

"The one on the right has a bow."

"The bow on the right is smaller."

"They look the same to me. I think they're two shoes from the same pair."

She rolled her eyes at me, "They're both left shoes!"

I looked more closely. "Maybe meant for a woman with two left feet?"

Another eye roll. "Alright," she tried again, "See? The one on the right has that little gold piece on the heel." She tapped, pointing through the glass.

"We can't even see that part of the heel on the other shoe from here. I bet if we go into the store and look at the back we'll see that same piece on that shoe as well."

"Bet what?"

"If they're different shoes I'll buy them for you."

"Which pair?"

"Both pairs. What do I care? They're the same shoe!"

We went into the store, and from the rear both pairs had the same little gold metal piece on the heel, though Valerie insisted they were different little gold pieces. A saleswoman came over and agreed with her. Women, they're all in cahoots, and she's probably on commission anyway. Good as my word I bought her two pairs of identical shoes, though they were somehow different prices. Go figure.

We looked at a big display in one window of mannequins all wearing rain gear: colorful gum rubber boots, raincoats, and umbrellas. It reminded us of what was waiting out in the real drowning world, so we moved on quickly.

We drifted past the Cinnabon. The big industrial fan behind the counter blowing the scent of warm cinnamon buns out into the concourse is torture to Valerie, though I myself am immune to its charms. I innocently led her on a quick loop out one of the mall's short arms and back past the Cinnabon shop again. On the third pass I bought a six pack of minibuns for myself. I'm not made of stone, you know. I managed grudgingly to split them with her.

"I thought you didn't even like these." Valerie said, sucking icing from her fingertips as she finished her third bun.

"I can take them or leave them."

"Can I have the last one?"

"Reach for it and pull back a stump."

"Uh-huh." She laughed.

It was in moments like these I felt that somehow the woman I had married was in there somewhere among the uncertainty and depression that my brush with death and our seeming infertility had created. But I knew that it wouldn't last.

Valerie locked up at a toy store, watching other people's children playing in the aisles. I gave her some time, standing next to her staring at my shoes, until it looked like she might start to cry and I dragged her away.

"Hey, I was looking at-"

I turned her around and hugged her to me. "I know. I know what you were looking at." She was stiff, cold, unyielding to my contact. I kept up the pressure, hoping she would thaw a little, looking over her shoulder at the window of a Target filled with cameras and picture frames.

Then I caught a glimpse of mustard yellow.

I released her suddenly and walked across the mall towards the display. I stopped in front of it, pressing my hands flat against the glass.

"Jack?" Valerie asked uncertainly as she came up behind me.

There were eight of them. Lucite picture frames were arranged on a series of stairs in a loose pyramid. Each contained a picture of the man in the mustard yellow cardigan and the woman in the dark blue blouse.

Unless Lauren's parents worked for a frame company, something very strange was going on. Something very strange indeed.

Eleven

Valerie remained outside the police department, waiting in the truck, probably steaming up the windows with her rising blood pressure. The conversation on the drive over from the mall to here had been a heated one as I told her about the woman in the Porsche. In her opinion I was risking my life, getting involved in a murder investigation that was none of my business while she was trying to have a normal life and a family. I didn't see any risk at all. There was no evidence that a murder had been committed. I was just bringing a picture frame to Bobby. Besides, how could she expect me to just forget that I may have been the last person to see Lauren alive and do nothing about it?

And, though I didn't say it, I resented Valerie's controlling attitude.

There we had drawn our immutable lines in the sand, agreeing to angrily disagree.

Bobby turned the frame that I had purchased at Target over, extended the hinged leg on the back, and stood the picture up on the surface of his desk. He folded his hands on the blotter in front of it. "Are you sure this is the picture you saw at the house?"

"One hundred percent. One hundred and ten percent."

Seated at his desk he looked at the picture, silent in thought. Then he said, "It could be a picture of her actual parents that they sold to an agency, and the picture frame company bought the image. I think that's the way that works. I don't think the frame companies hire models and shoot their own pictures."

"It's possible, but not likely."

"Not likely," he agreed. "Fake picture of her parents, no driver's license, no registered car. I wonder how much about her was true." He turned to his computer. "How old do you think she was?"

"I don't know. Twenty? Twenty-five? I'm near that age where everyone is starting to look young to me. Maybe Garrison West knows."

He pecked at some keys and waited, then pecked some more. "If I'm spelling her name correctly, I don't see a social security number for her either. There's an Ellen Wilkes who's twenty-two."

"He said her name was Lauren."

"Maybe that was her middle name, though Ellen is listed as living in Georgia." He shrugged. "I'd have to do a lot more searching to convince myself that she was faking her whole identity." Bobby pulled at his lower lip. "You said that Garrison had a key to the house?"

I nodded.

"I'm going to give him a call and see if he'll let me take a look at the place myself. Care to tag along and see it again?"

"Love to."

After checking the number in his notebook he called Garrison and made arrangements for him to meet us at the house. He put the picture frame back into the bag I had brought it in and then grabbed that and his hat and we went out to his cruiser. It was a shiny new Dodge replacing the one that had been destroyed in our last little adventure together.

While he got into the car I veered off and knocked on the passenger window of my truck. Valerie, a shape behind the fogged glass, turned to me and powered it down.

"I'm going to go check out Lauren's house with Bobby. See you at home?"

There was a soft look of hurt on her face for just a second that then hardened to a steely anger that flushed her cheeks and creased her brow. Wordlessly she buzzed up the window. I could see her through the haze scootch over to the driver's seat. She started the truck and drove away.

It was going to be fun fun fun in the Fallon household tonight.

I thought about telling Bobby to go without me and following her home, but then felt a spike of anger of my own. I was a grown man going to look at an empty house with the sheriff standing right next to me; a sheriff almost as big as a grizzly bear, I might add. What harm could possible come to me? After months of physical therapy and lying at home watching endless daytime television shows, I was going to walk around and exercise my brain a little. I would not let my life be ruled by her paranoid fantasies about my imminent demise.

I walked back across the lot and got into the passenger side of the cruiser, slamming the door perhaps a little harder than I intended.

"Everything OK?" Bobby asked.

"I don't know. Long story."

On the drive over I tried to talk about it. I found it difficult to articulate our different positions well, which was probably part of the reason Valerie and I were having trouble communicating.

Bobby was a good listener, which I think is a quality required to be a good sheriff.

For his part, he could understand my desire to help, first to solve Patricia's murder last year and now Lauren's disappearance. It was in some ways the same imperative that drove him as well. At the same time he tried to convey the difficulty this presented for women he had dated in the past; the essential uncertainty in what he did for a living. Ninety-nine point nine percent of what he did was absolutely routine, but that last one tenth of one percent could be a bitch. Any given traffic stop could very quickly become, without hyperbole, life or death.

Valerie, he reminded me, had married a physicist, which was definitely not a career that faced life or death decisions frequently.

It was a viewpoint that I had not considered before and Valerie had been unable to explain to me. In that light I looked at myself and saw someone selfish and uncaring to the one person I should be caring for above all others. His perceptiveness left me speechless. I choked up a little, and at that moment I had serious doubts about what I was doing in that police car, and why.

While he left me to stew about that, we arrived at Lauren's rental place. Garrison was already there standing under the front door overhang, his green Porsche parked at the curb.

"Nice car." Bobby said.

"I think his parents had to die for him to get it."

Bobby frowned and got out of the car. I followed him up to the front door.

"Garrison West? I'm Sheriff Bobby Dawkins."

Garrison hesitantly held out a hand, which Bobby swallowed in his own.

When he released it Bobby opened up the bag and removed the picture frame, handing it to Garrison. "Does this picture look familiar to you?"

Garrison looked at the picture for only a moment. "Did you take this when you were here?" He asked me.

"I bought that at Target."

He looked at the picture confusedly. "I don't understand."

"Mr. West," Bobby addressed him, "you told Jack that picture was of Lauren's parents."

Garrison nodded, a little bob of his head, "That's what she told me."

"I'd like to go inside and see if the picture in that frame is like this one."

"Do you have a warrant?"

Bobby shook his head, "No, and I doubt that I could get one. I'm just trying to find Lauren. You have a key, and if you let me in it might help."

Garrison thought about that for a moment, then shrugged to himself and unlocked the door. He swung it open and gestured us inside like a spokesmodel.

"Thank you," Bobby said as he passed him in the doorway.

Inside the front door Bobby scooped the mail off the floor and riffled through it quickly. It was all circulars and catalogs addressed to Lauren Wilkes. There was no personal mail or bills at all. Bobby looked for somewhere to put it, and, lacking any sort of table in the front hall, he put the small stack down in a pile near the archway leading into the livingroom.

From there we made a beeline for the bedroom. The picture and frame in the bedroom were identical to the one that I had gotten at Target. The picture inside Lauren's frame was not a photograph at all, just a color print on lightweight paper. There was even a copyright statement on the bottom that had been covered by the matting.

After comparing the two pictures Bobby reassembled Lauren's frame and put it back on the dresser. He put the one that I had bought back into the bag, folded over the top, and handed it to me.

He headed back towards the front door and stopped in the hallway, between the arches leading to the living room and kitchen. He took a deep breath through his nose, as if trying to get a scent of the place.

While Bobby did his breathing exercises I asked, "You have a key to her house. Did she have one to yours?"

He nodded.

"What about the car keys?"

"They're at the house. She could come get them anytime she wanted."

"Was she in any kind of trouble that you know of?"

"No."

"Do you know where she might have gone?"

"No."

Bobby watched the exchange with interest, and when I left him a gap he asked, "Has she ever gone away for several days without telling you where she was going?"

Garrison shook his head, bewildered, "No."

Bobby looked to me and I shook my head as well.

"Thank you for your help," Bobby told Garrison as he opened the door and headed outside.

We stood on the front porch while Garrison locked up the house. He had some problems getting the swollen front door to close well enough to set the dead bolt. After a few minutes of fiddling, Bobby offered to help. The door jamb was warped, and he had to lift the door on its hinges to get the deadbolt to align with its slot. He twisted the key in the lock, pulled it free, and held it by its ring out to Garrison. He noticed two keys on the ring.

"What's this second key to?"

Garrison took the ring from Bobby, "The side door I think. It was on the ring when she gave it to me."

Bobby took the keys back and looked at the other one. "It's not a door lock key. It's too small. Maybe a bike lock or a padlock."

He held the keys up for me to look at. I noticed tumbler ridges on both sides of the key body, as well as tumbler depressions on both faces. "That's a pretty complicated key for a bike lock." I caught a glint from the key. "Is something stamped on it?"

Bobby held the key by the shaft and angled it in the gray light. He squinted. "Uhh, the letters B and A, and the number three one five."

"BA? Bank of America?" I guessed. "Could it be a safe deposit box key?"

Bobby considered this. "Huh. Maybe. Did she have a safe deposit box?" he asked Garrison.

"I don't know. She never said anything about one. She didn't mention the second key on the ring at all."

"Mind if I borrow it?" Bobby asked him. "We'll get it right back to you."

Garrison shook his head, and Bobby wound the unknown key off the ring and gave the other key and the ring back to him. He wrote out a quick receipt and gave that to him as well. "Come on, Jack," he gestured to me towards the patrol car with his head, "Let's see if we can find out what this key goes to."

Twelve

Back at the police department Bobby and I split up the phone book that he had pulled from the lower drawer of his desk and started dialing. Southern New Hampshire isn't Zurich, and there aren't more than a couple of dozen banks and credit unions around. I sat at the desk of one of his officers dialing, chair springs tipped back to the end of their travel, feet propped up on the corner. I must confess to a certain visceral thrill as I opened the phone conversations with "Hello, I'm with the Dunboro Police Department…"

It didn't take much time to determine that the key didn't belong to any safe deposit box locally. The description of the key didn't even match. Ours was too complex.

I sat in the chair rolling the shaft of the key between my fingers looking much like a medieval soothsayer trying to read chicken bones.

"You getting anything?" Bobby asked wryly.

"It's a complicated key," I said, ignoring his tone. "Expensive." I rapped it on the edge of the desk where it sounded heavily. "Serious metal. Steel. Maybe stainless."

"So?"

I chewed on my lip while I thought about what all those facts added up to. When the answer came to me, I felt stupid that it had taken so long.

"It's to a safe."

"A safe?" Bobby sounded doubtful.

"Yeah. Not a bank safe, and not a lockbox from Staples or Walmart. A real safe. High end. Toss me the phone book."

He threw it to me and I flipped pages until I found a local locksmith in Milford and dialed. I gave a description of the key to the man who answered, who handed me off to another man so I could repeat it.

"Huh, doesn't ring any bells," the man said. "You sure it's not a safe deposit key?"

"I've tried all the local banks and credit unions. It doesn't ring any bells with them either."

"Just a sec." He left me for a moment and I heard the buzz of a conversation with the other man, then he came back. "I'm sorry. It's like nothing we've handled. You might want to try the big safe companies. Mosler and Brinks. Maybe Centurion or Honeywell. I've got their numbers if it would help."

I told him that it would and he gave them to me. I jotted them on the corner of the desk blotter.

From there I got lucky. The key was to a Mosler, which was the first company I had called.

"Oh, yeah," the guy on the phone said after I introduced myself as from the Dunboro Police Department. "That's one of ours. Give me the numbers off it."

I did.

I heard him flip some paper. "That's from one of our luxury boxes, three or four years out. No keys anymore, you see; everything is going to digital keypads. Those units came with either an internal drawer system or unfinished open space interior."

"How large a safe are we talking about?"

More paper. "Exterior dimensions are six inches by ten inches by twelve deep. It's a fire rated safe. The walls are double layered with water-infused mica in between, so the interior is smaller. This sheet doesn't say how much, but I'd guess an inch or so in every direction."

I did the math. Even with two inches of wall thickness there were over three hundred cubic inches of storage. Renting that tiny house in Dunboro, what could Lauren possibly have had of value to store in such a high-end safe?

"Can I trouble you and ask one more question?"

"Shoot."

"What would such a safe cost?"

I heard him blow out his breath. "Hard to say exactly. Wholesale? Retail? Installed or carry away? New or used? No less than two thousand dollars. And if you're curious, all that steel, plus the water and mica for the fire rating, that safe weighs over three hundred pounds, so it's not exactly trivial to install it yourself."

"Thanks very much. You've been a big help." I put the phone back in its cradle.

"So it's a safe," Bobby said after I had hung up.

"A pretty big one. Heavy. Three hundred pounds. Worth two thousand dollars or more."

"So where is it?"

"It's got to be in the house, right? It's the only place she had."

"That you know of," Bobby said.

"Point taken," I admitted, "Still, care to give the house another look?"

"Me? I've got no cause to go back into that house. Truth be told neither do you."

"But she's missing," I insisted.

He shook his head. "I don't know that. You say she's missing. Garrison hardly says anything at all. She's an adult who doesn't have to report to either one of you. If you can find a relative who will say she is missing or find out where she worked and they haven't seen her, or hell, even come up with a landlord who will say she missed a rent payment, then I could push it a little further. As it stands I've got nothing."

"Swell." I paused, then decided to try a different angle. "If Garrison lets me back in, then can I look for the safe?"

He bobbed his head, "Sure. She gave him the keys to both the house and the safe. Provided he didn't steal them, and there's no way for you to know that, that's tantamount to having her permission."

I got up from the desk and headed for the door, "I'm going to give him a call."

Bobby pulled a fanfold sheaf from the stack on one side of his desk, already moving on to other work. "Let me know what you find," he said to my departing back.

Thirteen

When I got to the house Garrison was already there waiting for me. He was standing under the front door overhang, his hands jammed down into the pockets of a battered pullover with Skullcrusher emblazoned on the front. I assumed that was the name of a snowboard company, but could have been a rock band or an energy drink or an advertisement extolling the virtues of blunt head trauma for all I knew. I pulled my truck to the curb behind his red BMW and jogged to join him under the overhang.

"Thanks for meeting me," I told him.

He shrugged, what I was coming to think of as his stock reply. Even so it was an odd response here. This was the third time he had come out to the house in just a few days. If it was interfering with other plans, if it was any kind of imposition at all, he didn't show it.

Perhaps he was genuinely concerned about Lauren, despite

his stoic exterior, and he was helping out in the only way he could think of. Maybe he was just bored and had nothing better to do. From either perspective his behavior was perplexing.

"The key on the ring is from a safe. Did Lauren ever mention a safe to you?"

"No," he said, shaking his head to emphasize his point. "You think it's inside?"

"Unless you can think of somewhere else it might be."

He appeared to give this question great deliberation before shaking his head again. "Uh-uh." His right hand came out of the pullover already holding the house key. He unlocked the door and went in ahead of me.

We stopped in the front hall after I closed the door behind us.

"Any idea where it might be?" He asked.

I had just been asking myself that very question. The house was just a single floor, without a basement. There would be a crawlspace underneath, which meant the safe could be in the floor. There was also likely a small attic accessed through a hatch in one of the closet ceilings, maybe with a drop ladder. I couldn't see anyone hauling a three hundred pound safe up a narrow ladder access and wasn't certain the ceiling joists would support it without some serious reinforcement.

"It's heavy," I said, "so it will be down low, in the floor or in a panel behind a wall."

We split up and I hit the bedroom first. I rolled up the area rug and knocked on the floor underneath then rolled it back into place. I tapped around under the bed. I walked the perimeter of the room, rapping on the mopboard, pulling furniture away from the wall so I could check behind it.

I had been saving the closet for last because I had really hoped it would be there; it's where I would have put a safe if I had one. Inside the closet I had to move two dozen pairs of shoes just to see the floor, which felt solid. I pushed and pulled on the molding, hoping to find a piece that would swing loose, a panel that would come out. No dice, and no access to an attic space. I replaced the shoes the way I had found them – in a large, disorganized pile.

I checked the bathroom next. It was a small room dominated by the shower with little space to hide anything. I tapped on the back wall of the medicine cabinet to see if maybe there was a hidey hole behind it. There wasn't.

I stomped my way down the hallway, checking the floor, passing Garrison on my way to the kitchen as he was headed towards the bedroom. Garrison had been presumably checking the front rooms while I was checking the back. It seemed unlikely that either of us would have missed a hidden safe in such a small space, and I was beginning to wonder about where else I might look as I disinterestedly pushed boxes of pasta around on the shelves in the pantry to see behind them. I was just considering moving the refrigerator, a beast from the late eighties that might weigh several hundred pounds, and how the hell could Lauren have moved it to get to the safe when she needed to, when Garrison called me from the back of the house.

"Hey, back here."

I found him kneeling in the bedroom closet near a dark opening in the back, the front of the safe exposed.

"How did you get it open? I couldn't get any of the

molding to move."

"I found a pull ring on the top shelf."

He demonstrated a small steel ring at the back of the top shelf in the closet behind a pile of folded sweaters. The ring pulled a hidden cable that released the catch on one side of the panel. It was ingenious. The carpentry skills required to put it together were minimal because the panel pulled out along perfectly natural molding lines, making the installation easy and practically invisible. Maybe I'd use the idea in my own house.

I slid the key from my pocket and inserted it into the keyhole on the front of the safe. It turned smoothly, the product of good lubrication and precision engineering, and the door hinged out silently.

The inside was dark, and I turned on a penlight that I had taken from my glove compartment. While I was at it I pulled on a pair of latex gloves. I carried a box of them in my truck for car accident scenes.

At first glance I thought the safe was empty. It was the model the man on the phone had mentioned which had the unfinished interior; it was just a dull gray steel box inside and out. Then I caught a glimpse of white near the back.

I reached in and scrabbled out a small white envelope, like the type a gift card might come in. I held it up to the light. The envelope was unmarked and unblemished.

The flap had not been sealed shut so I folded it back and tipped the contents into my palm. Four cards fell out and I fanned them with my fingers like holding a poker hand one card short.

They were four driver's licenses, all for the same woman,

though with little changes to her appearance from license to license. Arranged in order, the most recent was for New Hampshire resident Lauren Wilkes, the picture that of the blonde woman who had been driving the Porsche. The one before that was from New York for Lillian Wainwright, and showed the same woman, only with longer hair styled in loose curls and dyed dark brown. Before that she had apparently called herself Leslie Wattley and lived in California, with a platinum blonde hair worn in a short pageboy cut like a young Annie Lenox. Finally the earliest driver's license was from ten years ago when she had called herself Lorraine Watson of Texas and sported dirty blonde hair hanging straight to her shoulders with bangs across the front.

"Any idea what this means?" I asked Garrison.

He gave me a shrug.

I had expected nothing else.

Fourteen

Back at the police department Bobby did his thing with a Dick Tracy Junior Detective Kit, carefully dusting various oxide powders onto the licenses with a fine, long-haired brush and then blowing off the excess with few puffs of air from a red rubber squeeze bulb. He examined the front and back of each with a large magnifying lens that he pulled from one of the side drawers of his desk. It was just a big fisheye lens made from float glass, without a frame or holder of any sort. He held it by the edges and, as he looked through it, it enlarged his eye grotesquely. Looking across the desk at him, his eye seemed like an alien sky, an expanse of white threaded through with red capillaries of lightning, the hazel arc of a rising iris sun on the horizon.

After several minutes of me examining his eye while he examined the licenses, he tossed the one he was holding and the lens onto the blotter in front of him. The lens spun on the apex of the convex face for several turns before coming to a rest.

"Nothing." He stripped off the latex gloves he had been wearing, wadded them up into a ball, and threw them into the wastebasket by his desk.

With prime time television crammed to the gills with derivative police procedural dramas I wondered if even the most careless of criminals are just careful enough not to leave fingerprints on anything anymore.

"You said she didn't have a driver's license. Are they all fake?"

"The New Hampshire one is." He picked up that license and wiped a thumb across the surface, removing the residue of the fingerprinting dust, and then leaned across the desk to hand it to me. "It's pretty good, but the hologram is messed up."

I held the card and angled it to the light, looking for the telltale rainbow flash of the embedded hologram, the images they created blurred and indistinct. Other than that it looked genuine to me, and I probably wouldn't have remembered to look at the hologram at all if he hadn't mentioned it. I realized that it might not have fooled someone who looked at IDs regularly. She could have been caught if she had been pulled over by a cop, and she probably couldn't have boarded an airplane with it.

"What about the others?"

"I'm not sure. I think California has had holograms for a very long time, and that license doesn't even have one. New York got them fairly recently, and maybe that license is from the pre-hologram days. Texas? Their driver's license could be stamped on a piece of leather or engraved on a bullet for all I know."

Bobby continued, "I'll need to actually call those other states and see if valid driver's licenses were issued in any of those names in any of those places. It's very likely that I'll get several hits from the wrong people who just happen to have the same name. It would take a while to sort it all out. Alternately I could try tracking down the addresses and seeing if those are even real places, let alone the place where that person ever lived. That would take some time too, and I'm not exactly rolling in free time here. It would probably be a waste anyway. If I had to guess, I'd say they're all fake."

"Why do you say that?"

"It's the only thing that makes sense to me. Why worry about fingerprints? Because the fingerprints would lead to the real person whereas these licenses do not. Whatever they represent, for whatever reason she had them, they're fakes and she left them behind. She took her fingerprints and her real ID with her. For all we know, there were a dozen other identities in the safe that she also took."

I tossed that around in my head for a few moments, and then leaned forward on the desk, my elbows on the surface. "Let's say for the sake of argument that she had other identities ready and waiting, and that something, some crime she committed using these identities," I waved a hand over the cards on the desk, "came back to bite her on the ass. Why did she keep them until now in the first place? Just holding onto the fake IDs is a crime, isn't it?"

"It's just a misdemeanor. College kids do it all the time to buy alcohol, and mostly they just get a fine if that. If you're caught with falsified IDs from several states that can be a federal crime, a whole different ball of wax. Still, that's usually not prosecuted. They're more interested in the crimes you commit with the identities, rather than the identities themselves. As for why she kept them," he frowned, "sentimentality? Besides, if you think the identity is still a good one, why get rid of it? Good fake driver's licenses, even with a crappy hologram, cost real money."

"Any idea what crimes she might have been committing?"

Bobby blew out a breath, "No way to know. Identity theft would be very likely, though there are usually credit cards and sometimes social security cards along with the driver's licenses, and you didn't find any in the safe. You can use fake IDs to pass counterfeit checks or money, or launder money, but most of that stuff is done electronically these days. There are also any number of scams you can pull off with a bunch of fake identities – insurance fraud, welfare fraud, false disability claims, bogus lawsuits. There are just too many possibilities to even hazard a useful guess."

"So what now?"

"Like I said, I'll make the calls. I'll be honest though; it's not really high on my list with everything else going on. The only crime I have here for certain is the ID stuff. Maybe someone is after her, maybe someone isn't. Maybe she just picked up stakes and moved on. The multiple identities make it seem likely that she's done that before."

"Maybe she's in real trouble." I countered.

He gave a little bob of his head that I took for a nod, "Maybe. You can't prove it. I don't have any leads to follow even if you could. Garrison West doesn't seem to have anything useful to tell me. I don't even know her real name. I don't have a fingerprint. Nothing. I'll throw a report on the wire, and maybe she'll turn up, but most likely if she does she'll have a different name. It's a long shot that another police department will even make the connection unless they arrest her for something and actually put that new identity to the test."

There probably was nowhere to go with it, but I wanted to try. I couldn't shake the feeling that the woman who fled the car accident had been very much in danger. I pointed to the licenses still on the desktop, "Mind if I make a copy?"

He thought about it for a moment and then hooked a thumb over his shoulder at the copier against the wall. "Help yourself."

He watched me as I gathered up the licenses and aligned them on the platen so they would all copy onto a single sheet. I pressed the start button, but the machine had gone into energy-saving mode and would take a couple of minutes to warm up.

"Jack, piece of advice. Whatever you're doing, whatever sense of chivalry or desire to make things right that drives you, it's not worth your marriage."

I didn't have an answer to that. I resented that those were somehow opposing things: that I couldn't do what I felt was right because it was some kind of a violation of my marriage vows.

Also, my rudderless meandering to fill time since my plans after graduate school had fallen apart was wearing on me. I suspected that lottery winners, and in a sense living off of patent license fees without having to work was a form of winning the lottery, must discover that doing nothing is not a viable option. Going day to day without any sort of goal, either long term or short term, is empty. Here was a mystery dropped in my lap, a pile of puzzle pieces without the solution on the cover of the box it came in, and I wanted to see what picture I could make out of it.

Poking around was harmless and most likely pointless, and I would not be at risk. Indeed doing nothing, then living with the understanding that maybe someone had been hurt and I could have done something about it but didn't, seemed the greater risk to me, to my sense of self and my feelings about me as a person.

Valerie's viewpoint, which had seemed so clear to me earlier today, was becoming hazy again.

The copier completed its warm up process and made the copy, the bright bar of the scanner wand tracking across my peripheral vision as I stared off into space. I took the page from the receiving tray when it slid out of the machine, the sheet of paper still warm. I collected the licenses from the platen and returned them to Bobby.

He seemed on the verge of saying something else, but the scanner on the small table in the corner of the office interrupted him, locking up on the fire department frequency and toning an alarm.

He sighed. "They're playing your song."

I was technically still on medical leave, but it was midday and coverage at the station was likely to be thin. I wasn't going to go into a burning building in my condition, but I could run a pump or drive a truck just fine, and I was right next door. I grabbed my jacket and headed out.

Fifteen

The police and fire departments are only separated by the driveway that gives access to the rear parking lots of both buildings. I crossed the driveway just as the rain was starting to think about falling again and entered the fire station through the side door, then stood in the darkness realizing that I had not waited around long enough to hear what the call was for. The radio in the station was now silent; I must have missed it. I wanted to pull out a truck and have it waiting on the apron for when the crew arrived, but without knowing the call I couldn't be certain what pieces of equipment we would need, which truck would be best suited for the job.

As I was standing there contemplating the silent trucks, the Chief came in the side door behind me and stopped short of bumping into me.

"Jack, what are you doing here? You're not active."

"I figured I would drive the truck."

"Uh-uh. No way. If something happened the insurance would never cover you."

"Come on, John. If something happens I promise that I won't sue."

"It's not a matter of your suing. What if something happens to the horse?"

That was so incongruous that it took me several seconds just to process it. "What horse?"

"That's the call. It's for a horse stuck in the mud."

"Stuck in the mud? Why call the fire department? Is it burning?"

"No, it's not burning. They called the fire department, and we're going to see if we can do something about it."

You might be surprised to find out that my previous residence in Manhattan and my youth in the New Hampshire north country gave me little opportunity to mix with the equestrian set. As I stood there in the fire station rummaging through my mental filing cabinet I found that I knew embarrassingly little about horses. They have four legs and, that's about it. What does a horse weigh? A thousand pounds? More? You'd need a tow truck to move one. Could a winch be used? You'd have to pad out the winch cable or it would just cut in – you'd end up with two halves of a horse.

"What truck do you want to take?"

"You're not driving."

"Come one, John, you can't expect me to miss a horse stuck in the mud! How often does that happen?"

He wavered.

While he was holding his internal debate the door opened again and Winston David came in. He almost ran into us. "Get the fuck out of the doorway..." he began, but then realized that he was talking to the Chief. "Sorry, Chief. What's the holdup?"

"We're trying to figure out which vehicle to take?"

"I couldn't hear the call on the way over here. What is it?"

"A horse stuck in the mud."

"Is it burning?"

I barked a laugh.

John shook his head sadly. "What is it with you people and burning things? No, it's not burning." He snapped into Chief mode and made several quick decisions. "We'll take the Rescue. Maybe we can use the winch on the front. Jack, you're driving."

Without giving him a chance to change his mind I disconnected the battery charger and scrambled up into the cab.

Before I pulled it out of the garage we were joined by one of the Jonet brothers. They are twins, Bruce and Robert, and I honestly have trouble telling them apart, but one of them got into the crew compartment. The final member of the crew was a new guy. His name was Justin, or maybe Jared. Joseph? Because he was a body builder with biceps that were as large around as my thighs, his given name fell by the wayside and he was immediately given the nickname Tank.

Most fire departments have a Tank, the name bestowed upon the largest firefighter. Every so often you run across the name Moose instead, often somewhere in northern New

Hampshire or Maine. I once saw a firefighter at a mutual aid call in Hudson who had the name "Ogre" stitched onto the back of his jacket, though whether it referred to the character from the movie *Revenge of the Nerds* or was a *Lord of the Rings* thing, I never knew. Anyway, ours was nicknamed Tank, and as soon as the crew compartment door was closed I hit the road.

"Dunboro rescue responding with a crew of four" John spoke into the radio from the officer's seat next to me.

"Dunboro rescue responding with a crew of four, fourteen thirty-two hours," the dispatcher echoed back at him.

On the way we discussed using the winch, maybe with a length of dry hose as a sling of some sort, but the problem became more complicated when we arrived at the location of the call, only to find that it was not where the horse was.

The woman who flagged us down wore skintight riding breeches, knee-high black boots, and a white shirt under a short fitted black jacket, broad at the shoulders, possibly padded, and narrow at the waist. A white riding helmet was braced under one arm against her hip and she had a crop held in that hand. She was certainly dressed the part of an equestrienne, though the effect was spoiled somewhat by mud caked and spattered up her legs to mid-thigh.

She said her name was Sara and she had taken advantage of the break in the rain, a break that was now well and truly over dousing us all with buckets from above, to take her horse Chance for a ride in the woods. When he had become bogged down in the mud and she had been unable to free the horse alone, she had left it. She walked out of the woods, calling from the first house she came to and in front of which we all now stood. She had dialed 911. It was the operator who had decided to give the call to the fire department.

"Where is the horse now?" John asked.

"Down that trail," she pointed, "about half a mile." She stopped to reconsider how far she had walked. "Maybe a little more."

"Super," John said under his breath. With the horse that far from the road, the winch on the Rescue would be of no use to us. Perhaps we should have brought the Forestry truck instead of the rescue, though it could only carry a driver and one passenger and it didn't have a winch at all.

We were going to have to do this one the old-fashioned way, with our backs.

After assuring Sara that we would do everything we could, John got on the radio and requested additional manpower from adjacent towns. We were going to need some help moving this horse. In response we got a mixed crowd of a dozen firefighters from three other departments in about fifteen minutes. With all the firetrucks parked on the road, you would have thought a large house was burning.

"Bruce, get a roll of inch and three quarter hose out of the upper bed."

Either John had some means of telling the twins apart or it had been a lucky guess on his part because Bruce Jonet nodded once and set off for the rear of the truck, returning moments later with the roll of hose. When empty, the hose would be a flattened strap of woven canvas and rubber capable of supporting considerable weight.

"OK, let's go." John set off into the woods with Sara at his side. She wore her brown hair in a ponytail, and it was soaking wet and hung straight down the middle of her back streaming water. The rest of the firefighters followed along in clumps of three or four, passing various ideas for freeing the horse from the mud back and forth. One thought that we should have brought a chainsaw with us and perhaps cut down trees to make a frame around the horse that could be used to lift it out. Others shot that idea down. It sounded too complicated, and how would we brace the logs in the mud? I was wondering if there was somewhere we could get old-fashioned pulleys, block and tackle systems, like those used in old quarries or sailing ships before the invention of powered winches, but couldn't think of any I had seen outside of an antique store. Maybe we could get a set from an antique store in Milford or locate a pair hanging around in some old barn?

Sarah led us to a clearing where we all experienced a Godfather moment. In the middle was a vast pool of mud near the center of which was the horse's neck and head; no more of the horse was visible. To call this horse stuck in the mud was accurate and yet a gross understatement at the same time. This horse wasn't just stuck in the mud; it was stuck in five or six feet of mud, possibly more, depending on the size of the horse.

Someone gave a low whistle through the gap between his front teeth, a sound like a bomb dropping.

John stepped to the edge of the bog and looked down at his boots, chewing silently on the inside of his cheek.

I stepped up beside him, "Wow."

"Yeah. I wasn't expecting to find a horse *this* stuck in the mud. I was hoping to use the hose as a collar and leash and pull the horse out that way, but that's clearly not going to work now. What do you think? That degree in physics giving you any ideas?"

"You have a crane on you?"

"Left it in my other pants."

The horse snorted and rolled its eyes. It was well past struggling, completely winded. I suspected that the sides of the horse, which we couldn't see underneath the mud, were blowing like bellows.

I toed the edge of the mud like someone at the beach testing how cold the water is and watched the rings roll sluggishly away before damping down to nothing just a few feet from me. The fresh rain was stirring it up pretty good. There was about an inch or two of muddy water on the top, with increasing density on the way down to the bottom, where it would have the sucking consistency of glue. I looked at the firefighters around us, most of whom were looking at each other, all of the ideas thus far having been tried and failed in their minds on the walk down. If each guy could provide about two or three hundred pounds of pull, Tank perhaps five hundred, I had almost two tons of pulling power for a horse that couldn't weigh more than fifteen hundred pounds. Could the mud cause twenty five hundred pounds or more of friction? I didn't think so.

"I think we can pull it out."

"You think so, huh?" John seemed skeptical.

"Yeah, I think so."

"And how do we go about doing that?"

"It's going to be dirty, I can guarantee that." I turned away from him. "Bruce!" I called out, "Give me one end of that hose line."

He came over and held an end out to me, which I took, telling him to feed it out as I went but to keep a hold on the other end.

I looked over the crowd and picked out the tallest guy, who was wearing Milford gear, "Hey, Milford!" I pointed to him.

"Paul," He said pointing to himself.

"Great. Paul, you love animals?"

"They're OK."

"Horses?"

"Sure, why not?"

"OK," I said, stripping off my jacket, "let's get in the mud and save us a horse."

Holding the end of the hose I waded out into the mud. I walked with my toes curled to keep the mud from sucking my boots off my feet. As soon as the level of the mud was deeper than the waistband on my night hitch I could feel it running down the inside against my legs. It became quite a bit deeper very quickly and by the time I was standing by the side of the horse it was high up on my chest. The ground was soft underfoot, but seemed to hold my weight. Still I realized that if I thrashed around a lot the next 911 call was going to be for a firefighter stuck in the mud.

"Come on in, Paul, the water's fine. I need you on the other side."

He didn't look happy about it, but he handed off his jacket and gamely waded in. He stopped and leaned over, "Fuck, I'm losing a boot."

"Curl your toes."

He adjusted his stance, setting his foot back into his boot, and then kept coming, arriving at last on the other side of the horse.

I looked at him over the place where the horse's back was somewhere under the mud. "We've got to get this hose under the horse. I'll push it from my end, and you try to get it on yours."

"Swell."

"Yeah."

I took a breath and pressed my cheek against the mud, blowing bubbles in the layer of muddy water on top, the rain spattering it into my eyes. I tried to feed the brass connector on the end of the hose line underneath the horse's chest just behind the armpits. Do horses have armpits?

When I looked over, Paul was doing about as well as I was, but at least neither of us was drowning.

That idea of course brought to mind the fact that if the horse picked this moment to buck or for some reason rolled over on me, I'd drown in the muck before anyone could get the horse off of me.

"Easy, Chance," I breathed. Do horses even know their own name?

Animal lover that she is, Valerie would have been the first person to tell me to get into the mud and save the horse had she not already gotten into it herself, and yet my desire to find what had happened to Lauren was upsetting to her. It was all right for me to risk my life for an animal, but somehow not for a person? I wondered how Valerie would respond if I pointed out that fundamental disconnect.

I shook my head to clear it of such extraneous thoughts and concentrated on getting the hose in place and getting back to solid land as quickly as possible. I reached. I scrabbled. I took a deep breath, closed one eye, and submerged half my face.

I was just becoming convinced that we couldn't do it when

I felt Paul's fingers bump against mine and then he took the hose coupling from me and pulled the hose through. When he had enough slack he threw the end up onto the shore. The guys on the shore adjusted the hose so the horse was in the middle, and then distributed themselves evenly on each end.

"OK, guys," John said "let's give it pull, but go easy."

As they leaned into it, I thought at first that the horse wasn't going to move – guys groaned and slipped to their knees or fell on their asses on the shore, finding very little traction – then he started to. He bucked once, weakly, and I stepped back about as much as the mud would allow. They kept pulling, and the horse kept moving. When it was knee deep in mud, or what I think is a horse's knee, they stopped pulling and the horse walked out the rest of the way under its own steam, Sara grabbing the reins before it could trot off.

"Oh, Chance. It's OK boy. It's OK now." She murmured in the horse's ear as she stroked mud from its neck and side. "Thank you all," she said, and started leading the horse up the trail back to the road.

"Little help here," Paul called, and a couple of firefighters reached out to pull us both in. Paul lost one of his boots and even the sock on that foot. Unless someone in Dunboro took up archeology, they were going to be in that bog forever.

We made our way back to the truck, my feet squishing in my boots, the mud sliding against my legs with every step like my pants were filled with slugs. Ick.

We caught up with Sara about halfway back, she and the horse moving at a very slow walk.

"Is he going to be OK?" I asked.

"I don't know. His blood pressure could spike and he could

have a stroke. He could go off his feed and get colicky. He could get a cold. I'll put him in a heated stall tonight with some classical music and warmed oats and see how he is doing in the morning."

Classical music? A heated barn? Warmed oats? How did horses survive until humans came along to take care of them?

"Best of luck," I said, and walked ahead of her.

The one good thing about the rain was that it was washing the mud off of me.

Back at the trucks hands were shaken all around and the other crews got into their trucks and left. Paul, not wanting to get mud in their truck, stripped off his bunker gear and threw it into their upper hose bed. That seems like a good idea to me, but when I stripped mine off I found the pants underneath just as muddy. I put my clean but wet jacket on the seat and sat on that. John drove the truck back to the station.

"I honestly didn't think that was going to work." He said to me.

"I wasn't sure it would either, but it seemed likely enough to be worth trying."

"Glad we did."

"Yeah, I'm glad we did too."

Sixteen

I'd been thinking about the four driver's licenses off and on for a week, carrying the Xerox sheet around in my pocket and pulling it out every so often to look at it. The paper was deeply creased and a little stained, but I wasn't really getting anywhere.

Google, which is probably very useful in the hands of a trained crimefighter like, say, Batman, to me returned thousands of pieces of data that I had no means of sorting. Finding the proverbial needle in the haystack sounded easy by comparison, because at least a needle is very clearly different. I felt as though I was looking for one particular piece of hay.

A search by name and state turned up thousands of hits. Who knew that so many people have the same name? Out of curiosity I Googled 'Jack Fallon NH' and that returned a shade over 5,000 hits. A bunch of those were newspaper articles about me solving Patricia's murder last year, me in the hospital and me getting out of the hospital, but beyond those were listings for other Jack Fallons in New Hampshire. There were so many of us! Maybe I should host a party.

Sifting through the various Laurens, Leslies, Lillians and Lorraines proved impossible. I wasn't even sure what I was looking for. Very few of the Google results came with photographs, and none of them looked anything like the Lauren/Leslie/etc from the driver's licenses. Then again, I don't look all that much like my own driver's license picture, so maybe that proved nothing.

The lack of measurable progress was maddening.

As a hobby I started dabbling in meteorology. I bought one of those miniature weather stations mounted on a lacquered pine board – barometer, windspeed indicator, and dew point – and I hung a rain gauge outside. I set up my computer to download Doppler radar images every hour from the National Weather Service. All of that data was automatically dumped into my own weather models as well as a mathematical picture of the structural integrity of Baxter's Dam.

Unhappily there I was making progress.

The National Weather Service and I were in complete agreement that the current weather system had stalled overhead. The rain wasn't going anywhere in the foreseeable future. The dam, however, very well might be. The Fire Chief was hoping I could come up with some way to keep that from happening. I wasn't sure that one existed short of a metric ton of hydrostatic cement, and maybe not even then.

I was seated at the kitchen counter with my laptop and all these papers spread out in front of me while I sipped tea from a Lake Winnipesaukee mug. The tea was a gunpowder green variety imported by a local store in Brookline one town to the south. I watched as the weather pattern on the laptop screen circled pointlessly, much like myself, and then was surprised to find that I had idly doodled a loose structural layout for an ark on the back of a page of flow field numbers.

As I considered the sketch, then added a truss line to improve the lateral stress relief, Valerie came in and poured a cup of hot water, selecting a green jasmine for herself. She sat wearily on the stool next to mine. Though far too soon for her to take a pregnancy test, I was certain that she somehow knew from some depths as yet unplumbed by medical science that we had again failed.

"You OK?" I asked.

She shrugged, unwilling to put into words what we were both thinking, that something was the matter with one or both of us. I couldn't imagine that two healthy adults could literally have sex until it hurt and not get a pregnancy out of it.

"What are you up to?"

"Just poking around."

She turned the sheet of driver's licenses toward herself with an index finger. "This is the woman you're looking for? The one from the car?"

I nodded.

"So these are, what? Aliases she's used in the past?"

"That's my theory, but I can't seem to find out anything about her under any of those names."

She leaned her head down close to the page, her hair forming a curtain between us as she studied each picture carefully. "What would you do if you could?"

"Talk to people who know her." I said to her hair, "She was afraid of someone. Someone in her past may know who or why."

She looked up at me, one eye peering through a break in the curtain. "Someone in her past may be the person she was afraid of," she said pointedly.

I knew where this discussion would go and so said nothing.

"You know how I feel about you getting involved in this."

"I do, but this is something I need to do."

She considered this for a moment, no doubt rehashing old arguments. When she opened her mouth to speak I felt that I could practically say her response in two-part harmony alongside her but she surprised me. She swept her hair aside and stared directly into my eyes. "I know who she is."

"What? Who?"

She tapped a maroon-painted fingernail against the New York license of Lillian Wainwright. "Her. I know her."

"Who is she? How do you know her?"

She tilted her head to one side. "Here's the deal," she said, "I'll tell you on two conditions."

I could tell from the way that she said it that I wasn't going to like either of them, but hesitantly nodded for her to continue anyway.

"I want us to go to a fertility clinic."

I practically choked on my tea. What about my health? What about our marital problems? We'd have to be nuts to add a child to this equation.

On the other hand I felt that my health was improving, and underneath our present difficulties I believed we still loved each other, deeply. We would provide a stable home filled with that love, my amateur snooping seeming like such a small thing in comparison.

We could have a child. How could that possibly be a bad thing? Also, part of me was genuinely concerned for our health. If there was some medical reason for our lack of success I wanted to know what it was.

Her eyes carefully watched mine. They danced left and right, focusing first on one eye, then the other.

"OK," I said simply.

Her shoulders slumped as she relaxed the tension she had been holding.

She took a deep breath, her shoulders climbing again. Somehow the second condition was, at least in her mind, equally important, and I couldn't imagine what it was.

"Two, if I tell you who she is," she paused, and then continued in a rush, "wherever you go, wherever your investigation takes you, you take me with you."

I blinked, stunned, completely off balance.

It was a perfectly reasonable request on her part and in a way one I was surprised that she hadn't asked before. I also hated it. Though I didn't see most of my poking around as intrinsically dangerous, there was the very real possibility that someone had been murdered, and the person who killed them wouldn't appreciate me looking into it. It could be very nearly fatal as I had already proven, and I didn't want her exposed to that.

She was shaking her head. "Damn it, Jack, I'm not going to do it. While you're out doing whatever I'm not going through my day like nothing is the matter only to get a call from some cop or a hospital-" she choked up a little, then cleared her throat and continued, "a hospital telling me that you're in the emergency room or the morgue. I did that, Jack. I did that, and I'm not going to do it again."

I considered briefly trying to do an end run around her. The fact that somehow she knew Lillian Wainwright was in itself a clue that I hadn't had before. It was just a question of figuring out how. If I could answer the how, I could find her myself.

Even as I thought about it however I realized that I still didn't know where to look. Did Valerie know her as in she had perhaps seen her on the news or read about her somewhere, or did she *know her* know her, like maybe she knew her older sister in college?

More importantly, I realized that if I refused her deal and went ahead on my own that it would be a catastrophic blow to our marriage, maybe one from which we would not recover. Waiting at home, waiting for the worst was both intolerable and unacceptable. It was patently unfair in her mind, and mine as well if I were being honest with myself.

There was of course a third option – to just forget about it. Let time pass. Maybe Lauren would show up, or maybe her body would. Bobby or some other police department would deal with it. Or maybe nothing would happen and Lauren's fate would slide into the past as an unsolved mystery.

As I considered my options I thought that was the path Valerie was hoping that I would choose. She wanted my investigation to stop and without her information it very likely would. She would find some other way to get us into a fertility clinic in the future. That choice was in a way tempting to me as well. I had little desire to end up in the hospital again, and even if Lauren herself had not met a violent end, there was undoubtedly something very illegal going on around her that could be risky to uncover.

But then as I thought about the look on Lauren's face, the fear in her eyes, and recalled how she had fled, becoming a smudge that faded into the rainy night, I knew that I couldn't do that. No one should feel that way, running as she did consumed with a feeling that no one could or would help her. And she likely had parents somewhere that had no more idea of where she was or what had happened to her than I did, perhaps much less. They shouldn't go to bed every night with that uncertainty, that hole, in their lives.

"Deal," I said quietly.

Valerie paused, and then held out her hand. We shook on it formally, very businesslike, devoid of emotion.

She left the room and returned a moment later with her purse. Valerie has perhaps a dozen purses in different colors and sizes, from a glittering little sequined bag that can hold, maybe, a tube of lip gloss and a little folded cash, to the one that she returned with now. It was big and black, a utilitarian square with handles that very well might be refused by some airlines as too large for a carry on. She dropped it on one of the stools and reached inside, disappearing up to her elbows, and retrieved a magazine that she put on the counter in front of me.

It was one of those celebrity gossip rags, glossy pages filled with pictures of people I never muster the stamina to care about. I noted the date, about three years old, June 2001, and wondered if Valerie had been doing a little investigating on her own or if she had possibly come upon such an old issue at random. On the cover was what was probably a copy of a picture of Tom Cruise and Nicole Kidman at their wedding. The photo had been torn in half, the tear separating them. It promised "Exclusive never before revealed details of their divorce inside!" in twenty-four point yellow gothic print.

"You think she's Nicole Kidman?"

Valerie gave me her patented eye roll.

"Tom Cruise?" I ventured.

She spun the magazine so it faced her and flipped through the pages rapidly in clumps, then slowed as she reached her destination. She stopped and spun it back to face me again.

The headline on the page read "Cupid's Notes" and featured a chubby cartoony baby at the top with wings and a bow and arrow. The border was red and pink ribbons with little red puffy hearts like clouds. The page was divided into quarters, each containing a small picture of a happy couple and quick blurb about them.

The one in the lower right showed a man named Joseph Ambrose. He was young, in his early twenties, and incredibly good looking – natural healthy skin tone, straight white teeth, an artistic flip of thick dark hair, and clear blue eyes. Wearing an excellently tailored charcoal suit with a white shirt and a modernistic multicolored tie, he was identified as the son of a man who owns a huge nationwide hotel chain, dozens of brands, thousands of locations.

The woman next to him was identified as his fiancé, Lillian Wainwright.

Her face was flushed and her smile was so wide that it squinched up her face and made it difficult in the small picture to tell the color of her eyes. She wore a pale yellow dress with a beaded bodice that sparkled in the camera flash.

They were photographed coming out of somewhere, an ornately etched glass and brass door closing behind them.

It was impossible to compare the woman in the picture to the pale, half-drowned creature caught only momentarily in the unsteady beam of my flashlight. None of the driver's license photos showed much of a smile, and the woman in the magazine had a lot of hair elaborately sculpted into loops and whorls. I looked back and forth from one picture to another. This might have been easier if I took the magazine down to the police station and looked at the licenses themselves rather than a copy.

I tried to concentrate on her nose, the spacing of her eyes, the shape of her face, the things that don't change much when someone smiles.

Maybe... Just maybe...

After a little while I looked up at Valerie. "I think you might be right."

She frowned and looked away, unhappy with my confirmation.

Seventeen

The fertility guy that Valerie had made an appointment with was named Dr. Andrew Layton and he had an office in one of the annex buildings to St. Joseph's Hospital in Nashua. As we were passing from the waiting room into his office the day after we made our deal, I found myself wondering how she had gotten an appointment so quickly. It occurred to me that maybe she had been planning this for some time and had just been looking for a way to get me in here, and that was why she had researched Lillian Wainwright and found the old magazine article. Devious, my wife is.

Dr. Layton came around his desk to shake our hands, mine with a hearty businessman's pump and Valerie's with a kindly squeeze and release. He certainly looked the part of the doctor with salt and pepper gray hair and a white lab coat. It was a long coat, hanging to mid-shin, with only the lower leg of dark slacks and dark shoes visible underneath. I felt as though I had seen him somewhere, perhaps on television peddling hemorrhoid cream.

Once we were all seated around his desk he got started. His opening questions were delivered in a soothing monotone. How long have we been trying to have a child? Do we have any health problems? High blood pressure? Diabetes? Is there any stress at work or home? Valerie answered no to that question, which felt a little like a lie to me.

"There can be many reasons why a couple may have difficulty conceiving a child, many of which are easily treatable, without surgery. Problems with acidity or low motility, such as boxers or briefs?" He asked turning to me.

"Boxers." I replied.

"Good, good." He nodded, and then addressed both of us. "Surprisingly often the problem is technique related."

"Technique related?" I asked, not quite sure where he was going with this.

"Yes. Sometimes the couple is having sex incorrectly."

Valerie and I looked at each other. It felt all right to us. And besides, who can possibly have sex incorrectly in this day and age when twenty minutes of watching music videos on MTV practically gives you step by step instructions?

"I don't think we have that problem," Valerie said.

He held his hands up in mock surrender, "I know. I know. You're probably doing everything just fine. But we can save ourselves a lot of time and embarrassment by getting that possibility out of the way."

He then proceeded to launch into an incredibly detailed and graphic description of sex. He had simple cartoonish drawings and far less cartoonish anatomical plates and many, many full-color photographs in all their glory. He might have been right about saving a lot of time, but he was completely off base on the embarrassment issue. His talk would have made Mr. Sulinski, my high school health teacher, blush.

While he spoke I came up with many clever zingers such as 'You want me to put my *what* in her *where*?' and 'I'm not clear on which one of us is supposed to be tied to the bed.' I wisely kept them to myself partly because I suspected that they were nothing he hadn't heard before from other men trying to get out of this office with some fragment of their masculinity intact and partly because I thought that Valerie would probably punch me in the kidney.

The good news for us was that it appeared that we knew how to use our various parts correctly.

Leaning back in his chair, his legs crossed at the ankles, he moved onto a discussion of ovulation, menstruation, masturbation, and post-coital positioning for maximum probability of impregnation. When did a Ph.D. become a requirement for having a child?

As he went on however it became readily apparent that all of his ideas were things that Valerie had previously hit on in her own research and that we had already tried. She told him as much.

He shrugged and spread his hands in a these-things-take-time kind of gesture, which he emphasized by saying "These things take time, but it does seem to me that you're trying all of the right things. I think Mrs. Fallon that I'd like to perform a pelvic exam and take some swabs. And Mr. Fallon, I'd like a sperm sample. Agreed?"

We nodded. Was refusal really an option?

An assistant led us to separate rooms. I was left alone with a small plastic jar with a screw top and a pile of pornographic magazines. Joy. Still, it had to be better than what Valerie was going through. I completed the task as quickly as humanly possible, which for me was about ninety seconds flat, and then passed the jar off to the woman who had shown me to the room. I think she was a little surprised at my speed.

I knew that Valerie's examination would take time, and while she was occupied I had another appointment to keep.

As I crossed the pedestrian bridge back to the hospital proper I realized that Valerie had gone behind my back by making an appointment with Layton, and here I was going behind her back. What the hell kind of a marriage were we running here?

The Department of Public Health had its offices in the basement of St. Joes, and its undisputed lord and master was Dr. David Frick, who had been probing the prostates of firefighters and cops since the Nixon administration. He answered my knock on his office door with a gruff "Enter," which I did, squinting slightly in the haze of smoke from the cigar clamped between his fleshy lips. He apparently came from the do-as-I-say-not-as-I-do school of medicine.

I marveled at that cigar, realizing that this could well be the last room in any state building in the entire country where smoking was still tolerated; such was the absolute nature of his power. It was entirely possible that he could, with the stroke of a pen, remove even the sitting governor from office by having him declared medically unfit to serve.

I was hoping that he would clear me for duty at the fire department.

Fat, gravity, and time had conspired to give him the appearance of a person made of wax, slightly melted, all his features softened and subtly blended. He was looking exceptionally melted today, his heavy eyebrows sagging over his eyes reducing them to narrow slits, the end of his nose curling down even with his upper lip. "Wadda you want?" He asked as I came in.

"I'm Jack Fallon. I called earlier about my reinstatement to the fire department." I removed the medical clearance form from my pocket and unfolded it, and then held it out to him.

He leaned forward and took it, then settled back in his chair with a motion that was strangely reminiscent of a wave rolling onto a beach and then receding. Watching him work the cigar in his mouth as he read, I recalled that someone had mentioned to me that he had started his career as an obstetrician. I pictured him in the delivery room with that cigar, perhaps blowing smoke rings at the baby.

"Fallon. I remember now. Trapped in that house fire in Dunboro. You weren't breathing when they pulled you out."

"Yes sir, that's me."

"Spent some time in a coma."

I wasn't sure if that was a question and so said nothing. My own memories of that period were a little sketchy, seeming to involve something as unlikely as a badminton game with God.

"You feeling OK?"

"Yeah, I'm good."

"The burn on your neck healing alright?"

"Fine." I pulled the collar of my shirt open and turned my head so he could see the three-inch line of twisted and puckered skin, my souvenir of the house fire.

He drummed his fingertips on the desktop and chewed his

cigar thoughtfully. "Seems to me you had something else going on, some kind of fainting spells?"

I was impressed. This guy must have five thousand public servants in his realm, probably a thousand of them firefighters, yet he could pull the minutia of my case from his mind. Maybe his seniority was well deserved.

"They were more like dizzy spells or periods of weakness."

"Uh-huh. You have one recently?"

"No sir."

"When was your last one?"

Six days ago while I was in the shower, and five days before that while standing in the rain at Baxter's Crossing watching Lauren drive the Porsche into the water, but I wasn't going to tell him that. I could take care of myself, and as I had shown last week with the horse, the fire department needed me.

"I'm not even sure. It's been at least a month."

He removed the cigar from his mouth and narrowed his eyes at me, to the extent that was possible, "A month, huh?"

"Longer I think."

He waited, wondering perhaps if I would break down under his squinty eagle-eyed scrutiny. I didn't.

He plugged the cigar back into his mouth. "OK." He took a pen from the desktop and signed at the bottom of the form before sliding it back across the desk to me. His fingers remained on the paper, pinning it to the desktop when I tried to take it. "No joke, Fallon. You came as close to being killed on duty as any firefighter in New Hampshire in the last ten years. Anything doesn't feel right, you get your ass to a doctor."

"Will do."

I grabbed the paper and hightailed it out of there before he changed his mind. On the way back across the connecting bridge I checked out his signature on the paper before I folded it and put it back in my pocket. It was the barest squiggle of pen, something that easily could have been made by a seismometer during a mild tremor.

I returned to Layton's waiting room, grabbed a magazine at random, and managed to take a seat just as Valerie came out of the exam room. I chucked the magazine aside and stood to greet her, noticing as I did so that it was a copy of Teen Beat. If I was lucky she hadn't noticed that.

"Mission accomplished?" she asked.

"Mission accomplished." I confirmed. Then, after a pause, added casually, "I fantasized about a young Michelle Pfeiffer, if you're curious."

"I'm not, but thanks for sharing."

"You?" I asked.

"Daniel Craig."

"Phoo!" I made a noise like I had been hit in the stomach. It figured that she picked the sexiest man alive. Valerie smiled to herself.

"Home?" she inquired.

"Home. We've got an investigation to get rolling."

Her smile turned to a frown in an instant.

Eighteen

"You got a minute?" I asked Bobby as I walked into the police station.

He was seated at his desk with stacks of fan-folded paper piled on the blotter around and in front of him. It was the old style stuff, eighteen inches wide with green and white striping that used to come out of tractor feed printers. I was surprised there remained printers of that style in functional use, and more surprised still that some paper company somewhere continued to find it profitable to churn that format out. He had one fanfold open in front of him and was making marks on the page with a highlighter.

"Sure," he said. He pushed the stack of paper that he had been working on away from him. With the other stacks on his desk it would only move about an inch so it was a symbolic gesture at best. "Just working the overtime budget. With the hours my guys have been putting in, the town selectmen are going to throw a fit."

"The fire department is probably in the same boat."

"Probably," he agreed. He capped the highlighter and held onto it, twirling it between the fingers of one hand, his elbows resting in what little open space there was on the desktop. "What's on your mind?"

"Check this out." I handed him the magazine.

He took it, looked at the cover, looked at the back, then looked at the front again. "So?"

"Page eighty-two."

He tipped back in his chair and flipped though the magazine, then stopped on the page. He glanced at it for a moment. "You can pull off the skirt and the top, but the heels will make you look cheap."

"How's that?" I leaned across the desk and took the magazine from him. Page eighty-two showed "Fun fashions for summer" - a slim denim skirt with a scoop neck floral top and high-heeled ankle boots being worn by Jennifer Garner. I flipped backwards several pages, then forward a few, finally finding the Cupid's Notes on page eighty-six. So much for my smooth delivery. I handed it back to him.

I saw his eyes check the four quadrants, pausing only for a second at the lower right. "Lillian Wainwright was the name on the New York driver's license."

"Yeah," I replied, though he had more or less said it to himself.

"You think it's the same woman?"

"Don't you?"

He gave the picture another second. "I don't know. You going to compare this," he pointed to the page, "to a crummy driver's license photo?"

"I think it looks like her."

"You do, huh?" he tipped his head at me skeptically.

"And she has the same name."

"Lots of women do."

"And Valerie thinks she looks like her too."

That sat him up in his chair a little straighter. "She does, huh?"

Why he trusted Valerie's opinion more than mine I chose not to dwell upon.

"What does," he paused and checked the magazine, "Joseph Ambrose have to say about it?"

"Don't know. Haven't asked him yet."

"Well," he said, "let's give it a go." He reached forward and picked up the handset off his phone.

"I'm going to see him in New York."

He stopped with the handset halfway to his head, and put it back slowly on the phone base. "You are?"

"Yup."

"What makes you think he's going to talk to you?"

"I don't know that he will, but if the woman from the car was his fiancé in the picture, now three years later his wife for all I know, I can't imagine he won't want to talk to me, and I'd like to see his face when he does."

"And what if she's not?"

"Then he'll probably tell me that and then tell me to get the hell out of his office."

He checked my logic in his mind, "What if he's not even in New York?"

"That's where the corporate headquarters is."

"The magazine says his family owns something like two thousand hotels. He could be in Maine or Hawaii or practically anywhere in between."

This admittedly was the one piece of my plan that was pretty shaky.

OK, to be honest the whole thing was shaky, but this piece was the shakiest.

He could be absolutely anywhere, and therefore just from a sheer probability standpoint the odds were low that he would be in New York. He could also, despite my reasoning, refuse to see me. But I was afraid that if I called him he would just demand to hear the whole story over the phone, and as I had told Bobby, I wanted to see his face as I talked to him.

Finding out that your fiancé has vanished while living in New Hampshire under an assumed name, with still other names stashed away in a safe, has got to be a shock no poker face can mask. Unless of course you know something about her aliases or were responsible for her vanishing.

I also didn't see it as so far a trip as not to be worth the risk. The absolutely worst thing that could happen from my point of view was that he wouldn't see us, Valerie and I would spend a weekend in Manhattan away from the rain, maybe take in a Broadway show, see some old friends, have a few nice meals, and come back.

"It will probably be a waste of a trip."

"Maybe," I replied.

"What does Valerie have to say about it?"

"She's going with me."

That gave him a moment's pause. I watched as he considered and rejected any number of responses. He knew of her dislike for my snooping, but didn't really see it as his place to delve more deeply into what kind of new twist this represented in our relationship. He finally leaned forward and handed the magazine back to me. "Good luck. Let me know if you find anything."

"Will do."

He picked up the fanfold he had been working on and uncapped his highlighter. When I didn't leave he asked "Anything else?"

"Well, there is one more thing."

"Shoot."

"Could you watch Tonk while we're gone? The kennel we usually use is flooded out."

"I'm really kind of busy here." He gestured vaguely at the piles of paperwork around him.

"He'll be no work at all," I promised quickly. "Just throw him a cup of kibble twice a day and give him a few walks, and except for his snoring you probably won't even know he's here."

He hesitated, the dog lover in him tipping the scales. "How long are you going to be gone?"

"Couple of days. Just through the weekend, tops."

"OK, I'll take him."

"Great. I'll go get him. He's in the car now. We'll bring you bagels when we come back."

"Outstanding." He said, without enthusiasm.

Nineteen

We were cruising along the New York Thruway about thirty miles from Manhattan, making great time in an easy mix of typical weekday midmorning traffic. We played slide and shuffle with light commercial vehicles, big eighteen wheelers, delivery vans, passenger cars, and the occasional limousine. Ours was the only pickup truck in sight.

The weather pattern that had been drenching New Hampshire for weeks didn't extend this far south and west, and we had emerged from under the cloud cover somewhere back in Connecticut. Overhead the clouds had turned from threatening charcoal to friendlier gray to genuine white, the continuous sheet tearing into ragged streamers, progressively narrower and more diffuse, until nothing remained. Above the thruway now the skies were clear, the sun was shining, and all was right in the world.

Or not.

I had been hoping to use the drive time to talk about us and our thoughts about the fertility testing, but Valerie wasn't interested. She was sitting as far away from me as possible without going to the trouble of stepping outside and clinging to the truck's running board. Pressed right up against the passenger door, she emitted a *leave me alone* vibe so powerful that it shimmered the air between us. She wouldn't have been more clearly isolated had she surrounded herself with Jersey barriers and traffic cones.

The drive down from New Hampshire thus far had been one hell of an uncomfortable, quiet ride.

Perhaps quiet is the wrong word. As if her body language wasn't sufficiently projecting her mood, she was also literally broadcasting her feelings with her iPod, playing a selection of music over the auxiliary jack input to the truck sound system that she thought I wouldn't like. She played country oldies – Johnny Cash, Patsy Cline, and Hank Williams. Songs full of betrayal and loneliness, lying and cheating.

Whatever symbolism I cared to read into the themes of her chosen music aside, for the most part I was OK with her selections, having surreptitiously developed a taste for classic country western songs while working in my woodshop. Something about Patsy Cline goes well with the banshee shriek of a surface planer. If she started playing Carrie Underwood we'd have problems.

The scary part for me was that after all the years of our marriage and the time we had lived together and dated before that, going on ten years all added up, I suddenly found that I didn't know how to talk to my wife. The foundation of our marriage was crumbling, shaken by forces I could feel as clearly as an earthquake but which I couldn't figure out how to dissipate.

I'm not clueless; I was aware that I could defuse the situation, make everything right, by turning the truck around and heading back to New Hampshire. Had I done so, Valerie's mood would have improved even as the sky above us darkened, comfortable in her perception I would somehow be safer by ending my investigation into what had had happened to Lauren on that rain-soaked night. Giving her the benefit of the doubt, it was possible I would have been safer, but I would also have been sacrificing some nascent facet of my personality that I was still exploring and trying to define.

That I myself didn't understand it made it all the more difficult to try and explain it to her, but I desperately wanted to find some way to bridge the growing chasm between us. I mulled it over, looking for an approach that might help me make some headway with her, while Loretta Lynn sang the final stanza of *Coal Miner's Daughter*.

I glanced at Valerie out of the corner of my eye. She was conspicuously ignoring me, her head down as she gave her iPod way more attention than it merited. She worked the wheel and Conway Twitty began singing about living fast and dying young. More symbolism?

I took a deep breath and opened my mouth. I didn't know what would fall out but wanted to throw some words into the gap, see what conversation might come of it. Almost anything had to be better than the wrenching silence.

Without looking up from the iPod Valerie cut me off. "Don't, OK?" She said tiredly, "Just don't."

Twenty

We hit New York City in time for brunch, which we had in the Manhattan Diner, one of our old haunts from back when we lived in the city. The place hadn't changed at all, right down to the neon sign in the front window on which the 'M' flickered intermittently and the 'e' was out entirely. It felt strange being here in this restaurant after all these years. Maybe like Eddy Money said, you can't go back.

I had called ahead and Steve, my best friend from graduate school at Columbia, was there with his latest Asian girlfriend whose name was Teri with one 'r' and an 'i'. That's how she introduced herself as she daintily held out one delicate hand, palm down as though she expected me to kiss the back: Teri with one 'r' and an 'i'. I took her hand in an awkward uphanded grasp and shook it gently. She probably also put a little heart over the 'i' in place of the dot when she wrote it down.

We could see that, along with the diner, Steve's taste in women hadn't changed.

Steve was a big boisterous guy about six foot four with lots of dark hair and a big head and a big loud laugh, and as long as I've known him all he dated were ethereal Asian women. Even among that diminutive club, it was possible that Teri was the smallest. She was literally two feet shorter and a hundred and fifty pounds lighter than he was, and my mind boggled at the complications such a coupling must present.

It was a nice day in Manhattan, and the Manhattanites were out and about in force. The diner was comfortably full, noisy busy with the rattle and clatter of dishes and flatware and that particular New York City patois consisting of a dozen or so languages including Greek, Russian, Spanish, English, Italian, and a little German. I recalled a newspaper vendor down near our apartment on West 79th who spoke Erdu and Latin fluently, though not a great deal of English. Even though I had studied Latin for several years in college, asking for a New York Times in that language was a challenge. It just wasn't something the Romans had run up against.

"How are you feeling, Jack?" Steve asked between shovelfuls of a lumberjack breakfast: eggs, pancakes, sausage links, bacon, hash browns, with a side of oatmeal, and not a tree to fell in sight.

"Good. Really good."

Steve knew all about the whole thing with the killer and my time in the hospital, though I had never told him about the dizzy spells. Despite my lies to Dr. Frick, I truly believed that they were becoming less frequent and severe. The most recent one in the shower had lasted less than a minute. Time healed all, I hoped.

"So, what brings you into the city?"

"He didn't tell you?" Valerie said with an underlying purr of barely controlled anger between sips of her too-hot coffee, "He's hoping to find another murderer to finish the job that the first one started."

"Murderer?" Teri asked uncertainly as if she had misheard it.

So I told Steve and Teri about the woman in the car, the driver's licenses in the safe, and how maybe she was the same woman engaged to the son of a hotel magnate three years ago under another name.

Teri was so engrossed that she let her four egg white omelet with organic sundried tomatoes and tofu cubes go cold in front of her.

"And the son," Steve asked as he mopped at his plate with a triangle of multigrain toast that he had stolen from Teri, "he's got an office in midtown?"

"Fifth Avenue in the forties."

"Does he know you're coming?"

"Nope."

"What if he won't see you?"

"We'll burn that bridge when we come to it. But it's a pretty good story, right?" I looked at Teri who gave me a nod, "And I think he's going to want to hear it."

"Were they married?" Teri asked.

"I couldn't find a marriage certificate in New York and that whole system is online. Maybe they got married in another state, or out of the country, or maybe I just missed it. I also didn't see any mention of a big marital splash in the society pages, and I'm pretty sure that the Ambrose family would get some coverage. In any case, I'll ask him when I see him."

For the first time I pondered what it meant if they were married. Why would his wife be living in New Hampshire, hanging out with Garrison West under a fake name?

Maybe I was looking at the mother of all bad divorces. A guy with resources like Joseph Ambrose could make your life pretty awful if he wanted to, and maybe he was the person she was running from. But if that were true where was she now, and where did the other identities fit in?

"It's all so mysterious," Teri said as she pushed away her half-eaten plate and folded her napkin over the top of it, "How do you catch a murderer? This guy you're going to see later today, how do you know what questions to ask?"

I shrugged. "I like to go in and kind of feel things out and let the questions come as a surprise."

She looked confused, "A surprise for him?"

"For me," Valerie said, pointing to herself.

I shook my head, "For all of us."

Twenty-One

On the way out of the diner, Valerie bought a plain bagel to go for Tonk. This was something she did out of habit, and she completed the entire purchase on autopilot. It was only after we stepped outside that she realized that Tonk was still in New Hampshire with Bobby. She rolled up the little takeout bag around the bagel and stuffed it into some niche in her purse. Tonk wouldn't care if it was a little stale.

We left Steve and Teri on the sidewalk in front and headed downtown. It was a really beautiful day and our first sighting of the sun in weeks, so despite the fact that it was more than twenty blocks to Ambrose's office we opted to hoof it. Valerie did the window-shopping thing along the way, reminiscing about stores she used to go to when we lived here. I enjoyed the sunshine, recharging my vitamin B cells. Like a large bird of prey I had the urge to spread my wings and warm my feathers in the sun, but figured I would risk clotheslining passersby if I did and so refrained.

Far too soon we reached the address and found ourselves outside a tall art deco building, the facade a checkerboard pattern of brushed steel panels and blued glass. I looked up the face and had a moment of vertigo, then steadied myself and quickly grouped the floors into chunks of ten, estimating the building at a little over fifty stories high. Who knew that hotels are such big business?

The entrance consisted of two oversized brass and glass revolving doors with a single auxiliary access swing door on either side. It was busy this time of day, and it took us several seconds to cue up. We stopped just inside the doorway, which upset the steady flow of foot traffic for a moment before it reached a new equilibrium around us.

The lobby had a high ceiling with ornate gilded moldings and a floor of polished marble that made the space echo sharply with the clacking of hard-soled and high-heeled shoes. Everyone seemed to know where they were going except for us, and I didn't see a building directory anywhere on the walls.

A woman wearing one of those headphone and microphone combos sat to one side behind a short arc of desktop. She seemed like as good a place to start as any. Valerie and I headed in that direction, cutting sideways across the stream of people like swimmers escaping from a riptide.

As we approached, the wood of her desk caught my eye. With a broad, deep grain and a warm color somewhere between walnut and cherry, it was like nothing I had ever put my hands on. South African maybe? With a grain that broad perhaps it had come out of the rainforest of Brazil or Guatemala. It was a stunning piece.

"Hello," I said when we reached the desk, "We're here to

see Joseph Ambrose."

Without even looking up from the computer screen mounted in the surface of the desk in front of her she asked, "Do you have an appointment?"

"No."

"Mr. Ambrose is very busy today," she said, giving us the standard gatekeeper brush off. "May I ask what this is in reference to?"

"Lillian Wainwright." I considered for a moment adding "his fiancé" but realized that I didn't know what their relationship was now and so left well enough alone.

She looked up at us, making eye contact for the first time. I couldn't read the reaction on her face, but there was definitely something there, wariness maybe, but genuine surprise as well. This was not a topic she had expected to encounter under any circumstances this morning, and I wondered again what the relationship between Joseph Ambrose and Lillian Wainwright was like today.

"Excuse me?" She asked.

"Lillian Wainwright. We'd like to see Joseph Ambrose about Lillian Wainwright."

"And you are?"

"I'm Jack Fallon, and this is my wife Valerie. I'm a volunteer firefighter from Dunboro, New Hampshire."

"New Hampshire," she repeated, then shook her head slightly. We had somehow cracked opened a doorway into her personal Twilight Zone. "If you'll wait for just a moment, please."

She typed on her computer keyboard, and it must have been linked into the phone system because a moment later she was talking into the mic. It had a good spatial filter and even three feet away I couldn't hear a single word of the conversation. She took a long time, and when she finally returned her attention to us all she said was "Someone will be down for you shortly."

Valerie and I stepped away from the desk to wait, finding a spot out of the press of people.

"Did you see the look on her face?" Valerie asked. "I thought she was going to have a heart attack. What do you think that was about?"

"I don't know," I answered, but given Valerie's earlier resistance to this whole trip I was pleasantly surprised to see her taking an interest.

Someone did come for us shortly. He was young and clean cut in dark slacks with a blue jacket that looked vaguely uniformish. There was a plastic rectangle clipped to the jacket that read 'Security' that I assume identified his function, but I suppose could also have been his last name. It would have been ironic if it were both. He took the handoff of us from the woman behind the desk with his eyes.

"Come with me, please."

He led us to the elevator banks and once inside used a keycard from his jacket pocket to activate the button for the top floor, which I noticed was fifty-five.

In a sense, I understand why management tends to select offices on the top floor. Not only is the view better, but it places you both literally and figuratively on top of the company. But I can also see several disadvantages to the top floors. For one, there's the extra time spent on the elevators, often with people who have no sense of smell concerning the magnitude of their usage of perfume and cologne. For another, should a fire break out, the last place you want to be is on the top floor, unless of course you've got an escape helicopter stashed on the roof.

The elevator dinged and the doors slid open revealing a waiting room a hundred times more ornate than the lobby. The walls were a flawlessly selected shade of cream offset by exactly the precise amount of indirect lighting to make them glow warmly. Abstract paintings in dark, soothing colors adorned the walls. Two dark wooden sofas covered in royal blue fabric with gold brocade formed a conversation nook around a black lacquered table inset with onyx, jade, and mother of pearl. Heavy oak double doors led off to the left, right, and straight ahead. Another man, identically dressed, sat at a desk to the right of the elevator doors. His badge also read 'Security.' Brothers?

The man from the elevator stayed inside while we exited, and we were again handed off. The man from behind the desk stood and came around it, showing us to the doors on the right. Our feet whispered across a thick Persian rug showing scenes of men with spears and bows and arrows on horseback hunting stag and antelope.

I found that I was more than a little bit nervous. I thought that whatever Ambrose's motivations for agreeing to see us that I was only going to get one crack at this. If I failed to get answers from him, was I really going to go to California or Texas to chase down Lauren's other identities? Would Valerie tolerate it if I did?

The guard stepped ahead of us, opened both doors with a sweeping motion, and gestured us inside.

Twenty-Two

The office we were ushered into was an Architectural Digest photo spread. A couple of hundred square feet of burgundy carpeting led up to a big mahogany desk where Joseph Ambrose and another man sat in front of a wall of tall windows with a panoramic view of uptown. Between the entrance to the office where Valerie and I stood and the desk was a long oval conference table and chairs made of black-lacquered wood with a vaguely Asian vibe.

The double doors behind us closed on whisper-quiet hinges and we were alone for our walk down the length of the office. We skirted the conference table, passing with the table on our left and glass-enclosed mahogany shelving covering the wall to our right. The shelving was filled with what looked like Samurai bric-a-brac: a sword in a display holder, a metal statue of a warrior on the back of a horse rearing up on its hind legs, small daggers, gutting hooks, pieces of pottery and painted tiles.

Pinpoint lights illuminated the displays like we were in a museum; all that was missing were the little description cards. At the end of the wall unit, just about level with the desk, stood a mannequin wearing full samurai battle dress, a tunic of burnished brass and lacquered steel disks with red leather straps, and a scary snarling face mask.

It took us thirty seconds to cross the length of the room – this place could maybe use a golf cart or a Segway – and Joseph Ambrose remained seated behind the desk the entire time, tipped back almost insolently in his big burgundy leather chair with little brass studs, watching us as we walked. The experience was much like that of a supplicant coming to request a favor from the king, which I suspect was very likely the aura he was attempting to achieve.

To his right the older gentleman had a narrow hawk's face, his gray hair parted left, wearing a dark conservative suit and muted red tie. I didn't think he was the elder Ambrose. I got a quick impression that he was playing the role of Sir John Gielgud in *Arthur*, something like Ambrose's man Friday. I had nothing to base that on, but it felt correct.

When we arrived at the other side of the desk Ambrose didn't seem to be in any hurry to do the introductions. There were two chairs on our side of the desk but he didn't offer us a seat. He was cold and dismissive, remaining slouched in his chair. He had a pen held between the thumbs and forefingers of both hands, which he flexed as though he was trying to snap it in half. It was an expensive pen with a polished rosewood barrel accented by bright bands of gold.

The silence stretched and that made Valerie uncomfortable. I could feel her discomfort shivering the air nervously around her. This would normally have had her talking nearly non-stop, but we had agreed coming in that this was my show, and I was depending on her to let me control the dialog.

I on the other hand was perfectly willing to wait all day for him to open the conversation; we didn't have anywhere else to be, and besides I'm pretty much immune to feeling nervous during awkward social moments. Valerie would say that I'm oblivious. Po-tay-to. Po-tah-to.

Past Ambrose's chair I could see the green tufts of trees in Central Park and various landmark buildings. To kill time I tested my architectural acumen by naming as many of them as I could. The Empire State Building, the Chrysler building, Pan Am, Citibank tower, the Flatiron.

I was doing pretty well when, finally, he spoke, "You told Stephanie that this was about Lillian."

"I'm Jack Fallon, and this is my wife Valerie. I'm a firefighter from Dunboro, New Hampshire."

"Uh-huh." He twirled the blunt end of the pen in the air for me to cut out what he thought of as small talk and get to the point.

The other man had yet to move. Except for the fact that he was breathing and his dark eyes followed us carefully, he could have been another mannequin.

So I told them about the flooding, the car in the water, the woman in the night. I told the story slowly and with plenty of detail, trying to read Ambrose's face as he heard me tell it. Was it a complete mystery to him, or did he know something more? Did he know that his fiancé Lillian Wainwright had been living in New Hampshire under the name Lauren Wilkes?

"I don't understand," he interrupted, as I was diverging into a fascinating sidebar on the possible future collapse of Baxter's Dam, "What does this have to do with Lillian?"

He had a great poker face. Either that or he didn't know anything.

I decided to connect the dots for him, so I continued with the discovery of the driver's licenses and the article in the gossip rag. I handed over the xeroxed sheet with the four licenses on it.

Ambrose looked at it for a moment and then skimmed it onto the desktop in front of the other man. He didn't move to pick it up. His eyes tipped down perhaps a whole millimeter and then back up at us, though it was difficult to be certain that there had been even that much motion.

They seemed less interested in the story than Teri did an hour ago, which made absolutely no sense to me. I mean, it was about his fiancé, right?

"And you're a police officer from Durham?" Ambrose asked.

"A volunteer firefighter from Dunboro. Dunboro, New Hampshire."

He nodded as if that somehow confirmed something for him. He leaned forward in his chair, snatched the paper from in front of the other man, and slid it with exaggerated precision over to our side of the desk using a single fingertip of his right hand. "That's not Lillian."

"But she looks just like her." Valerie said.

He turned his attention to her, his gaze suddenly hostile,

withering. "Nevertheless, that's not her." He emphasized.

Valerie held her ground under that gaze, which I gave her credit for, "How can you be so sure?"

"Because Lillian was killed on nine eleven."

Twenty-Three

Dead? Of all the things he could have told us, that she was dead hadn't even been on my radar. My brain got stuck on the idea, like a chicken bone caught in my throat. She was dead.

If Lillian Wainwright had died on nine eleven, then who was the woman in New Hampshire? I realized that I didn't have a clue.

I couldn't see as there was anything left for us to say. Ambrose and the other man sat on their side of the desk while we shuffled our feet on ours. Then I collected the paper, mumbled an "I'm sorry to have taken your time," and Valerie and I were off on our trek back across the burgundy expanse.

We opened the double doors on our own and closed them behind us. The man behind the desk in the anteroom conspicuously ignored us as we pressed the button and waited for the elevator to arrive.

On the elevator riding down to street level Valerie said "I really thought it was her."

"So did I." I said, swallowing, trying to get my ears to adjust to the change in pressure as we went down, "I wouldn't have come all this way if I hadn't." My ears finally popped. "Interesting that he said she was killed."

"How so?"

I shrugged. "I don't know. You and I didn't know anyone who died on nine eleven."

"Jackie's husband," she replied.

Jackie was the friend of a friend. Her husband had been a paramedic on the forty-ish floor of the North Tower when it collapsed.

"I mean directly."

"Oh."

"Anyway, I think most people say died."

"Jackie says that her husband was murdered." She pointed out.

"Right. Anyway, Ambrose said she was killed."

"What does that mean?"

"Probably nothing. I'm just ruminating."

The elevator slowed to a stop and the doors slid open and a woman got on. She wore a gray skirt that stopped just below the knee and a cream silk blouse. A narrow black belt matched her sensible black mid-heel shoes. She radiated a certain sexuality and it reminded me of when Valerie and I used to play boss and secretary, back before we started having sex exclusively for reproductive purposes. I sighed at the memory.

The doors closed and the elevator continued down.

"I didn't like him," Valerie leaned over and whispered.

"I didn't either," I whispered back, "but you have to see it from his point of view. We showed up with this crazy story about his dead fiancé vanishing into the rain in New Hampshire." I admitted to myself that in that light his behavior had been incredibly well restrained. Likely far more than I would have been in his place.

I let her chew on that while we rode the rest of the way in silence. The elevator dumped us into the lobby and we crossed to the big doors leading to the street. On the way by the front desk I noticed that Stephanie was on the phone. She gave me a look as we went by. That was probably Ambrose on the other end, and clearly we'd worn out our welcome.

Outside we both squinted and blinked in the sunshine. Valerie dug around in her purse and came up with a pair of sunglasses which she put on.

She looked at me, and I could see myself mirrored in the lenses. "What if she didn't?" She asked.

"Didn't what?"

"Get killed on nine eleven. What if she faked it?"

I had heard some rumors of that kind of thing going on after nine eleven. The heat of the fire and the forces of the buildings coming down had left even modern forensic science with little or nothing to go on, bones pulverized to dust and DNA baked by the fires to an amino acid slag. To this day many remains had yet to be identified and several of the missing were assumed dead without so much as a single bone fragment to substantiate it.

Urban legends had cropped up that some people had supposedly used nine eleven as an opportunity to leave their lives behind; let themselves be declared dead and get away from whatever problems they may have had. To my knowledge, none of them had ever been proven true.

"Why?" I asked. "For what purpose? To avoid marrying an incredibly wealthy guy?"

"He's also very good looking," she smiled at me.

"I'm so glad you noticed."

"I still don't like him," she added, almost as an afterthought.

"Nice recovery."

I was blinded momentarily by a flash of sunlight reflected off a passing taxicab and re-reflected off of Valerie's sunglasses, the optical equivalent of a multi-cushion shot in pool, and I turned away. When my vision cleared I was looking down the length of 5th Avenue. The day was flawless and the typical haze over the city had lifted, which made me feel as if I could see all the way to Ground Zero. "So she faked her own death to avoid marrying a rich and good looking guy?" I said it aloud, just to see where this train of through would take us. "Wouldn't it have been easier to just walk away? Just stop returning his phone calls?"

"Maybe he doesn't handle rejection well. Maybe he

threatened her."

"That still doesn't explain the other driver's licenses."

She didn't have an answer for that one and we stood there with the flow of Manhattan foot traffic parting around us like a river past two stones. She shook her head slowly, but not as a denial. It was more like she was trying to physically shake off her confusion.

"Where to now?" she asked.

I paused, trying to think of where this information about Lillian Wainwright might lead us. "The library. You've given me an idea that I want to check out."

Twenty-Four

I love libraries. I always have. From the seventies-era split level in my hometown in northern New Hampshire, to the tiny converted church that is the Dunboro Public Library, to the somewhat antiseptic engineering library at Columbia University. They all have books in common, in orderly rows and columns of shelving. You can stand in the stacks and feel them thickening the air around you, waiting like patient messengers for you to pick them up and hear what they have to say.

I could spend all day sifting through one. Searching, sorting, looking for some specific piece of information amongst the mountains available. It's part of how I got through graduate school. Students today are missing something by simply asking Google to find whatever it is they are looking for. In a library, the journey is half the experience.

We settled into a quiet corner of the Dewitt Wallace

Periodical Room on the first floor of the lion-flanked monument that is the New York Public Library branch at 42nd and 5th. Valerie's thrill of the hunt doesn't run as deeply as mine, but she did manage to find some magazines to occupy herself as I dug in.

The first piece of information that I was looking for didn't take all that long to find. It was a small blurb in the New York Times Metro Section dated October 13, 2001, which discussed the discovery of personal effects belonging to one Lillian Wainwright, fiancé of Joseph Ambrose, who is the son of Emerson Ambrose, a national hotel magnate.

I think that was the first time I had seen the elder Ambrose's first name. Emerson Ambrose. What could it possibly have been like to be a child saddled with such a grandiose name?

The article went on to describe a partially burned appointment book with her name on the inside cover as well as a damaged monogrammed pocketbook that was identified as a gift from Joseph Ambrose.

I found a second piece written almost a full year later stating that the nine eleven forensic team had concluded the identification process as far as current science allowed. The condition of the rest of the remains was too poor to work with, though they would be carefully stored for any future advancements in forensics that may occur. The article ended with a list of those who had been definitively identified and those who were suspected lost but had not. Lillian was among the had nots.

An hour later I looked away from the screen to find Valerie flipping through a copy of Modern Bride. Maybe she was trying to figure out why Lillian Wainwright would fake her own death to avoid a wedding. Either that or she just liked looking at pictures of elaborate place settings and expensive cake designs.

Valerie must have sensed some difference in my mood because she looked up from the magazine she was reading, holding her place with her index finger poked between the pages. "Getting anywhere?"

"I don't know. I found an article that said they found Lillian Wainwright's purse on the pile, no identified body, no driver's license."

"So she could be alive."

I made a face. "Seems farfetched, doesn't it?"

"You tell me; you're the one who got us here. What are you looking for now?"

"I'll let you know when I find it."

The next piece I sought took a good deal longer to locate. Most of the back issues of the California newspapers were still on microfilm, and as the afternoon wore on the piles of the little spools grew and became unsteady, threatening to topple over and roll around on the floor. I didn't have much of a starting point. The address on the driver's license was in Los Angeles, but I struck out there. I proceeded to San Francisco, Santa Barbara, and Palm Springs. I pulled newspapers from Monterey, Malibu, Fresno, and Palo Alto.

Valerie went out onto 5th Avenue and returned, smuggling two hot dogs with everything and bottles of soda in her purse. We ate surreptitiously among the stacks of microfilm spools.

I was tired and my eyes were hot and grainy and I was thinking of giving it up and heading for a real dinner, the hot dog having served only to get my appetite rolling. Maybe I'd come back tomorrow. Maybe I'd give it up and just drive back to New Hampshire. Then I got a hit in a newspaper called the Napa Valley Daily Register. I read it over twice before convincing myself that it meant what I thought it meant, as crazy as it seemed.

"What did you find?" Valerie asked me as she picked pieces of onion off of the hot dog wrapper and popped them in her mouth.

"Maybe something, maybe nothing. How do you feel about a trip to Napa Valley?"

Twenty-Five

"California?" Valerie asked.

I nodded.

"You want to go to California?" she asked again, a raw edge in her voice.

I nodded again. She had already asked more or less this same question in half a dozen different ways. I knew that she wasn't being dense or purposefully obtuse, but she was trying to understand my motivations, trying to make clear to me how unhappy she was with that decision. There was a world of difference between an overnight trip to New York and a sojourn to Napa Valley, about three thousand miles worth, and it was likely to test the bonds of our marriage to the breaking point.

"California," Valerie said again, less like a question and probably more to herself than to me.

I nodded again anyway, then reached forward and took an individually-wrapped saltine out of the basket on the table. I unwrapped it noisily and popped the whole thing in my mouth. As I chewed, it achieved the consistency of tile grout on my tongue.

We were seated at a booth in a restaurant near the public library called Diner King, the sign outside lettered in an old-English font heavy on flair. Inside it looked like most diners: suspended acoustic ceiling tiles, a long counter running down one side, and a line of narrow booths against the opposing wall. The red vinyl seating was worn, but not to the point that duct tape was needed to hold it together. It wasn't a five star establishment, but diner competition in Manhattan was fierce, and consequently they were all, ambiance aside, pretty good. Darwin rapidly winnowed out the bad ones.

When I had been a graduate student, I had found a certain comfort in the fact that you could walk into any diner in the five boroughs and get more or less the same uniformly pleasant food. Staple meals, like chicken parmesan or turkey club sandwiches, were virtually indistinguishable from place to place. It is, I mused, likely some of the appeal of a chain like McDonalds where, Phoenix, Arizona or Bozeman, Montana or Caribou, Maine, you were guaranteed to get the same exact crappy Big Mac every time. Many people find comfort in predictability, even if the status quo sucks. Becoming a firefighter had for the most part separated me from that herd. As time went by, I found I was more and more thriving on the unexpected, though not without consequences.

Between the two of us we had littered the table with saltine wrappers. When the waitress arrived, she scooped them up in a crinkling double handful. Valerie ordered a salad while I got some funny looks ordering hot dogs off the children's menu, because the one from the street vendor earlier had gotten me in the mood. I would have been perfectly happy eating our whole dinner from a street cart, but Valerie had insisted she wanted something green in her diet. Picky, picky. When the waitress asked me if I wanted something called smiley fries with that, I threw caution to the wind and accepted.

Valerie, California on her mind but uncertain how to begin, took another saltine from the basket. Instead of opening it she just turned it this way and that in her hands. I was willing to let her come to the conversation at her own pace. I picked up the fork from the table and, noticing the tines were bent up a little, straightened them out. Why did all the silverware in diners look like it had just come from a party at Uri Gellar's house?

"You want to go to California," Valerie said for the ninth time by my count. This time, however, was different. Her eyes were on me. She was past the shock and absorption phases and looking for real answers. No simple nod on my part was going to cut it.

"I do. I think it's the only way *we're* going to find any answers." My use of the word 'we're' was intentional, trying to remind her that she was as much a part of this as I was.

Sharper than a pointed stick, Valerie picked right up on it. "When I offered to come along on *your* investigation," her emphasis on the word 'your', "I was honestly hoping you would choose to give it up instead."

As I remembered it, her offer had seemed more than a smidge like blackmail, but instead of prying open that can of worms I answered, "I know."

She sighed. "I'm trying to figure you out, Jack. I really am. But I don't understand why you're doing this. You almost died last year looking for Patricia Woods' killer, and now you want to do it again. This woman, whatever her name is and whatever she was up to, you met for a grand total of fifteen seconds. Is she worth risking your life for?"

Our food arrived and it gave me some time to formulate my response. Smiley fries turned out to be processed potato disks about the size of a fifty cent piece molded with a smiley face and then deep fried. They seemed pleasantly mindless, their jumble of simpleton smiles beaming up at me from one side of the plate. I thought, momentarily, how nice their lives must be, unaware of murder and death and nine eleven. Oh, to be reincarnated as a potato.

I am, on the whole, not a particularly introspective man. The depths of my motivations, like those of most people I suspect, go unplumbed. I do things because they feel like the right things to do. The complex arrangement of past events which formed the lodestone for my moral compass, I rarely felt the need to examine. In this instance, however, the event from my past which drove me was absolutely clear, and I was lying to myself and Valerie if I didn't admit it.

"Does the name Sharon Bishop mean anything to you?" I asked.

Valerie wiped away a small dollop of salad dressing from the corner of her mouth with her thumb. "I don't think so. Should it?"

"She was a graduate student in psychology who lived down the hall in the same apartment building I did my first year at Columbia."

"Girlfriend?"

I gave an involuntary laugh through my nose, though there was nothing funny about it. Perhaps, I thought, we never really know why we do certain things, even when we think we do. "No, just a friend." One of the fries seemed to be smiling at me in a particularly mocking manner, so I flipped it over. Naturally the image had been molded onto both sides. "She was the original drama queen. A pattern of poor judgment, an endless chain of bad boyfriends. Her life was a soap opera."

"A psychology major," Valerie noted, pointing out the irony.

"Yeah, well, doctor heal thyself," I commented, then continued my story. "I would be in my apartment ankle deep in quantum electrodynamics homework and she would come in and bemoan that her current boyfriend wanted her to get her labia pierced."

"She wanted to date you," Valerie said with a sly smile.

I frowned without giving her an answer. Steve and I had debated that very point many times, mostly with alcohol involved, after the fact. We had never reached a conclusion. I dipped the offending potato round in ketchup and ground it up with my molars. *Smile about that.* "She came to me one evening and told me that her boyfriend was acting crazy jealous because he had seen her with another guy at some bar. She said that she was a little scared of him, and could she spend the night hanging with me? She'd get pizza and rent a movie, her treat."

"Your first date," she sighed, making big moony eyes at me.

I shook my head. "It never happened. There was a huge storm rolling in, lots of lightening predicted. I had a lab full of delicate electronics that I wanted to get wrapped up and buckled down. Besides, it seemed like more of her same old drama, and I had had more than enough of that. I told her she was on her own."

My mood darkened considerably at the memory and Valerie picked up on it. She put her fork down in her salad and leaned forward. Jack Fallon, master storyteller.

"So what happened?" she asked quietly.

"It took several hours to get the lab packed up. After that I went out and got a bite to eat. I got back to the apartment, I don't know, midnight? It might have been a little later. More or less on a whim I knocked on her door as I went by. There was no answer. I knocked louder and called her name. No answer. Something felt seriously wrong. I pounded on the door, really whaled on it. Nothing. The guy across the hall opened his door to see what the noise was. I told him to call the building superintendent. After some wheedling the super opened her door, and she wasn't inside. I called the police. A graduate student missing for all of five hours didn't merit a blip on their radar. They told me to call back in two days if she was still missing."

All those little smiles looked up at me. I would have thrown the plate through the window if I hadn't been pretty sure it would cause a scene.

"What did you do?"

"I called Steve and we went out and looked for her. Sounds pretty daunting, right: finding one particular person in Manhattan? But we figured given her concerns she wouldn't have gone far from Columbia, and that area is pretty built up. If she had been roughed up and left by her boyfriend somewhere, and I couldn't shake the feeling that was what had happened, there were not very many places that she wouldn't be found quickly. Riverside Park is just a couple of blocks over. Today that park is beautiful; the area completely gentrified. A single mom could wheel a baby carriage through there at midnight unmolested. But back then it was a pit, a collection of cracked asphalt paths and weeds littered with used condoms and discarded hypodermic needles. I don't know how true it was, but it was said that cops wouldn't go into that park after dark unless they were in pairs. Steve and I might have been taking our lives in our hands going into Morningside at 2AM, but it was raining, and I guess criminals don't like to get wet."

My voice started to sound very strange to me. I received some kind of echo of it back, as if I were listening to someone else narrate the story using my voice.

"We found her. It didn't even take very long considering the size of the park. She had been beaten to death and dumped just off a path in some bushes." I remembered, actually found it extraordinarily difficult to forget, the way the rain washed over the pale skin of her face, pooled in her open eyes, and ran down her cheeks like tears.

"She had asked for my help and I had been too fucking wrapped up trying to save a few thousand dollars in electronics to give it, and she had been murdered. If I can do anything to stop that from happening again, no matter what the risks or the cost, I will." I curled my left hand into a tight fist on the tabletop, the knuckles white from the effort.

Valerie reached across and cupped her hand over mine. "Alright, Jack," she said, massaging my fist, trying to get it to unlock. "We'll go to California."

Twenty-Six

"You're going where?" Bobby asked.

"Napa Valley." I had to shout to be heard.

The connection was crap. The phone lines in New Hampshire were damp to the core and the conversation was filled with pops and crackles like someone was crushing a handful of wax paper near the mouthpiece. Alexander Graham Bell had probably had a better connection for the very first phone call.

"Back up a second," Bobby said, "What did Ambrose say?"

"He said that it's not her. That his fiancé died on nine eleven."

"And you think he's lying?"

"No, I believe that he thinks it's the truth."

"So you think he's wrong."

I shook my head even though Bobby couldn't see it. "No. Look, I don't know what I think. I'm going on a hunch here."

"To Napa Valley."

"Yeah. Napa Valley is beautiful this time of year." I said cheerfully.

"Better than New Hampshire, I'll give you that." Bobby muttered. "By the way, I got a chance to check on the address on the New York driver's license. The address is real."

"It is?" I was surprised. I had been so certain that it was fake that I didn't even bother to look it up. "Maybe I should go by her apartment and check it out as long as I'm in New York."

"It's not an apartment."

"It's not?"

"It's a Starbucks. So unless you think a Grande mocha half decaf latte constitutes a clue there's nothing there for you."

I gave myself a point for being right.

"So, what's in Napa Valley?" Bobby asked.

"Leslie Wattley was engaged to marry a dot-com millionaire named Alex Nidal who lives there. She vanished when she fell off a yacht the night of their engagement."

"A yacht?"

"A boat, a big boat. He had rented it in San Francisco."

"I know what a yacht is. You think she's the same woman?"

"She matches the name on the California driver's license."

There was silence except for the hiss and clicks, and then Bobby asked "That's it?"

"Yeah, so far."

"So the woman who disappeared in New Hampshire has a fake driver's license in the same name as a woman who died on nine eleven, only her fiancé says it's not her, and a second fake driver's license in the name of some woman in California who fell off a yacht."

"When you say it like that it does sound a little implausible."

"Implausible? Try crazy." He changed tack. "How many Leslie Wattley's are there in California?"

"I don't know."

"I assure you, there are lots."

I sighed, "Look, I didn't call to ask you to check my logic exactly. I'm wondering if you wouldn't mind keeping Tonk for a few more days."

"Sure, I love the little guy. He rides shotgun in the patrol car, though he does have a habit of hitting the siren controls with his paw."

I chuckled, "That's my boy."

"Let me know if you find anything in Napa Valley."

"Will do."

As I took the phone from my ear and had my thumb over the disconnect button I heard Bobby say, "Wait, one more thing," so I pressed the phone back against my head.

"John wanted me to ask you, just a sec, I have it here somewhere." There was a pause and a shuffling of paper and then he was back, "John says that we got an inch and a half of rain in the last twenty-four hours, and he's wondering where that leaves the dam."

I closed my eyes and tried to visualize the math in my head. I added one and a half inches to the volumetric calculation of the lake, figured out the extra mass of the water, and tried to recall what my models would have to say about it. "I don't have my computer in front of me, but do you want my best guess?"

"Yours more than anyone else's."

"I think there's a thirty percent chance that the dam is already stressed past the failure point."

I heard him sigh what must have been a very loud sigh given the quality of the connection. "I was afraid you were going to say something like that. Have a good time in Napa Valley."

"We'll talk when we get back."

"Safe travels." Bobby replied.

I killed the call.

"How's Tonk?" Valerie asked.

"He's fine. Bobby made him a deputy."

She laughed, "And what does he think of Napa Valley?"

"He thinks I'm a genius."

That earned me a patented eye roll. "Uh-huh."

Twenty-Seven

We caught a flight from JFK to San Francisco, landing in a cloudy but rainless dusk, and then rented a car and headed north and east, likely driving through a bunch of miles we had flown over just an hour ago.

Valerie's Ipod provided our soundtrack, a steady stream of eighties dance hits: bouncy, peppy, and utterly forgettable. Something about the nineteen eighties culture lent itself to music that was inherently shallow, but it filled the time, both then and now.

The rental car passed through acres of grape arbors, reminding me of a trip I had taken across the country with my parents in our station wagon. Lying in the back cargo area as we drove through Kansas, I looked out the long side windows at wheat as far as the eye could see. I recall falling asleep, and waking up several hours later, to the panorama of wheat. My father joked that it was the same wheat field that I had fallen asleep in, hundreds of miles across. Maybe he hadn't been joking.

Napa Valley felt like that.

Far from the roadway, frequently at the top of a small rise, were the wineries themselves. They were massive structures, designed like Italian villas or English Tudor estates or French mansions or modern structures of steel and glass. While there was no unifying architectural theme between them, the thing that they most clearly had in common was that there was lots and lots of money to be made in winemaking, though occasional foreclosure and for sale signs indicated that it's not foolproof. The grapevines themselves were in neat rows, each vine trimmed and carefully trellised, with fat bunches of grapes covered in glistening beads of water from the irrigation misting nozzles.

Valerie did a little gardening in New Hampshire. It was all we could do to maintain a hundred square feet of tomatoes, cucumbers, and summer squash. I couldn't imagine the amount of manual labor involved in cultivating a hundred acres of grapes with such precision. Perhaps there are specialized machines that do some of the work.

In a lull in the soundtrack, while Valerie was fiddling with her Ipod, I told her, "I'm glad you're here."

She looked up at me out of the corners of her eyes, most of her attention still on the Ipod. "You are?"

"Yeah. One, I like having you around. You're a better conversationalist than the Onstar woman who just keeps asking if I need assistance over and over."

This won me a small smile, one that was almost

microscopic. It might have been a grimace.

"Two, I'm hoping that you're starting to understand why I'm doing this."

She blew out a breath, "Honestly, I'm not."

"But I-"

"Let me finish." She paused to see if I was going to interrupt and then continued, "This is an adrenaline rush for you. You're traveling around and you're talking to people and you're playing Jim Rockford."

"I have better fashion sense."

"Just barely. Anyway, I get that. I also understand that you can't do physics anymore and carpentry and firefighting don't occupy that great big brain of yours, and maybe this does."

I waited to see if there was more, but there didn't seem to be. "That's it?"

"What else is there?"

"Then I guess you don't understand at all."

She turned sideways in her seat, the arbors a green blur behind her head when I glanced in her direction, one leg folded underneath her at the knee. "Then help me."

I thought about how to discuss this with her, hoping to find some new angle that we hadn't hashed over a dozen times before. "Let me try it this way. Do you know why I became a firefighter?"

"Because it's cool and it's fun and you like the guys?"

"It is cool and I like some of the guys," I thought, not adding that some of them hated my guts and the feeling was mutual, a vision of Fiske floating in my mind's eye. "But very little of it is fun or exciting. Most of it is what guys in the military call the four D's – Dull, Dirty, Difficult, and Dangerous. Oh, I know it's not dangerous in the same way that this can be dangerous, driving around Napa Valley aside," I gestured out my window at the passing scenery, "but firefighters get killed in amazingly random ways. Don't kid yourself; it's dangerous."

"Then why do you do it?"

"Because I can. Because it needs to be done. Because of the people. They're losing their homes and their lives and they need someone to help them."

"And that someone is you?"

"Yeah, if I can, that someone is me."

Her eyes tilted down to her lap where her fingers were tracing the lines of her Ipod – the edges of the screen, the curves of the control wheel, the seams of the case.

"Understand?" I asked.

She looked up at me for just an instant, "Let me think about it."

"That's all I can ask."

It was silent for a while except for the hum of the motor and the thrum of the tires as Valerie resettled herself straight in the seat, then she turned on the Ipod and the car filled with the sounds of late-arc Beatles. Music from the period past the bubblegum silliness of *Love Me Do* and the experimental chaos of *The White Album*. Valerie played *Let it Be* and *Hey Jude* and

156

The Long and Winding Road. All songs that showed a melancholy side of the Beatles, as if they knew that internal stresses were building between them that would shortly tear the band apart. They are songs full of the realization that they, at least as a group, wouldn't be on top of the world forever.

It was also some of my favorite music, which I took as a sign that Valerie was coming around. Or maybe I was reading too much into it and she had just wanted to hear some Beatles.

Forty minutes later it was full dark. With the only light provided by the distant buildings, we experienced a level of darkness beyond even what we typically see in Dunboro. The cloud cover had broken up at some point and the sky above lit up with the brilliant pinpoints of Deneb and Vega, the confection sugar dusting of the Milky Way, and a billion stars in between. We were down to the last of the *Let it Be* B sides, the final chords of *Get Back* dying out, as we pulled into the gravel lot of the bed and breakfast that Valerie had reserved while we were standing on the sidewalk in front of the New York Public Library three thousand miles away.

I got out of the car and stretched, cracking my back, then popped the trunk and yanked out our bags. While I did so I took in the enormous stone building, long and squat, with deeply inset windows and heavy timbers poking out from under the eaves. Spotlights mounted on the ground pointed back at the structure illuminating the rough cut gray stone blocks, making the building glow like a ghost in the darkness.

The interior was decorated in a kind of rustic hunting lodge winery motif; heavy, oversized furniture, lots of exposed wood, and a big stone fireplace with a stag's head mounted over it. Against one wall was a tall wine rack loaded with bottles and a stack of oak casks with thick black iron bands. While Valerie checked in I looked at a glass display case containing ancient bungs next to an early-vintage wine press that looked like it could moonlight as a medieval torture device.

It had been a long flight and a lot of driving. We managed to scrounge up a late snack with the help of the hosts and called it an early night. I hardly remember what I ate and didn't even look at our room as we went inside and dropped our luggage. I went to sleep without ever turning on a light.

I dreamt of being harassed and bitten by a pack of small, vicious animals; rats maybe, or weasels, possibly angry ferrets. I tried not to read too much into that.

Twenty-Eight

When I awoke the next morning I had no idea where I was.

I lay on my back in the unfamiliar bed, a regal king-sized affair with thick hand-hewn maple corner posts, and looked at the exposed timber frame ceiling above me. The light in the room was dim, the furniture vague humps and lumps shaped like a nightstand, a chair, an armoire, a wide dresser. The walls looked like heavy plaster in some light color – white or pale yellow or baby blue.

I realized then that Valerie was asleep beside me, so at least wherever we had ended up, we were there together.

I got out of bed and stepped to the window, parting the thick drapes just a crack with my fingers. I was greeted by sunlight slanting across a field of grapes and I remembered where I was.

Valerie stirred behind me and I turned to see her looking at me, lying back in the bed with the blankets pooling around her waist.

"Welcome to Napa Valley," I said.

"Come back to bed," she smiled at me languidly.

I let the drape settle back and did, and it was wonderful. Just two kids rolling around and sweating up some sheets without worrying about positions or timing or thermometers. It was soft and tender and urgent all at once. When we were younger we might have broken that bed, but we're older now and the bed was very, very sturdy. Perhaps if I had brought some power tools.

We leisurely ate an extremely late breakfast, or a slightly early lunch depending on your point of view, at the buffet in a room off the lobby: fruit and yogurt, cottage cheese and coffee.

I had called Alex Nidal prior to booking our flight out of Kennedy. It had seemed like a good idea before we bought plane tickets only to have him refuse to see us or be away on travel; we were talking about a lot more than a quick drive to New York after all. Somewhat to my surprise he had readily agreed to meet us at his vineyard, but not until that evening. We had the bulk of the day to kill ahead of us.

Valerie suggested we play tourist by taking a tour of a winery operation.

We joined a group at the winery right next door and Valerie and I walked hand in hand down the narrow rows between the grapes, a trail of round paving stones demarking the path. The guide discussed soil moisture and acidity and the ways in which various grape stocks are interbred to bring out certain characteristics of each type. My memories of high school biology class are faded but it seemed to me to be pretty much the same thing Mendel had done with pea plants three hundred years ago.

The tour then moved into a prefabricated green building set farther back on the property. There were big polished steel tanks the size of backyard swimming pools for fermenting and oak casks as large as Datsuns for aging. The guide talked about the balance of grape sugars and alcohol, the modulation of temperature and pressure required to create a consistent wine.

The last part of the tour was the tasting. Everyone loves the tasting. Let Valerie loose at a wine tasting and we could have missed our meeting entirely, but I kept an eye on the time and pulled her out of there just in the nick of time.

"Are you OK to drive?" she asked me as we buckled into the rental car.

"I'm good."

"You had a lot to drink."

"I'm fine."

"I thought we were going to miss our meeting until I managed to drag you out of there."

"Do you want to drive?" I asked, shoving the key into the ignition slot.

"Yes."

"Fine."

So we did the Chinese fire drill thing and headed off to our meeting with Valerie driving.

I got my revenge from the passenger seat by setting the Ipod for Pink Floyd.

Twenty-Nine

The Magellan winery was only about twenty minutes from the bed and breakfast. It was a small operation, nestled between two enormous ones, looking no larger than the grounds keeping operations of either. Alex Nidal had named the place after his internet company which had made some chunk of code fundamental to how maps are created and displayed on the web. Mapquest had bought him out seven years ago for one hundred and thirty million dollars.

Valerie piloted the rental car between two pillars made from flattened brown river rocks and up the white gravel driveway. Grape arbors crowded the road closely on both sides. The main house looked more like it belonged in New England than Napa Valley. The design was essentially Adirondack, long and low, with a green metal roof and trim offsetting the dark brown siding. A multitude of high windows across the front warmly reflected the rays of the westering sun.

It was lovely; exactly the kind of place I'd buy if I ever managed to sell the Jack Fallon carpentry business for a hundred and thirty million dollars. Though as I thought about it, that price seemed a little bit steep for a one-man job shop operating out of a modified garage. Perhaps if I added 'dot com' to the name.

Valerie parked the car in a wide turnaround in front of a wooden sign with letters scorched into the surface like a branding which read 'Welcome to the Chart House.'

Mapmaking, Magellan, Chart House – nerd humor. I got it.

Alex Nidal came out the front door and down the steps, opening Valerie's door for her before she had a chance to open it herself.

"Valerie, Jack. Thank you for coming." He greeted us like old friends. "I hope your trip was a pleasant one."

"Fine, thank you, Mr. Nidal." Valerie said as she climbed from the car.

"Please, call me Alex." He met me at the back of the car with a casual, non-competitive handshake.

Alex Nidal looked just like he had on the cover of Time magazine, the issue about Indian entrepreneurs taking Silicon Valley by storm. He had a cap of black hair in a soft wave, a thin face, a narrow nose, and intense black eyes. His jeans were clearly brand new, with an ironing crease on the front of the legs, as was his blue work shirt, which he wore with the sleeves rolled to the elbows. He looked uncomfortable in his clothing, awkwardly trying to emulate what advertising or perhaps some style consultant had told him comfortable should dress like.

"May I offer you a tour?"

"Please," Valerie smiled at him.

He led us past the house to a smaller structure behind it that too looked like it had been lifted here from New England. The exterior was vertical barn board over a timber frame structure, albeit with truss work of a distinctly Californian flavor. The floor inside was crushed stone, but otherwise his place looked like a miniature of the winery we had toured earlier.

He was very enthusiastic about his wine, and Valerie returned his enthusiasm, holding her own in a fairly technical discussion of body and finish, and the pros and cons of infusion with black currant or peach. She must have paid a lot more attention during the earlier tour than I did.

I'm really more about the wine drinking than the wine making, which left me as a kind of conversational third wheel. I was fine with that. Valerie had worn a pair of tight faded jeans and a short fitted denim jacket that accented her shape. I was happy just trailing behind them admiring the view, thinking about this morning, and wondering if maybe our relationship was headed to a better place.

Thirty

The shadows lengthened outside the barn's double doors which were rolled back on their tracks revealing a magnificent view of the sky as it shifted from pink to purple to dusky blue. Valerie and Alex were still at it, kibitzing about the finer points of humidity control during aging, when Alex looked at his watch, something with a big stainless steel face.

"I'd like for you both to stay for dinner," he announced. His housekeeper had prepared a pork loin and mushroom sauce, patti pan squash, and saffron rice, and he assured us, over Valerie's protests, that it was no imposition and that there would be plenty of food.

Inside the house was essentially one big room with a loft at one end that held the bedrooms. The living room, kitchen, and dining room formed a ring around a central fireplace made of the same type of stone as the pillars at the end of the driveway.

Dinner was served at a large butcher block trestle table, the top a splined expanse of southern yellow pine three inches thick that must have weighed two hundred and fifty pounds. He waited for our approval before serving himself and sitting down, uncorking a bottle of his own white.

The cobalt blue bottle appeared to be hand blown, or at the very least manufactured in small quantities, the bubble of the pontil visible on its base. The label was printed on a home ink jet featuring a line portrait of Magellan against a background of an old cartographer's map of the world, one where the globe has been flattened into two dimensions and all the landmasses are elongated and distorted. A careful hand had written the lot and date of the wine into the blanks provided with a thin black felt tip pen. The wine was quite good, and though he didn't at that time have his health department certificate or his vendor license, Alex promised Valerie that he would have a case shipped to our home.

We kept the conversation light during dinner, an unspoken agreement that we would leave the discussion of Leslie and what had happened to her for afterwards.

He told us of his childhood in India, coming to America, and expanding his former company from the corner of his small apartment living room to a company with revenues of seventy-five million dollars before he sold it. Valerie told him about growing up in Kentucky, the mountains, the forests, and how it was nothing at all like the Dukes of Hazard. I told him some of my firefighting stories. He laughed at the funny ones; a big booming laugh that echoed through the immense, open room and sounded like it should have come from a much larger man.

Afterwards, we moved our empty plates to the kitchen and stacked them on the counter where he told us to leave them. In the living room he gave us some variety of Indian tea, a dark blend not unlike some high-octane version of coffee, so stratospheric in caffeine that I probably wouldn't sleep for a week. We settled onto various pieces of a big poofy beige sectional. Valerie pulled her boots off and placed them on the floor, curling her feet under her on the couch as she sipped her tea.

"So," he said, clearly a little disturbed at what lay ahead, "you wanted to talk about Leslie."

"Maybe," I replied, then launched into the story about the woman in the car in New Hampshire, handing him the wrinkled page of driver's licenses at the appropriate time. I added to that the element of Ambrose and Lillian, and his insistence that the woman in the car was not his dead fiancé.

When I was done Alex seemed visibly shaken. He stared at the photocopy for a long time. Finally he responded, "I don't understand."

Valerie leaned forward, her elbows on her thighs, like some kind of yoga position. "Is it possible that Leslie is the woman in New Hampshire?"

"But how could it be? Leslie has died."

Valerie looked to me for how to continue. I recognized that we were in something of an emotional minefield, and she is better at that stuff than I am. Also, she and Alex seemed to have a connection, so I shrugged and let her go forward however she wanted to.

She took some time crafting her approach. I could see it in minute adjustments of her body language as she composed the questions she wanted to ask and then played with the order in which to ask them in her head.

Alex didn't register the subtleties of our married language, and looked from her to me for an answer.

Valerie shifted her position on the couch, setting her teacup on the coffee table. "How did you and Leslie meet?"

It was the perfect approach, and Alex relaxed visibly on less mysterious ground. "The office Christmas party," he smiled at the memory, "nineteen ninety seven."

"She worked for you?"

"No, those parties were huge. That year we had rented the Carnelian Room. You know it? The restaurant at the top of the Bank of America building in San Francisco?" He didn't wait for us to answer. "We had gone public earlier that year. There were employees, friends, families, friends of friends, probably a few crashers, some celebrities. Kevin Bacon was there," he added with a laugh.

What's a couple of hundred people at two hundred bucks a head. Ah, the heady and unrealistic dot com days.

"Do you know who she came with?" Valerie asked, leaning forward, engrossed in the story.

"No, as I said, maybe no one. It was just a party. Did you know that all of this," he twirled his finger in the air, "is because of her?"

Valerie shook her head.

"Wine was her thing first. We came out here, did a Napa Valley tour and visited a friend of mine who owns another winery nearby, on the anniversary of our first date. I loved all of it, and when the time was right I came out and bought in."

"Can you tell us about the night she disappeared?"

He frowned, taking a deep breath through his nose and letting it out, "I had rented the *Cabernet Sauvignon*." He noticed our confusion and clarified, "It's a yacht, one hundred twenty four feet, out of San Francisco." He nodded shyly and continued, "I held a party, told her it was a surprise birthday party for a friend of mine. My friend even agreed to stand in as the fake birthday boy. She had no clue. At midnight a cake was brought out. Everyone sang *Happy Birthday*, but instead of 'happy birthday' they sang 'happy marriage.' I proposed and gave her a ring."

Valerie made an *awww* noise. I had to admit that it was a pretty romantic scheme, but it's not like I had proposed to Valerie at a bowling alley between frames.

"So what happened? When did she fall overboard?"

"No one knows. No one actually saw it happen. We were with a lot of other people on one of the upper decks, looking at the lights of the Golden Gate Bridge, and she excused herself to go to the bathroom. Then sometime later, I'm not honestly sure how long, I realized that she hadn't come back. I looked for her and couldn't find her, and asked people if they had seen her but no one had. I spoke with the captain who made an announcement over the PA system, and the crew members pulled out plans of the boat, broke us into search parties and assigned us to different areas. We looked everywhere, but," he shrugged, a helpless and futile gesture, "when the boat got back to the dock everyone got off and she just wasn't there."

"And the Coast Guard never found her," Valerie said softly.

He shook his head, "They didn't even know where to start looking"

We were all silent then, not sure where the hell this had all been going and not all that pleased with the destination we had found. After a few moments he said, "Please, excuse me." He placed the photocopy he had been holding all this time carefully onto the coffee table. He got up and crossed the room, climbing the stairs and heading for the back of the loft area out of our sight.

Valerie waited until he was gone. "He hasn't gotten over her."

"No, I guess not," I answered quietly.

"So what are you thinking?"

"I don't know," I admitted, running an open palm across the stubble on my cheek. "If Leslie and Lillian and Lauren are all the same person, maybe she's just afraid of commitment."

"But why be so weird about it? Why fake your own death instead of just walking away? Were she and Garrison even engaged?"

"I don't know, but I'll tell you what I do know. She didn't have to fall off the *Cabernet Sauvignon*. She could have just walked off when it got to the dock. Maybe she wore a jacket and a baseball cap so no one recognized her. Or maybe she stayed on the boat and hid until everyone else was gone. They searched for someone incapacitated, not someone hiding."

"But why," she asked again, and I still didn't have an answer for her.

Alex came back then, plodding down the stairs slowly, shuffling across the floor, and taking his seat like an old man. "I'm sorry, this has all been," he struggled, grasping with his hands, trying to find the right word and finally settling for, "a lot."

Valerie unfolded herself from the couch and went around the coffee table to sit next to him. She put a hand on his arm. "Do you think it's possible? Do you think Leslie could be Lauren?"

He leaned forward and picked up the photocopy again, studying each of the four images, moving his head from one to the next. "I think," he began, then stopped and checked the page, then began again, "I think she is." He said this almost to himself, then looked up at us, "But why?"

That was the sixty-four thousand dollar question, and one that none of us had the answer to.

Thirty-One

Alex seemed like he might want to excuse himself again. The realization that maybe his fiancé had decided to fake her own death rather than marry him was a shattering blow, regardless of the fact that it appeared that she had done the same thing again since.

Valerie turned sideways on the couch, "Is there someone we can call? Someone who could be here for you to talk to?"

"No." He looked down at his clasped hands hanging between his knees. Then he looked at her sideways, out of the corners of his eyes, "Do you know what it's like being rich?"

"I haven't had the pleasure."

He turned in his seat to face her, animated, talking with his hands. "Don't get me wrong, it's better to be rich than poor. Believe me, I know; I've been both. But wealth can be very," he paused, "isolating."

I had a sudden insight then. It wasn't a bolt of lightning or anything, but I saw Alex and Garrison as the same in many ways. They were both young, wealthy, and essentially, in all the important ways perhaps, alone. If Ambrose was wrong and Lillian was Lauren, I wondered if he fit that pattern as well.

I realized that Valerie had reached the same conclusion, only with her it was accompanied by the meshing of gears and the rumblings of a large motor, the sounds of the Valerie Fallon matchmaking machine spooling up. He was polite, good looking, well-spoken, and very rich. Among Valerie's single friends the three thousand mile trip to California would seem insignificant. I could imagine Valerie passing his phone number with the same self-assured aura of success as a realtor holding the last multimillion-dollar listing in Beverly Hills.

Alex looked at his watch, "Well, you have a long drive back to your hotel, and I wouldn't want to keep you too late."

I remembered Valerie telling him about where we were staying and he must have known that it was nearby. He was instead telling us that he wanted to be alone.

Valerie wavered internally before relenting, realizing that her desire to provide comfort however well-intentioned would have been an intrusion.

I collected the photocopy from the table, folded it, and put in into my pocket. "You mentioned that a friend of yours owns another winery nearby. Was he on the boat that night?"

He nodded, "He was the one who pretended that it was his birthday party."

"Do you think we could talk to him," I checked my watch,

"if it's not too late? I'd like to ask what he thinks about all of this, get his perspective."

"I'll call him." He pulled out an iPhone from a holster on his belt and dialed. He held it to his head as it rang, turning away when it was answered. "Brian," we heard him say as he went around the fireplace into the kitchen area.

"What are you thinking, Jack?" Valerie asked me.

"Is it just me, or does her disappearing act seem odd?"

"In every way. I don't understand what you're driving at."

"Put yourself in her shoes. You're in this relationship and somehow you're unhappy – you'd have to be or why would you leave? Why pick that moment to go?"

"Maybe it was the proposal that made her unhappy," she countered.

"Maybe, but to try and leave at that exact moment? Off a boat filled with people? And all of them were looking for her. What would she have done if someone had found the closet she was hiding in or whatever?"

Valerie considered this. "So you're saying that her whole plan was to be declared dead, and the party and the boat provided her the opportunity?"

"Is that what I'm saying?" The whole idea was so twisted, but it was also somehow strangely compelling. "Maybe that is what I'm saying."

Valerie just shook her head in bewilderment.

Alex came back from the kitchen with a sheet of paper that he handed to me. "He said that he would talk to you. These are the directions to his place."

I gave them a quick read over. It was actually just a little ways beyond the bed and breakfast, no more than thirty minutes away. "Thank you for your time, Alex."

"And dinner was wonderful," Valerie added.

"No, thank you. If there is anything I can do to help, just call me. I'd really like to hear what you find out."

He led us to the front door and outside, but stopped at the edge of the porch as we went down the three steps and to the car. Valerie still had the keys so she went around to the driver's side.

"I'm curious," he called from the porch, "how are you getting home?"

"We have a flight back to New York in the morning. We'll pick up our car and drive back to New Hampshire from there." I replied as I opened the car door.

"We left our baby at home," Valerie added.

His eyes widened in surprise, "You left your child home alone?"

"Our dog," I told him. "She means our dog, and we have a friend watching him."

"Oh," he nodded. "What airline are you flying?"

I looked to Valerie for this. She had made the reservations while I talked to Bobby on the phone.

"American," she answered.

"No, please. Come back here tomorrow morning and I'll

have a driver take you to my jet."

Valerie was stunned and I had no idea of the etiquette for turning down an offer of a private jet, and so accepted with a simple thank you.

That settled, I was just lowering myself into the car when he called out, "Wait!" he came down the steps to the car. "May I see her driver's license again?"

Without comment I unfolded the paper and handed it to him.

He pulled out the iPhone again and, with the paper held between his hand and the phone, danced his fingers across the screen. It downloaded the page he wanted while he waited, and he used finger gestures to enlarge the screen. He gave a mirthless chuckle.

"What?" Valerie asked from where she stood in the open door on the other side of the car.

"The address on her driver's license," he waved the piece of paper in the air like a flag of surrender, "it's a Starbucks."

Thirty-Two

The home of Alex's friend looked like a big brother to Garrison's house; same California modern architecture, same chaotic roofline, same stone chimneys. It was simply bigger in every direction.

It occurred to me then that everywhere we seemed to go on Lauren's trail we kept finding mansions and wealth.

There were half a dozen luxury cars parked in front of it and lights blazed from many windows. Some kind of small party underway. Scared that even a minor dent in one of the Ferraris or Bentleys or whatever would bankrupt us, I had Valerie park well away from them.

The doorbell rang with the tolling or heavy bells, like we had set off Big Ben, and it was answered by a man in his late twenties. He had a tussle of blonde hair and friendly blue eyes and a sharply-boned stern, almost military, face. Aryan nation meets surfer dude. He was dressed in an Italian-cut dark suit over a cream-colored shirt with no collar.

"You must be Jack and Valerie," he said.

California, the land of the first name basis.

"Yes. And you're Brian?"

"That's what the tag in my underwear said when I put it on this morning. Come on in."

He led us into the entrance hall, through an arch to the right, and down two stairs into the living room. This place really was just like Garrison's place, so much so that I wondered if it were possible that the same architect had designed both of them. This living room however was carefully arranged with matching furniture positioned to create detached conversation clusters that nonetheless worked to tie the whole room together. Instead of the giant television, Brian had hung an enormous canvas that looked like a Jackson Pollack, sprays and slashes of paint in blotches and swirls. I counted seven other couples scattered around the room, the men in hand-tailored suits, the women in designer gowns, as if a red carpet might roll out at any moment.

"We didn't mean to interrupt your party," Valerie said.

"They're just some friends over for a few drinks." He announced to the room, "We'll be back shortly. You know where the wine cellar is."

We passed through, feeling somewhat conspicuous as the other couples appraised us with undisguised curiosity, into a corridor beyond. The flooring in the hallway was something really exotic, a banded wood like bamboo but in a darker color like cherry. I had an urge to get down on my knees and feel the grain.

The third door on the right opened into another living room. At least I thought it was another living room. There were two brown leather couches on the opposite sides of a coffee table and a fireplace in the wall. How many living rooms can one house need?

He closed the door and the silence in the room was absolute, like there was some kind of sound dampening material built into the walls.

"Is there anything I can get you? A glass of wine?"

Valerie laughed, "We've been at wineries all day."

He smiled in return, "Coffee, then?"

"Really, we're fine," I assured him, "but I would like to talk to you about Leslie."

He walked past us and sat on one of the couches, right on the edge of the seat, gesturing for us to sit on the other one which we did. "Alex said you thought that she was alive. Where is she?"

"We don't know where she is. But a woman named Lauren Wilkes who disappeared after a car accident in New Hampshire had driver's licenses in other names, one of which was Leslie Wattley."

He leaned back suddenly into the couch as if blown away by the information. "Oh, wow. That is trippy. Does Alex think it's the same woman?"

Instead of answering his question I unfolded the page of driver's licenses and handed it to him, "What do you think?"

He sat up and took the paper from me, and looked carefully

at the photos. "Who are these other two women?"

"I think they're all the same woman. The licenses were in a safe in the house rented by Lauren Wilkes. Lillian Wainwright is maybe the name she used when she was engaged to marry a man in New York."

"He believes she was killed on nine eleven," Valerie completed the thought for me.

"And Loraine Watson?" He asked.

"We don't know anything about her yet."

He shook his head slowly. "It was almost five years ago. I can't tell from these pictures." He handed the page back to me.

I decided to try another angle. "Can you tell us about that night, the night of the party? I'd like to see if your memory can add anything to what Alex told us."

He got up from the couch and walked to the windows, but it was dark outside so he was looking at nothing at all, just a black square of glass. He turned back and sat with his butt on the narrow windowsill, his hands resting on the sill. "There's not much to tell. She just vanished. We looked. The crew of the boat looked. The Coast Guard looked. And the next day the police looked. Everyone concluded that she fell overboard."

"But they never found her body," Valerie noted.

"They also never found those guys who escaped from Alcatraz either. The water is cold, and deep, and there are sharks. And the current; the Coast Guard thought she might wash up in Canada."

"What do you remember about the party?" I asked.

"Oh," he blew out his breath, "it was a big party. How often does a guy like Alex get engaged? So he went big. The boat, great food, a lot of alcohol; I provided the wine." He gestured at the room, the winery, around him. "The setup was that it was a surprise birthday party for me, but it was a surprise engagement party for her. A surprise within a surprise. She had no clue. She freaked."

"What do you mean by that?" Valerie asked.

"The look on her face when he proposed. Like her eyes were going to fly out of her head."

"But was she happy? Was it what she wanted?"

"She said yes."

Valerie gave him a look, the one she had that made a man realize he had just said something stupid.

He came back, slumped on the couch. "I don't know. I wasn't in her head."

"But you didn't think so. It wasn't what she wanted."

"Look, Alex for all his money is a pretty quiet, shy guy. He doesn't want to be on the front page. He'd rather be home watching a movie than at a red carpet premiere for one. Understand?"

"That's what you meant when you said 'a guy like Alex?'" I asked.

He nodded. "But with Leslie he wanted to be a different person. He would go out to clubs. He would snag invitations to glitzy events. They were at the Oscars in 1998. He told me that Harrison Ford was at the next table."

"I don't understand," Valerie interrupted, "what does this have to do with Leslie being happy about the proposal?"

"She and Alex got all hooked up in that lifestyle, galas, concerts, big crowds, but I think she wanted the quiet Alex, the one she started dating at first. When she looked around at this giant party the pressure to say yes must have been incredible, but it wasn't what she wanted at all."

"So she faked her own death?" I couldn't help keep the skepticism out of my voice.

"I don't know anything about that," he replied, "but do you know what I thought when I first heard that she was missing? The very first thing that popped into my head?"

Valerie and I both shook our heads.

"I thought that she had jumped off that boat and swam for her life."

Thirty-Three

Private jets, let me tell you, not to state the obvious, but they're nice. Not only do you have more or less one on one service from the flight crew and real silverware with your meal, but you don't have to worry about being sandwiched in the middle seat between two people with the bodily dimensions and hygiene of Sumo wrestlers straight off the mat. As an added bonus the seats are bigger, they never lose your luggage, and you get to avoid the whole pointless Kabuki theater production that is modern airport security.

After landing at JFK we picked up my truck and headed for home. The first raindrops, fat and lazy and as big as dimes, spiraled out of the sky and hit the windshield in Connecticut, and by the time we were back in New Hampshire they had been joined by friends to produce a steady, raw downpour. We stopped at the police station to pick up Tonk and update Bobby.

While Tonk danced around Valerie's feet and mashed his face against her shins in some incomprehensible display of doggie affection, I told Bobby about Ambrose and Lillian, Alex and Leslie, and her possible pattern of engaging and then abandoning wealthy men.

"But why?" Bobby asked.

"Don't know. Popular question, though. Of course, Ambrose insisted that Lillian was dead."

"You think he's wrong?"

I shook my head in bewilderment. "I don't know what to think. If Ambrose's Lillian is dead, then I've got another Lillian Wainwright out there somewhere that I haven't even identified yet. And if he's wrong and Lillian and Leslie are both Lauren, then..." I let the thought trail off. I didn't know what that meant either.

"I did get a chance to look up the address on Lauren's New Hampshire license." Bobby said.

"Don't tell me, let me guess." I tented my fingers on my forehead like a fortuneteller for a dramatic pause. "It's a Starbucks."

"Yeah, in Amherst."

"Her address in California was a Starbucks too," I informed Bobby.

"She must really love their coffee to live there," Valerie joked while scratching Tonk behind his ear so that one of his hind legs rapped against the floor.

"Alex looked up the address on the Texas driver's license before we left this morning." I added.

"A Starbucks," Bobby guessed.

"Uh-uh. A private residence way out in the boonies. So far off the grid even Google Earth doesn't have a picture."

"Who owns it?" He asked.

"He's working on that and will let us know when he finds something."

The room was silent except for the sound of Tonk's foot as we considered what it all might mean. I hoped the fact that this last residence was something of a mystery itself was significant, because it was the last driver's license and lead we had left. It was also the first driver's license chronologically, at which time Lauren then Lorraine would have been about nineteen, if the dates on the licenses were to be believed, for whatever that was worth.

Bobby's cell phone rang and he answered it.

While he talked I looked at the map on the wall behind his desk. There were a lot more pink-highlighted roads on it, a lot more roads out, and plenty of blue as well. It had turned the town into something of a maze, and I played a game with myself trying to draw routes between the fire department and other locations.

After he folded up his phone and returned it to his pocket he grabbed a couple of markers and made two more blue lines and one more yellow one on the map. I still hadn't managed to figure out his whole color scheme. I supposed I could have just asked him, but what would be the fun in that?

"You're using cell phones?" I commented.

"The repeater on Tomkin's Hill went down. Cell phones

still work, though there are big dead spots, and the radios are out over most of the town."

"Excellent," I said dryly.

"When do you want to go out there," Valerie asked me.

She meant the address in Texas. "A couple of days. I want to see what Alex can turn up. I also want to talk to Garrison, do a little research on Lorraine Wattley formerly of Texas, and maybe take another shot at Ambrose." As I considered that 'to do' list it sounded like a very ambitious couple of days, so I reconsidered, "Maybe a week."

She nodded, not thrilled but expecting nothing less. I didn't know what she had to complain about; no one had tried to kill us, and she gotten to ride on a private jet.

Valerie snapped a lead onto Tonk's collar and we were all ready to go when the horn on the top of the fire station sounded.

"I'm going to take this," I told her with a quick peck on the lips, "I'll see you at home."

Thirty-Four

Surprisingly I wasn't the first guy to reach the station house. With the high volume of calls we had been receiving some of the guys had taken to divvying up the day into unofficial shifts.

When I got there a truck was already idling on the apron with Tom behind the wheel and Tank in the back.

"Jack, long time no see," Tank said when I climbed in with my gear. He rapped on the back of the driver's headrest, "Hey, Tom, Jack's back here."

"Welcome back, Jack," Tom half turned in his seat, "you've missed a heck of a lot of calls."

"I can imagine," I replied. "What have we got?"

Tom's face darkened, "Car off the road into the water. Family's still inside. As soon as we have an officer we're out of here." He revved the big diesel engine in neutral to emphasize his point.

The officer's door opened and Roland Fiske got in. He scanned the rear compartment to let him know who he had on his crew. His eyes locked up on mine and I thought about getting out just as surely as he thought about telling me to get out, but a family was in the water and we silently agreed to put our mutual animosity on the back burner. He turned straight in his seat and said a single word to Tom: "Go."

Tom stomped his foot to the floor and the big truck spun the four rear wheels on the rain-slick pavement before grabbing hold and pressing us all back into our seats. He did a power slide out onto Route 13, the siren shivering droplets of water from the leaves on the trees near the road.

I was fumbling with my gear like a rookie as the truck accelerated into the straightaway.

"What have you been up to, Jack?" Tank asked as he pulled the Stokes suit, a full-body coverall made of buoyant, reinforced rubber, out of its bag and unrolled it.

"Same old, same old." I paused, then added as casually as I could manage, "I flew on a private jet."

He did a double take, "Seriously?"

"Uh-huh."

"Nice?"

"Hell yeah."

I was suddenly thrown against the back of the officer's seat as the truck's brakes locked up. I managed to get myself turned around and took most of the impact on my side. I heard "Steer to the left! Steer to the left!" from Fiske and "Whoa! Whoa! Whoa" from Tom, as the truck came to a sudden and shuddering stop. Between the front seats out the windshield I saw that the hillside had slid onto the roadway, a mix of small boulders, trees, and dirt that formed a barrier six feet high or more from one shoulder to other.

"Go back," Fiske said, "take Milborne!"

Tom started to back up the truck to make a three-point turn.

"Stop!" I shouted.

Tom banged on the brakes, thinking from my shout that he was about to hit something. "What?" he said with no small amount of panic in his voice, as the truck skidded to a stop diagonally across the road.

"Milborne's closed."

"Where?" Fiske turned on me angrily. Talk about killing the messenger.

I tried to visualize the map on the wall in the police department, but I hadn't spent all that long looking at it. It took a moment to dredge it up from the depths. "Near Addison." I closed my eyes and zoomed in on that area in my mind. "Between Addison and Fletcher."

"Bullshit." Fiske snarled, "I drove that road not an hour ago. Tom, go."

"Call the PD," I said, "It's on their map."

Tank pulled out his cell phone, which looked small in his big hand, and dialed. This earned him a black look from Fiske that he either didn't notice or chose to ignore.

Tom had the truck turned around and was headed towards Milborne when Tank closed his phone. He leaned forward and tapped Tom on the shoulder, "Jack's right. That road's out."

"Crap," he said dejectedly and eased off the accelerator.

The lights and siren were still going, but our speed wasn't more than a leisurely fifteen miles an hour.

189

"Where to, Jack? How do we get there?" Tom asked

"Um, hold on." I zoomed the map back out, but found when I started to concentrate on it that big pieces of the picture were missing. I simply hadn't looked at it long enough.

"For fuck's sake," Fiske said as he pulled the road book off of the dashboard and tore into it angrily.

I was trying to play the game that I had played back at the police department, but without the map in front of me it was hard. I had a can't-get-there-from-here moment, but then thought that maybe I saw a way, but it was long and not pretty. "We've got to go around the lake, come at it from the south."

Tom nodded and slowed the truck for another three-point turn.

"Call Brookline," Fiske told Tank because his phone was still in his hand, "they can get a truck there faster by Old Milford Road."

Tank started dialing.

With the truck turned around Tom headed down Baxter's Crossing and the long way around the east side of the lake.

Tank closed the phone. "Brookline already has two trucks out on mutual aid, one to Mason and one to Pepperell. They'll roll a truck now, but it's going to have a short crew and little equipment."

The mood in the truck darkened considerably. Brookline, with only a couple of guys and lacking equipment, would likely be unable to do much and we were maybe, if we didn't hit another blocked or washed out road, ten minutes out. If the car were actually submerged, we would be too late. The only hope for that family was if the car was only in the water, not under it, or if they managed to get out on their own or with help from bystanders.

There was none of the usual banter between us as we got ready. I helped Tank struggle into the Stokes suit. One size fits all rarely has someone like Tank in mind.

"You're on Tank's safety line, Fallon." Fiske said.

Of course I was on the safety line. Tank was in the suit and there was only the two of us back here, but I understood what was on Fiske's mind. In a sense we were over prepared, with too much time on our hands before we could get to the scene and do our job, and we were all conscious of the fact that it was likely time that we didn't have, that the family didn't have. We went over the steps to take when we arrived again and again though we already knew them by heart, because the alternative was staring off into space and thinking about that car filling up with water.

We were doubly damned because, while we knew the Brookline unit would reach the scene in just a few minutes, we had no way to get any feedback from them because all the radio repeaters were down.

So we waited, tensely, and Tom drove.

Tank and I were both hanging between the seats, trying to get as early a look at the situation as possible. The Brookline truck, their utility vehicle, was pulled over to the side of the road. Two firefighters stood in front of it just staring out at the water. We couldn't see a car.

Tank was out the door before the truck came to a complete stop. He slid, then regained his balance and ran to the Brookline crew.

"Where is it?" He shouted, as if he wanted to grab them and shake them.

"You tell us. There are the tire tracks." One of them answered, pointing at the ground where the thick mud had preserved the record of the car's passage into the water. "But there's no sign of the car. We would have gone in, but all our suits are out with other trucks."

"It must be completely underwater," I said, locking a safety rope onto the back of Tank's suit with a carabineer. "Tank, see if you can find it."

Tank started where the tracks ended and gamely waded out, swimming on his back when it got too deep to stand.

"Try to your right," Fiske said from the shore beside me.

The Brookline guys took the other suit from the back of our truck. One of them put it on and the other got on their own safety line. They fanned out to the left.

It was the worst sort of duty because we knew that it was completely hopeless. Though we had been trained never to admit it out loud, we knew that the car had been in the water far too long. We were no longer part of a rescue but a body recovery.

Tank paddled out to the end of the safety line, bobbing with his feet down, hoping to feel the top of the car roof or the antenna.

Time passed. Where the fuck was this car?

A man carrying an umbrella came out of his house across the road and walked up to us. "They're gone," he said.

"What?" Fiske asked, startled.

"They're gone," he repeated. "They hit the water, a big SUV, went in real far," he considered, "halfway up the door line. But they managed to back it out after a couple of tries, and they left."

"You're sure?" Fiske wasn't going to give up the search if there was any chance that the car was still in the water.

"Ay-yuh," the man replied, revealing a strong Maine accent.

So that was it.

Tank hadn't heard way out on the end of the line, so I shouted to him, "They got the car out."

"They what?" he yelled back.

"There is no car. They got it out and drove it away."

Tank settled back in the water and floated on his back. Jazzed on adrenaline with nowhere to dump it he bellowed up at the sky, a vast, wordless, and primal sound that startled birds from nearby trees. They burst into the air as a group, wheeling away into the low dark clouds hanging over our heads.

Thirty-Five

I was in my shop the next day experimenting with hidden dovetail joints for the drawers of the china hutch that I'd been building off and on for the past six months. The high humidity made precision woodworking more or less impossible; no matter how snugly the pieces fit, it would be certain to rattle like the joints of an elderly athlete when the wood dried out and shrank. I was really just playing around with scrap pine, making big pieces of wood into little pieces as the old-timers would say.

I had never made a hidden dovetail before, and my first two attempts thus far had failed to mesh at all, even accounting for the swollen wood. In that sense it was just as well that I was working with scrap. Maybe I should have asked Jonas, a friend of mine who was a talented woodworker and retired firefighter, for a few pointers.

My failure to create a joint correctly aside, the simple manual labor gave me an opportunity to clear my head and play with the pieces of the Lauren puzzle to see what I could make of them. It really wasn't much of a picture unless Ambrose was wrong and Lillian Wainwright was Lauren Wilkes. Though even if true that still left the sixty-four thousand dollar question untouched.

A thought occurred to me, as I backed out the router bit and blew the fluted blades clear of sawdust. By making it appear as though she fell off of the yacht she was presumed dead, even without a body. Ditto for being in the World Trade Center on nine eleven. Driving a car into the water didn't fit that pattern. By doing so, the fact of her death remained unclear, and questions went unanswered. Someone trying to vanish would likely be interested in leaving as few unanswered questions behind as possible, right?

That train of thought became even more convoluted when I considered my role in it. If I hadn't been there to see her drive the car into the water, someone would have found the car some indefinite time later, and it wasn't even her car. No one would be looking for her at all unless Garrison reported it. Or maybe her landlord would have said something when he went to collect the rent and found her missing. More likely not; he would probably just have moved her things into storage and rented it out again, then sold the stuff on Craigslist three months later if she didn't show up to claim it. But I had been there, and I saw her, and I reported it.

So, by witnessing the accident did I help her in her plan to vanish or ruin it, and had that been her plan at all?

Some flaw in the piece of wood that I was working on, a knot or twist, failed spontaneously with a loud crack that made me jump and sent a shard of wood flying across the shop to bounce off the far wall. Pulling the work block from the clamps, I shook my head and threw it onto pile in the corner that Valerie and I would burn in the fireplace over the winter. I took a new piece off of a shelf, put it into the clamps, and was back at it again in minutes.

I felt as though I simply didn't know enough to have a hope in hell of figuring out the answers. Maybe Garrison could add something to the puzzle. I was certain that Ambrose knew something, if only I could figure out another way to approach him, one that wouldn't get me thrown out of his office in the first five seconds.

The last piece of the puzzle, the address on the final driver's license, may hold the key, but I was hesitant to go out there unprepared. I would likely only get one crack at it as I had with Ambrose. Blowing it was not an option.

I was happy with most recent joint; it fit without being so tight that it had to be forced. I spun the clamp locks and pulled the piece out of the jig, sweeping little bits of wood debris out of the slots with the side with my thumb as I did so.

In fact the joint was so perfect that I found myself wondering if I could be wrong about the swelling and shrinkage of wood. Was it possible that the entire joint would shrink uniformly, resulting in a good fit when it was dry? I wanted to try assembling it and put it in the oven to dry and find out, but then was torn between using glue or nails to hold it together. Modern wood glues are amazing materials, but classically, and I considered myself a classical woodworker, the pieces would have been joined with nails. As I had that thought, I wondered if maybe I was wrong about that. I turned my attention to the shelf that ran above the workbench, looking for a book that might answer that question, when a change in pressure in the room told me that the exterior door had been opened.

Valerie came in leading the man who had been seated next to Ambrose in New York. He was dressed in a long gray

London Fog trench coat and a black bowler hat. He looked so much like a spy from a John LeCarre novel that if he tried to hand me a micro-cassette I planned to scream and run away.

"Jack, this is Mr. Jeremy."

"We met at Mr. Ambrose's office in Manhattan last week," he said, as if I needed to be reminded. Naturally he had a slight English accent. How could he not? He extended his hand.

"I remember," I said, giving my hand a quick swipe against the leg of my jeans before shaking his hand. It was cool and smooth and dry, and the whole experience was vaguely reptilian. It sent shivers up my spine. "What can I do for you?"

"Upon further reflection, Mr. Ambrose has decided he would like the opportunity to discuss Lauren Wilkes with you again."

"I don't recall a whole lot of discussion the last time we met," I replied, "except that he didn't think Lauren was Lillian Wainwright."

"Mr. Ambrose regrets his earlier behavior and now believes his statement might be in error."

"In error?" Valerie asked. "So he thinks Lauren could be Lillian?"

"Yes, he thinks that is a possibility."

"*He* thinks?" I asked, emphasis on the he.

"Yes sir."

"Mr. Jeremy, did you ever meet Lillian?" His English accent was very addictive, and I had to concentrate to keep from imitating him.

"Yes sir, I did. On several occasions."

"Do you think she could be Lauren Wilkes?"

"I'm certain I don't know."

"But what do you think?" I pressed.

That question gave him a moment's pause. "Mr. Ambrose thinks that she might be, and that's all I need to know."

His loyalty was admirable, but at the same time the cynic in me wondered at the annual salary necessary to buy it.

"Sure," I shrugged, "I'll talk to him. Is he here now?"

"Mr. Ambrose's schedule would be better accommodated if you would come to Manhattan."

"Ah, I see."

"For your convenience, his Gulfstream is ready at the executive terminal at Manchester Airport. I'm prepared to drive you there now."

It's nice to be liked by rich people.

"Valerie," I asked, "That OK with you?"

"Two trips in a private jet in a week? A girl could get spoiled."

"Mr. Jeremy, we accept, but I'll need some time to get cleaned up and leave our dog with a friend."

He nodded. "One of the wonderful things about a private plane is that it is impossible to miss your flight."

Thirty-Six

My second trip on a private jet was just as nice as the first, perhaps even nicer. Whereas Alex Nidal's jet was more or less set up like an ordinary airplane with seats, big comfy ones, and a couple of tables, Ambrose's plane was more like a hotel room. The most surprising thing was that the airplane lacked any sort of normal airplane seats at all, unless you counted those in the cockpit, and even those looked exceptionally luxurious.

A rear compartment, sectioned off from the rest, held a queen-sized bed, oak dresser, closet, and bathroom complete with a shower the approximate size and shape of a telephone booth. There were no seatbelts or restraints on the bed. I had no idea what the FAA regulations on that were but made a mental note to check them out of curiosity. Next to the bedroom was an office area dominated by a desk that could have been the twin of the one in the Manhattan office with a wet bar off to one side. Forward of that was a lounging and sitting room with couches (these had seatbelts) and tables. Then there was another bathroom, the galley, and the cockpit.

The flight crew was accommodating and obsequious almost to the point of obsession. I suspected that if I asked them to try a touch and go landing on 12th Avenue so I could pick up some bagels at H & H that they would have. I almost asked them to. Never underestimate the glory of a fresh, hot cinnamon raisin bagel.

That level of pampering continued, bordering on the ridiculous, as we landed at Kennedy and taxied to a private corner of the airport. There we were ushered down the steps onto a rectangle of carpeting, imperial blue not red, that had been rolled between the bottom of the stairs and the door of a stretch limousine, lest our feet tread upon the same earth as mere mortals.

The limo whisked us into Manhattan where it seemed that every light magically turned green ahead of us. Perhaps it wasn't magic. I know that in some cities the fire trucks have a device that can turn red lights green in their path, but I didn't know if New York was among them. I was pretty sure it was illegal to use those devices on private vehicles, but I suspected that the Ambrose family was largely unconcerned with such trivialities when stacked against the inconvenience of waiting at a red light for ninety seconds.

We glided to a stop in front of a restaurant called Prairie Fire that I had heard about on the Food Network. It had been opened by some guy from Maryland who went to cooking school in France and had come to New York to open a southwestern-themed restaurant serving Kobe beef from Japan. Only in New York could such a restaurant immediately shoot to the top of the haute crowd A-list.

Mr. Jeremy hopped out carrying a small leather satchel and

held the limo door open for us, then trotted ahead to hold the door to the restaurant open for us as well.

"This place is supposed to be impossible to get reservations for," Valerie whispered to me.

"So I've heard."

Inside we were greeted, not with the expected hum and bustle of a popular midtown restaurant, but with eerie silence. The hostess lectern was empty as it appeared were all of the tables. It was jarring, in a creepy post-apocalyptic kind of way, and caused Valerie and I to come to a halt just inside the doorway.

Mr. Jeremy was forced to step around us as he entered, which he did smoothly, the door audibly sighing closed behind us.

"Mr. Ambrose has reserved the restaurant for lunch so that he may speak with you privately."

As he said that I scanned the room and noticed that one table was occupied. Joseph Ambrose was seated in the far corner of the room, his back to the wall like a Mafia Don afraid of a hit.

Valerie, Mr. Jeremy, and I crossed the restaurant, sidestepping heavy oak tables surrounded by blocky straight-backed chairs covered in coarse wool upholstery in jagged, brightly-colored patterns. There was a scattering of sawdust on the strategically-worn wood floor, and above our heads the ceiling had been built up with some kind of fiberglass foam into peaks and waves, like meringue, lit from within by red and orange lights. It took me a moment to realize that it was supposed to look like fire. Coming from a guy who had been in room where the ceiling was burning, it didn't, but it did make the scar on my neck tingle.

Ambrose watched us approach, rising from his chair when we arrived with a smile as fake as the fire above our heads. "Jack. Valerie. Thank you for coming. I hope your trip was pleasant. Please, sit down."

There were two place settings across the table from his. Apparently Mr. Jeremy didn't get to eat.

Valerie and I exchanged glances on how to proceed. It was clear that we were being glad handled, but whatever it was that Ambrose wanted, we didn't have a clue. She gave me a little shrug and we both sat.

Mr. Jeremy turned a chair at the next table a little bit towards this one and sat down on Ambrose's right, the satchel on the floor by his feet.

Satisfied that we were all adequately seated, Ambrose continued, "Order whatever you like. The Kobe beef is a specialty."

A waiter appeared magically from somewhere, either through a trap door in the floor or via a Star Trek style transporter, and handed us menus. They were immense things with thick parchment paper pages and wooden cover boards and hinges made of strips of leather that could have been used to beat a man to death. He waited patiently while we chose, though with the whole restaurant empty it wasn't like he had anywhere else to be.

I settled on the southwestern salad with grilled sliced beef and Valerie ordered the filet mignon. She spent a very long time pouring over the wine list, entering into a complicated discussion with the waiter, who actually had to leave and return with reinforcements to answer all of her questions, before she settled on a California Pinot Noir. I hoped she didn't expect me to open a winery any time soon.

Ambrose looked on approvingly as he swirled his own glass of wine. I seemed to recall some discussion between Valerie and Alex Nidal about how you weren't supposed to do that, something about bruising the grapes. Though how you could bruise a grape that had already been crushed to juice was beyond me.

"I love this restaurant," Ambrose said as he let his gaze roam lovingly around the room, "great wine, great food, great service."

That last bit was not exactly surprising when you reserved the whole place.

He leaned towards me, "This will interest you as a carpenter," he said, his voice adopting that tone and cadence guys use when discussing guy stuff. "That's Oklahoma sawdust on the floor."

I looked down at the floor and toed some of the sawdust with my shoe. Was there some wood or wood process that created Oklahoma sawdust, and was it somehow different from regular sawdust? I didn't think so. Or did he mean that the sawdust was actually bagged and shipped here from Oklahoma, and for what possible advantage? As far as I knew, and I had made a lot of it, sawdust was sawdust. It sounded like promotional bullshit from the restaurant, but I nodded anyway, then said, "How did you know that I'm a carpenter?"

"I checked up on you," he said with startling frankness. "I like to know who I'm dealing with. I assume you checked up on me as well."

In truth, I had. Joseph and his family – his father, mother, and younger sister – have filled a lot of pages in a both newspapers and magazines over the years: business deals, charity events, wedding announcements, graduations. Of course, entangled in the murders last year I had spilled no small amount of ink myself. Still, his investigation into me felt like a violation. Valerie is far more sensitive about that kind of stuff than I am, and I could feel her doing a slow burn in the seat next to me. I put a restraining hand on her knee under the table.

As if sensing my concerns he swept them away with a wave of his hand, the one holding the wineglass, which would have slopped over had it been more full. "When you showed up on my doorstep with your story about Lillian, I figured you were either crazy or after something, maybe both. You can't imagine the stories that people come to me with."

"So you think we're telling you a story?" Valerie asked, an ominous purr in her voice that Ambrose didn't pick up on but that I heard loud and clear. Her fuse was lit, and the tight bundle of dynamite was nearby.

I hoped she held off exploding at him; I still wanted to hear what he had to say.

He made a pained face, turned and locked eyes with Mr. Jeremy for a moment, and then looked back at us. "It's nuts, right? It makes no sense whatsoever. But you solved a murder last year."

Three murders, I thought to myself, but who's counting?

"And you're not crazy. You came from New Hampshire on your own dime, said your piece, asked for nothing, and left. So I figured there might be something to this."

Reassuring as it was to discover that he didn't believe us to be crazy, I couldn't see as this was getting us anywhere. "Mr. Jeremy said you wanted to talk to us about Lillian?"

He nodded, "I do, but I thought it would be more pleasant to wait until after lunch was served."

As if on cue, and perhaps it had been on cue, lunch arrived. Three separate waiters presented our meals to us simultaneously, like a precision military drill team, and then melted away.

While we ate Ambrose told us about how he had met Lillian at a shareholder meeting. Typically frequented by crackpots and troublemakers, people with an axe to grind with the corporate board, Lillian seemed normal, pleasant. They parted without plans to meet again, but he bumped into her at a charity event just a couple of weeks later, he couldn't recall for what charity. Then a short time after that she phoned him at his office and asked him to lunch.

"She pursued you?" Valerie asked.

"Of course," Ambrose nodded, spreading his arms wide as if to add 'Hey, look at the prize.'

I could see from the look in her eyes and the set of her jaw that the Valerie Fallon matchmaking machine had no desire to process Joseph Ambrose, but she would have gladly fed him into a wood chipper if given the chance.

"You had her investigated," I said, spearing a piece of beef from the salad with my fork. The beef was probably world class, but the company was making it taste like two-day-old meat loaf from a greasy spoon.

"I had to, right?" He lamented, the poor rich boy relentlessly pursued by unscrupulous women. "But there was nothing to find. She told me that her parents were dead. A couple named Wainwright from Connecticut was killed in a car accident on the New York Thruway in 1998. They had a daughter named Lillian who went to Wellesley. Without a social security number it was impossible to prove it if was her or not."

Difficult maybe, but not impossible. I had stumbled across the same information while looking at dozens of Lillian Wainwrights across the country. One had led me to a Wellesley yearbook photo of a Lillian Wainwright that bore little resemblance to the one on the driver's license. I thought that interesting, but hardly definite, considering that Wellesley women are often given plastic surgery gift certificates as graduation gifts. What did convince me was the alumni association, which was kind enough to put me in contact with their Lillian Wainwright who was a law clerk with the superior court in Connecticut.

The investigative skills of Ambrose's people aside, I pictured his dates becoming a lot more fun in the future, perhaps starting with a rousing game of twenty questions and ending with a cheek swab for DNA sample collection.

"So," I said, "let's say for the sake of argument that Lillian didn't die on nine eleven and ran off to New Hampshire instead. Any idea why she would so such a thing?

"I've been thinking a lot about that," he replied lifting his napkin from his lap and tossing it on the empty plate which was removed seconds later by an agile waiter. "I have an idea, but first I'd like to hear what you were doing in Napa Valley.

"How did you know we were in Napa?" Valerie demanded, an angry flash in her eyes that made me want to yell 'Fire in the hole!' and duck under the table. She was just about at the end of her patience with Ambrose and his attitude of entitlement.

"Let me guess," I said, "your father owns the bed and breakfast, and it flagged our names for you when we checked in."

Ambrose nodded, pleased "They're a growth industry, B and B's. We're buying them up in lots of destination cities. Napa Valley, Aspen, Cape Cod. We own one in the White Mountains in New Hampshire. Anywhere people want to see the landscape unspoiled by corporate chain hotels."

I made a mental note to check on hotels I stayed at in the future and to avoid the Ambrose family brand.

While I certainly could have told him about Alex Nidal and Leslie Wattley I found that I didn't want to. I didn't really trust him, and I'd be damned if I had to quid pro quo with someone like Joseph Ambrose to find out what had happened to Lauren. If it came to that, I'd find what I needed some other way.

"Nothing," I said, "At least nothing to do with this. We needed a vacation from the rain, and my wife is very into wine."

He didn't consider this for long given her performance with the wine list earlier. "Fair enough. Lillian had some things with her when she disappeared. They've never been recovered."

It was interesting to note that he was using the word disappeared now instead of killed. "What kind of things?"

Without looking at him Ambrose held a hand out to Mr. Jeremy with a gimme gesture. When whatever he had been expecting didn't end up in his palm quickly enough he turned.

"Really, sir, I," Mr. Jeremy began.

Ambrose cut him off with a look of such pure condescension that Mr. Jeremy closed his mouth with an audible snap. He dug into the satchel, removing a thick three-ring binder, which he handed to Ambrose.

Ambrose thumped it down on the table and began flipping through it. It was filled with 8x10 color photographs in protective plastic sleeves. I caught pictures of cars and boats, paintings and statues, rugs and antiques. Was it some kind of insurance binder?

After passing a king's ransom in treasures he stopped at a particular page and spun it to face us.

The sleeve held a photograph of a blue diamond ring against a black velvet background. If the ruler next to it in the picture was accurate, the central stone in the ring was as large as an eyeball.

"The Star of Kashmir," Ambrose narrated for us, "the seventh largest blue diamond in the world."

"How nice to be in the top ten," Valerie muttered in my ear.

There is a point, for me at least, beyond which a diamond is so large that it looks fake. This rock was way past that point. It dwarfed the simple platinum ring behind it, and its mass required a complicated arrangement of corner clamps and restraining loops to hold it in place. A tiny engineering marvel, it was nonetheless the single ugliest piece of jewelry I had ever seen in my entire life.

"She wore this?" Valerie asked in disbelief, likely thinking as I was that she would need a backpack to haul it around. Then again she could have always pushed it ahead of her in a wheelbarrow.

Ambrose either misunderstood her comment or chose to do so. "She was wearing it on the morning of nine eleven. The ring has never been found. I think she took it with her."

I couldn't understand his logic. "When the towers fell over two million feet of office space spilled into the Trade Center Plaza, and not so much as a single desk, filing cabinet, or phone was found intact. They didn't even find her body, so why should the ring have survived?"

"That's not all she had," he said, pointing a finger at me. He used his other hand to flip more pages in the book.

The page he had stopped at was not a photograph, but a Xerox copy of a certificate. Across the top in elaborate script it read *Deutsche Bank* and below that were paragraphs of text in German and a column of numbers and maturation dates. I had taken only a single semester of German in college a long time ago, and had forgotten pretty much everything but the obscenities since then, but the columns of numbers told me what I was looking at.

"Bearer bonds."

"Exactly," Ambrose nodded, "she was retrieving them for me from a holding company in the North Tower."

"How much?" Valerie asked.

I was already doing the math in my head using some notes in the margins of the certificate about bond issues and certificate numbers. My calculation was complete a few seconds before Ambrose gave his answer.

"One million dollars."

Heilige Scheiße!

Thirty-Seven

"I never had a reason to suspect that she hadn't died on nine eleven until you showed up." Ambrose said a short time later over coffee.

"Did she cash the bonds?" I asked as I watched Valerie stir a spoon around in her tea, ringing it against the sides of the mug. Why she kept mixing it after she had drunk more than half was something that I never understood. Maybe she liked the ringing sound.

"There's no way to know. Bearer bonds aren't tracked by the issuing institution."

"And the diamond?" Valerie added.

"She hasn't sold that. There probably is no way to sell it. The Star of Kashmir is known the world over."

I thought that maybe she could get it cut up into smaller stones or sold to some private collector under the table, but he seemed certain of what he was talking about. Maybe I had been reading too many caper mysteries.

The waiter delivered the check to Ambrose. He made a big show of drawing his wallet from the breast pocket of his jacket and sliding the credit card from its appointed slot using his thumb with the practiced motion of a Vegas blackjack dealer. The card was an American Express Platinum, and when he dropped it on top of the check it clanked like it was made of metal. Perhaps in Ambrose's league platinum credit cards were made of actual platinum.

After the waiter had scooped up the card and left, Ambrose put his elbows on the table and folded his hands in front of him. "I'd like to hire you to find it."

His use of the pronoun it threw me for a moment. "Lillian?" I asked uncertainly.

He shook his head, "The diamond," he paused, then added "and the money," almost as an afterthought.

"What about Lillian?" Valerie asked.

He shrugged, a gesture that conveyed such blatant disregard for the welfare of another human being, one that had been his fiancé no less, that I immediately pushed back my chair and stood to leave. Valerie, no doubt as enraged as I, stood with me.

Ambrose remained seated but pressed his case, framing the argument with his hands. "Look, I can hire any investigations firm in the country, but I thought to myself: *This guy cares. This guy is invested.* You can't buy that."

He was right and he was wrong. I did care, but not about

the diamond or the money. He was also right in that he couldn't buy me.

"Mr. Ambrose, I'm looking for Lauren Wattley who may or may not be Lillian Wainwright and may or may not have your diamond," though after all I had found so far I was nearly certain she was and she did. "I'm not a private investigator and I'm not interested in your property, and we most certainly are not for hire."

He refolded his hands in front of him and looked down at them and ran his tongue around inside his mouth. Not used to being told no, I was curious how he would take it. I was hoping he would give me a glimpse of that behavior, maybe a flavor of what Lillian might have experienced if she had told him no.

He didn't give me much to work with.

He closed the binder with a clap, "I hope you enjoyed lunch, and thank you for coming," and just like that we were off his radar.

I stood behind the chair that I had pushed back into the table, wondering if perhaps there would be some offer of returning us to New Hampshire. When it was clear that one was not forthcoming Valerie and I left.

The air outside the restaurant, agitated in a swirl of foul diesel fumes by a recently departed bus, nonetheless tasted light and sweet after the confines of the restaurant, which had seemed somehow thickened by Ambrose's presence.

Valerie pulled out her cell phone and dialed our travel agent, a number she probably by now knew by heart.

Mr. Jeremy came out of the restaurant. "I'm sorry about that."

"It's not your job to apologize," Valerie said caustically without removing the phone from her ear.

I thought that maybe it was, but didn't see it as my job to point that out.

Mr. Jeremy looked to me, perhaps seeking a more sympathetic party. "He really did love Lillian, in his own way."

"Nice qualifier, in his own way," Valerie snorted, and then turned her back on us as she said "Yes, one way flight from Kennedy or LaGuardia to Manchester Airport in New Hampshire, two adults."

"He did love her." Mr. Jeremy emphasized.

"But he loves the money more." I said.

He didn't have an answer to that except to sigh tiredly.

"Boston would be fine as well," Valerie said into the phone.

"I'd like to offer you the jet for the return flight to New Hampshire."

"You're offering, or is Ambrose offering?" I asked.

"Mr. Ambrose would need never know." He smiled slightly.

Tempting as it sounded to sneak a bill for ten thousand dollars or more into Ambrose's In box, I didn't want to risk any blow back on Mr. Jeremy. It also didn't fit in with my plans. "No thank you, Mr. Jeremy, as you can hear, we're making other arrangements."

"I understand, sir."

"Mr, Jeremy, may I ask you a question?"

"You may ask," he replied with the same smooth delivery with which politicians say 'no comment.'

"What did you think when we talked to you about Lillian? You must have had some insight into the relationship between her and Joseph. Does her leaving make any sense? Did she give you any idea that she was unhappy?" I realized that I had gone way past my one question allotment and so shut up to give him a chance to answer.

"Lillian was an extraordinary woman. Poised, confident, stunningly attractive. When she and Mr. Ambrose were photographed somewhere together they made a striking couple."

"But," I prompted.

He frowned, "But it wasn't her. The big parties, the photographers, were not what she wanted. All of that made her very uncomfortable."

"So you think it's possible that she wanted to leave?"

"Possible, yes, and I honestly didn't expect the marriage to last." He paused and rubbed his upper lip with the side of his index finger, "Still it was very hard on Mr. Ambrose when we learned that she had been killed. It was hard on me as well; I was quite fond of her. And now to think that she might be alive. And with a million dollars!"

He drifted off, his eyes open wide in awe. I couldn't help but wonder if his awe was due to the thought that Lillian might be alive or if he was thinking that he himself might abscond if given a similar set of circumstances.

"So you think Lillian could be Lauren?" I asked.

His eyes came back to me from wherever they had been and focused on me, "To fake her own death like that? Yes, she was unhappy, but... I really don't know."

"That makes two of us."

"I wish you luck in finding *her*," he said, emphasizing the pronoun. "Please let me know what happens."

"I will."

He held out his hand and I shook it. He turned, hesitated, and then went back into the restaurant.

Whatever Ambrose was paying him, it wasn't enough.

On the plus side, I had learned how to refuse an offer of a private jet should it ever come up again in the future.

Valerie hung up her phone. "We've got return tickets to Manchester from Kennedy this evening."

"That's great, but we're not going back to New Hampshire."

"We're not?"

"No, we're going to Texas."

She opened her phone, hit redial, and held it to her ear. "I had a feeling you were going to say that."

Thirty-Eight

We called Alex Nidal from Kennedy airport.

Despite his best efforts he had been unable to find out anything about the owner of the address on the Texas driver's license. The property was contained within a township that had let progress slip by. Shunning such modern conveniences as computers, their property records all remained on paper in the town hall and the woman who had answered the phone there had refused to look up the property, despite a promise from Alex to build the town a new library if she helped him.

"I would have, too," Alex said to me. "Perhaps she didn't believe me."

While I had him on the phone I decided to ask a difficult question. "Did Leslie take anything from you?"

"Take anything? What do you mean?"

"When she left, did she have anything of yours, something of value?" I didn't want to get into the whole story of Ambrose and the million dollars and the Star of Kashmir, not over the phone, not while we were standing in the airport waiting to catch our flight.

"What? No, nothing. I don't understand."

Valerie tugged on my sleeve and mouthed the words "engagement ring" slowly and carefully.

I nodded to her indicating that I understood.

"Alex, it was your engagement party. You said you gave her an engagement ring."

"I did."

I gave Valerie a thumbs up.

"Was it expensive? What was it worth?"

"Money? Not much."

Of course 'not much' to a guy worth hundreds of millions of dollars probably meant something very different to him than it did to me. "How much?"

"It was just a gold band. I'm not even sure it was gold. It might have been gold plated."

"Gold plated? Now I don't understand."

"The ring. It was my grandmother's."

Damn.

"I'm sorry for bringing it up," I told him.

"It's OK. I'm," he paused, "It's OK. Have a safe trip." He hung up on me.

After I folded up the phone and put it away I told Valerie about the ring.

"Damn." She said.

Six hours and two thousand miles later we picked up a rental car from the Rent-A-Wreck at the Midland, Texas airport, which apparently ranked neither a Hertz nor an Avis. It was a two-thousand-something coke-bottle green Chevy Impala sedan with a soft suspension, slushy steering, and an industrial-grade disinfectant reek that was engaged in take-no-prisoners guerilla warfare with the joined forces of fresh mildew and ancient cigarette smoke. Otherwise it ran well, the tires were in good balance, and the air conditioning literally put a fine furring of frost on the vent slots, even on the low setting.

We drove west of Fort Stockton about an hour off of I-10 on a road with the picturesque name of State Route 432. The army corps of engineers had really outdone themselves. SR432 was as straight as a laser; two hundred foot strips of latex-modified concrete laid end-to-end and spliced with rubberized expansion joints that gave a solid double thump as the car tires passed over them. The roadway extended to the horizon, shimmering with heat haze under the mighty Texas sun. Thermal layering caused index of refraction disparities that bent the light, creating optical illusions that looked like pools of water in the low spots ahead which vanished as we approached only to reappear again in the distance.

I was surprised how difficult such mundane driving was without significant geographic or architectural features to break up the landscape. In New Hampshire there probably isn't a road in the entire state that is straight for more than a hundred feet. On

SR432 it was almost impossible to stay focused on driving. Lulled into a false sense of security, I felt as though I could tie the steering wheel to the brake pedal, drop a brick on the accelerator, and climb into the back seat for a nap without risk.

Valerie was providing the soundtrack for this leg of our journey, a collection of seventies easy listening rock ballads including *Horse with No Name* and *Dust in the Wind*. They felt somehow appropriate, in harmony with the desolate and somewhat alien landscape through which we passed.

The road was a single lane each way bisected by a faded dashed yellow line. I couldn't help but wonder, with a quick peek at the speedometer which told me that I was doing eighty-one, about high-speed head-on collisions. What would be the response time for emergency crews out here? When was the last time we had passed a police or fire station? The GPS mounted on the dash, which we had rented for the low, low bargain price of nine-ninety-five, showed us nothing at all; a single thread of roadway without a documented crossroad for more than ten miles in either direction. Perhaps emergency services arrived by helicopter, but who would call them? An accident might go unnoticed for hours.

The 'No Service' message on my cell phone screen completed the picture. We were off the grid here, way beyond contact or help should the need arise. I made a mental note to try my best not to say anything that would make someone want to shoot us.

I had thought that I was starting to get a handle on the pattern of Lauren's life and was expecting to come upon the South Fork Ranch. There would be acres of manicured lawn and miles of white split rail fencing, horses or perhaps cattle, all dominated by an enormous plantation home. There would be another lonely rich man who had been left in her wake, poorer for the experience in more ways than one.

That was until Alex had told me about his grandmother's ring. Now I didn't know what to think.

"Turn right ahead," the GPS announced in a feminine voice with a vaguely southwestern twang.

I tapped the brakes and slowed.

"Turn right now."

I let the car coast to a stop.

I looked out the window and saw... nothing. There was scrub brush and rocks as far as the eye could see. The road was edged both left and right by a triple strand of barbed wire mounted on weathered wooden stakes, every fifth one topped by a No Trespassing sign. The marching line of utility poles on the right hand side was unbroken.

I checked the address on the sheet of driver's licenses, now deeply creased and with a little tear out of one corner from five trips in my luggage. The address and the GPS marker matched.

"There's nothing here," Valerie said to the GPS in that tone of voice she uses for arguing with inanimate objects that have displeased her.

I frowned and leaned forward, stretching my back, my forearms resting on the steering wheel. A glance at the rearview mirror showed the road behind me empty. I hadn't seen another car in the last twenty minutes. Shifting the car into park, I opened the car door and stepped out. The exterior felt blistering in comparison to the car's glacial interior. It must have been over a hundred degrees, but as they say in hell, it's a dry heat. I shielded my eyes with my hand and squinted.

Valerie got out of her side of the car and spoke to me over the roof. "Are we in the right place?"

I began to shake my head uncertainly and then thought I saw something ahead, but in the heat shimmer it was difficult to be certain. "I think-" I began, and got back into the car.

Valerie got in and I shifted back into drive and lifted my foot off the brake to let the car roll slowly forward on the idle. In fifty yards we came to a gap in the barbed wire on the right. A narrow dirt road, little more than two wheel ruts, threaded its way between cactus and mesquite bushes and headed around and behind a small hill to the North.

Valerie shrugged.

I shrugged back, hit the turn signal for no particular reason, and eased the car down the shoulder and through the gap. The clearance of the rental car was low, and an occasional piece of rock or fallen branch scraped the undercarriage with a sound like fingernails on a chalkboard. A plume of dust followed behind us.

Around the corner of the hillside, in a shallow valley between that hill and the next, a silver Airstream trailer rested on cinderblocks. It was a classic design with rounded corners, built perhaps in the early sixties or late fifties. It had a weathered green awning midway down its length that shaded four aluminum lawn chairs with pink nylon strapping and a pale yellow wrought iron table. A crooked television antenna sprouted from one end like a Christmas tree without needles. An empty clothesline was strung between a corner of the trailer and a nearby pole jammed into the ground.

I pulled to a stop behind a faded red Jeep Cherokee.

As the dust settled, I tried to reconfigure the story I had been constructing in my head to encompass this little trailer in the west Texas badlands and found that I couldn't do it.

I opened the door and got out. The sand beneath my shoes was coarse and gritty; the air was hot, dry, and still. Valerie and I met in front of the car, where we held hands like teenagers in a horror movie about to confront the psychotic killer.

The door to the trailer opened and a woman came out. She climbed slowly down the three aluminum steps to the ground, wiping her hands on a yellow dishtowel with small blue flowers.

She was wearing a men's blue denim work shirt tucked into blue jeans. Her hair was grown long and drawn back in a ponytail, blonde shot through with threads of silver. She was perhaps fifty, though her age was a little difficult to determine. The skin on her face was smooth and unlined but looked tough like worked leather. Her eyes were a very pale blue as though bleached, perhaps the palest blue I had ever seen.

She took a deep breath and let it out as a sigh, "You're here about my daughter."

I looked at Valerie who looked as blank and confused as I felt.

"Yes, ma'am," I replied, "I think that we are."

Thirty-Nine

We sat on the pink lawn chairs underneath the awning.

After Valerie and I had introduced ourselves she told us that her name was Arlette Watson, and she was Lorraine's mother. She served something she called sweet tea over ice in big white plastic cups. The name was apt; there was so much sugar in the mix that it made my teeth ache.

I sat in the chair facing up the length of the valley. A jackrabbit loped among the brush about a hundred feet away, then through some sixth sense knew that it had been spotted and took off in a blur. I lost sight of it in the uneven landscape. A bird of prey, something large that I couldn't identify, wheeled on the rising thermals in the sky overhead.

I was trying to figure out how to begin when Arlette cut right to the bone.

"She's dead, isn't she?"

Valerie swallowed audibly.

Without answering her question I decided instead to ask one of my own. "What makes you say that?"

She seemed to consider her response for some time, and then asked, "Do you have children?" She directed that mostly at Valerie.

"No," Valerie answered simply, but there was a husky quality to her voice. Our failure to conceive was never far from the forefront of her mind.

"I just feel..." Arlette let the thought trail off and hugged herself as though she was cold.

"I don't know that she's dead," I said as kindly as I could, choosing my words carefully.

"But you think she is." She said quietly.

I shifted uncomfortably in my chair and looked to Valerie for help, but she had picked that moment to fixate on the bird of prey above. I put my cup down on the wrought iron table in front of us. Clasping my hands and resting my elbows on my knees I said, "I don't know, but let me tell you what I think I do know."

So I started at the beginning, taking the page with the driver's licenses from my pocket at the appropriate time, unfolding it, and handing it to her. She glanced down at the paper for only a moment and then back up at me, as if she didn't want to miss a second of the story. I kept going, without a single comment from either her or Valerie, right up until we had pulled up outside her trailer.

"And that brings us to," I paused, "now."

Told all at once, start to finish, the story sounded wildly implausible even to my own ears, but the thread that held it all together was undeniable.

She was silent for a moment as she furrowed her brow. Then she opened her mouth and Valerie and I actually leaned forward in our chairs to catch every word, but she closed her mouth instead and turned away. Her eyes misted and her mouth worked but she made no sound.

Valerie and I waited patiently. I was prepared to wait all day for her to speak, without any pressure from us. We had just driven up in the middle of the day without any warning and blown a big chunk out of her world.

She spoke to us without looking back from whatever out in the scrubland had her attention. "I'm sorry, I-" She broke off.

"It's OK," Valerie said in her gentlest tone. "Take your time."

"We're sorry," I insisted, "It would have been better, fairer to you, if we had called first, but I had truly had no idea what we were going to find when we got here. It certainly hadn't been this."

"Just as well; I never answer it. Nothing but telemarketers and bill collectors." She said distantly.

I tried to look out in the same direction she was, see what she was seeing, and noticed that the jackrabbit had reappeared, or maybe it was a different one. It's not like they wear nametags.

Arlette turned back to us slowly. She lifted her cup from the table, took a drink, and then replaced the cup carefully as if it were made of the most delicate china. She cleared her throat. "Living out here is very peaceful; at least it is to me. There's no rush to get caught up in. You can do things at your own pace."

"Did Lorraine like it here?" Valerie asked.

Arlette snorted a small laugh at some memory she chose not to share with us. "She had what my mother would have called a wild hair up her ass. I knew she'd leave here just as soon as she could, same as her father."

"Where is he?"

"He moved to New Jersey just after Lorraine was born, then went to cancer." She said it as if cancer was somewhere you could move to, like a particularly bad suburb of Newark.

"I'm sorry."

She waved Valerie's apology away with her hand as though scattering a cloud of gnats. "A lot of years, a lot of water over the dam."

My mind flashed to Baxter's Dam back home for a moment, then I refocused. "Does any of this make any sense to you? Is that your daughter in the driver's licenses?" I asked her.

"Without a doubt." Arlette nodded, "She changed her hair a little, but that's Lorraine." She looked at the page of the driver's licenses for another moment before putting it down on the table. "Excuse me for a second," she said. She stood up and went into the trailer.

"Do you think she's dead, Jack?" Valerie asked me softly.

"I don't know what I think," I replied, shaking my head. "It would be nice to find that she pulled up stakes and moved on after Garrison like she had in the past and is now living in some other place as Loretta Wilson or Louise Wojciehowicz. I really hope it's true."

"But it doesn't feel that way," Valerie finished the thought for me.

"No," I agreed. "It doesn't."

Arlette returned carrying a slim hardcover book, which she handed to me. She sat down and scooted her chair around so I was sitting between her and Valerie. It was a yearbook from the Plainview High School class of 1996. The cover helpfully informed me that it was the home of the Falcons.

The inside cover had a landscape photograph of the graduating class, twenty-seven students in all. I wondered how much geography the school district had to encompass to gather together even that meager number.

The next four pages were devoted to color pictures of the seniors. Lorraine was easy to find. They were in alphabetical order, and she looked almost exactly like she did in the Texas driver's license.

Two photos down and one to the right was a man with the unlikely name of Digby Utt. Digby was what would unkindly be referred to as a buckethead. His neck muscles were so overdeveloped that it looked like his head was welded directly to his shoulders. He had drawn a heart shape next to his picture and added 'From, Digg' inside.

Valerie reached over and touched the heart with her fingertip.

"That's Digg, Lorraine's boyfriend from high school. He's still local if you'd like to talk to him – works in his father's lumberyard in Telejo – but I'm sure he would have told me if he had heard from her."

Valerie withdrew her hand and rested it on my thigh. "When was the last time you heard from her?"

"Not long after she left. She wrote me from Los Angeles and told me that she was working as a secretary. She was also taking night classes at UCLA."

"Nothing since then?" I asked.

"No," she replied, then, because she probably knew how that sounded quickly added, "we hadn't had a fight or anything. This place just wasn't for her and I guess she felt it was best to make a clean break. I didn't want to cling. She wanted to do her own thing in the world. You know, kids." She summarized with a shrug.

We were all quiet then, thinking our own thoughts.

I took the opportunity of the lull in the conversation to summarize for myself what we had learned so far from our two-thousand-mile trip to the Middle-of-Nowhere Texas: nothing. OK, so it wasn't nothing; I had, for example, confirmed that all the driver's licenses were for Lorraine Watson. But I was disappointed in that I was no closer to finding out what had happened to her. I wasn't even certain whether I was investigating a murder or not. And I didn't know where else to look.

"Would you stay for dinner," Arlette asked suddenly. "I haven't been shopping in a while and I can only offer you hamburgers, but I really don't want to be alone right now. I can invite Digg over to give you a chance to talk."

"We'd be happy to," Valerie said with a smile.

Forty

Digg arrived in a primer gray Dodge pickup that was so dented it looked like someone had systematically worked it over with a ball peen hammer. He was even bigger in person than the picture in the yearbook had led me to believe. His blue jeans were heavily abused, like the truck, but his work shirt was relatively new, sporting the logo of the lumberyard sewn onto the left breast pocket with his name below that. After introductions he settled into one of the lawn chairs which creaked alarmingly under his weight but held.

True to her word Arlette served hamburgers. She cooked them over a mesquite-fired grill and served them with roasted green chilies and pan-fried potatoes.

The dinner was amazing, far surpassing the Kobe beef at Prairie Fire yesterday. Maybe that was because the company was better.

After the meal Valerie and Arlette talked about Lorraine. Arlette broke out a family photo album and Valerie vicariously experienced the daughter she would likely never have. I flipped through the yearbook while they spoke, finding the last several pages devoted to advertisements. "Katy lumber salutes the class of 1996' and 'Kelso's Feed and Grain congratulates the Falcons for their undefeated season!"

The Falcons were apparently a football team, and to look at the team photo every boy in the school had played.

Digg caught my eye and gestured off into the distance with his head, then got up and began walking down the valley away from the trailer and cars. I trotted to catch up with him. He walked with an easy long-legged stride which I realized covered about six of my steps for every four of his. I was also expending a lot of extra steps avoiding rocks and ruts and snagging mesquite and cactus plants, and I was more than a little concerned about tripping over a rattlesnake, while he seemed to somehow naturally flow along the landscape avoiding all of it effortlessly. If we kept up this pace, I'd be winded before too long.

"Arlette told me why you're here on the phone. About Lorraine and the driver's licenses and the other guys." His voice was rough and gravelly, not quite a rumble but close to it.

"Have you heard from her?"

"Recently?" He looked over and down at me, then shook his head. "No."

"How about not recently?"

He reached out and snapped a branch off a nearby bush and started pulling the bark off of it in long strips, letting them drop

230

to the ground as we walked. "For a while after she left I got letters from Los Angeles about school, about work, and I'd write back."

He stopped there, but clearly that wasn't the end of the story. How and when did they lose touch? I waited to see if he would continue on his own, but he didn't. He finished denuding the stick and dropped it on the ground at his feet. Without breaking stride he bent over and scooped up a rock the size of a softball. He grunted and I flinched, afraid that he was going to use it to bash my head in, but instead he turned and hurled it way off into the distance, so far that I saw it land but didn't hear it. It raised a plume of dusty sand where it had hit. He stopped walking and stood with his hands on his hips looking out that way.

"What, Digg? What is it you're not telling me?"

"She got in trouble out there," he said softly. So softly that in his rumble of a voice it was tough to sort out the words.

"Drugs?"

He shook his head vehemently. "Money."

"Her mother said she was a secretary?"

He nodded. "She was, at a small bank, but she lost it when they were gobbled up by some bigger bank. Her rent was high. Everything in Los Angeles was expensive. School cost a small fortune. She got a loan from some government agency, but it only covered part of her tuition and did nothing about her living expenses. A couple of years of that and she had more debt than she could handle."

He again stopped, but I didn't see it as an invitation for me to speak. I felt that he was just organizing his thoughts or replaying old memories, and I was willing to let him get it all out at his own pace.

"I sent her some money. I work at my dad's lumberyard. The construction industry is in the shitter and all the lumber has to be hauled in from Canada or South America. The transportation costs are eating us alive. It's a hard way to earn a living, but I sent her what I could. We talked about her moving home again, but she couldn't see as there were any opportunities out here that would let her pay off her debt." He sighed, "I think that was only part of it. I think she was worried what people would think of her if she moved back, the smart girl who went away to college and came crawling home a few years later with her tail between her legs."

He started walking again in that curious flowing gait of his. I tried to imitate it for a few steps but somehow my joints just didn't seem to move that way. I returned to my ragged and awkward scramble.

"It all got to be too much for her. She looked into declaring bankruptcy, but the laws don't let you get away from student loans. She wrote me that some friends of her at UCLA, illegal immigrants I think, were going to get her a new identity. We sort of joked about it in the letters, that she'd change her name to Lillian Wainwright and pretend that she was some upper crust, trust fund, Ivy League graduate."

"Lillian Wainwright? She actually mentioned that name in the letters?"

He nodded, "Yeah. But I didn't really think that she would go through with it. How would she finish school? What would she do for work? She'd essentially become an illegal alien in her own country. I thought that she was just, I don't know, blowing off steam or something."

"Did she ever mention the names Leslie Wattley or Lauren Wilkes?"

"The other names on the licenses? No. But once you've thrown away your own name I suppose one is as good as another."

He had a point, but I still wondered where she had gotten them. Did she just pick them out of a book of baby names?

"When did you lose touch?"

"Not too long after that. Her letters stopped coming, a few of mine came back, returned by the post office, and that was more or less that."

"More or less?" I panted, starting to suck wind.

"I got a postcard from somewhere every so often. San Francisco, New York, Denver, New Orleans, Chicago, Florida. The last one was maybe a year ago give or take. I didn't keep them or I could check for you."

"Where did the last one come from?"

"New Hampshire. The Old Man of the Mountain was on it."

"Did she tell you what she was doing?"

He shook his head, "Nah. She didn't really write anything on the postcards. Just 'Thinking of you, Saw Fisherman's Wharf,' or 'At the Statue of Liberty, miss you.' Never more than a line or two."

"Did she?"

"Did she what?"

"Miss you?"

He stopped suddenly, and I stumbled a few steps before managing to come to a halt. "What's that supposed to mean?" He became agitated.

"Whoa. Nothing," I held my hands up in a calm-down kind of gesture, "I'm just, uh," in truth I didn't know what I was doing. I was just running my mouth hoping that something that sounded like a clue would turn up. "She was engaged to marry other men, but she kept sending postcards saying that she misses you. Do you see where I'm going with this?" I was hoping he did, because I sort of didn't.

He nodded a little but his shoulders remained hunched and he started walking again, his pace if anything faster than before. I was practically jogging. "Lorraine," he said and blew out his breath.

"Unfinished business between you two?"

"After all these years?" He paused a long time, the only sounds the scuffing of our feet in the coarse dirt and my increasingly labored breathing. Finally he continued, "No. But Lorraine was, is I guess, a hard woman to forget. It wasn't just that she was beautiful and smart, which she was, but she had a natural attraction about her, something innate, like a magnet. It was like a tug at your insides." He shook his head. "It's hard to explain if you never met her."

I had met her if only for a moment when she drove the Porsche into the water, and I suppose even then, her looking like a drowned rat and terrified, I had felt some fragment of what he was trying to describe. "Did she ever mention Alex Nidal or Joseph Ambrose or Garrison West in the postcards?" I puffed out.

"No."

"Can you think of anyone else I should talk to around here who might have heard from her?"

"Not if Arlette hasn't heard from her."

"And you can't think of anyone who would want to hurt her?"

"I don't know. She signed all the postcards Lorraine, so I didn't even know that she had gone through with changing her name until Arlette called." He shook his head in frustration. "Roaming all over the country, changing her name all the time. There's no telling who she pissed off along the way."

I was starting to think that he might be right about that. Was there any way to sort all of this out?

I had just about run out of questions and either we were in the middle of a meteor shower or I was starting to see spots before my eyes. I came to a stop hoping he would too, which he did in half a dozen steps. I had a strong urge to put my hands on my knees and suck up some air, but instead managed to ask, "Did you ever tell Arlette any of this?"

"Would you have?"

I didn't answer him, but thought to myself that no, I probably wouldn't.

We started walking again, more slowly this time, and shortly came upon the cars and the trailer from the other side. Our route must have taken us all the way around one of the low hills.

We settled back on the lounge chairs and watched the

sunset, which with the land so low and flat took a long time. The sky streamed an incredible palette of colors, so full of reds and oranges and purples that it looked a little like some fanciful animation and not real at all.

Afterwards Arlette turned on white Christmas lights that she had strung around the edge of the awning, and we drank coffee and ate Chips Ahoy cookies in silence looking out at darkness so complete that it felt like I had gone blind beyond a range of ten feet. We had to leave just a little while later; it was a long drive back to the hotel by the airport.

Arlette and Valerie hugged like sisters and Digg shook my hand, a little roughly, I thought. I might need an MRI when we got back to New Hampshire.

"Will you find out what happened to my girl?" Arlette pleaded.

"We will," Valerie replied, "I promise."

And with those last two words Valerie had hung a millstone around our necks that was almost certain to drag us to the bottom.

Forty-One

The flight back to New Hampshire was mostly empty but it was a bad one, the plane tossed all over the sky by turbulence. The flight crew was effusively apologetic, like the atmospheric thermoclines were somehow their fault. They also ran out of peanuts. How you manage to do that with so few passengers onboard was beyond me, though in truth I think I ate ten little bags.

Bounced around on the outside like ball bearings in a clothes dryer, we were also torturing ourselves on the inside; the promise Valerie had made to Arlette weighing heavily on the both of us.

"We have to find out what happened to Lorraine, Jack," Valerie beseeched me from across the aisle where she sat white-knuckling the armrests.

"I know." I mumbled, sucking the last peanut fragments

out of my seventh bag.

The problem was that I didn't know what to do next. I had seen the trip to Texas as the last stitch in the tapestry that I had had to pull. It had led me, not to the end of the thread, but the beginning. Sure, I had a better understanding of how Lorraine had become Leslie et al, but that didn't tell me what had become of her. Whatever had happened to Lorraine, it was likely that Garrison, Ambrose, or Alex or perhaps even Digby was responsible, but how could I know which?

If you got right down to it, the alternative still remained that she had moved on again as she had done in the past, which opened whole new avenues of possibilities. The next person after Garrison, someone we as yet had no knowledge of, could be to blame. She could also be perfectly fine and well wherever it was that she had moved on to. Though in my heart I didn't believe that was true and I didn't think Valerie did either.

Valerie, never having discovered Ambrose's good side, if he had one, wanted to drive into Manhattan and beat the answers out of him. I gave her points for spunk, but didn't see Ambrose as a man you could beat anything out of, and I wasn't sure he had answers to give us in any case.

We landed unsteadily in a steady downpour, collected our luggage, snagged a taxi, and headed for home.

My rain gauge had overflowed three days earlier and I had yet to empty it. I had also ceased adding new data to my dam models. Whatever was holding that structure together was a mystery itself. And to top it all off we hadn't been through the door thirty seconds when my pager went off.

"You're exhausted, Jack. Don't go."

"I'm fine."

The call was for a single home structure fire caused by an electrical short in the flooded basement, and it was screwed up before the first crew even made it to the scene. We lost the fire engine ten feet from the bottom of the unpaved driveway, a ribbon of muck that devoured it halfway up the wheel wells. With the truck trapped there, and the driveway blocked by its bulk, we were forced to haul a thousand feet of hose line through ankle-deep mud just to reach the house.

When two crews were down in the basement, Tank and I being one of them, the pump panel on the Tanker blew with a shower of sparks. Tank and I found ourselves suddenly holding an empty hose.

"Back it up! Clear the building!" I yelled to Tank as the fire rolled over our heads.

We called in two trucks for mutual aid, and managed to keep the fire contained to the basement and put it out, though the house had heavy smoke damage throughout.

It wasn't exactly one for the highlight reels.

An hour later, soot streaked and covered in mud, absolutely weary to the bone, I was on my way home when I saw something in the road ahead. I lifted my foot off the gas and hovered it over the pedal. Had I switched it to the brake, even if I hadn't leaned on it, the outcome would likely have been very different, but you can only guilt yourself over such things for so long. It's unproductive.

It was difficult to identify what I was seeing through the rain-streaked windshield. It looked like nothing more than a patch of black slightly darker than the night around it. At the last moment it turned its head in my direction and there was a ghostly green flash of my headlights in its eyes.

Bear! I thought, and spun the wheel to the left as I moved my foot to the brake. By the time it got there, the weight of the truck was unbalanced, the suspension crushed forward and right. I hit the brakes and felt the rear begin to lift. A moment later the entire truck was essentially riding on one tire, threatening to roll or flip. I released the brakes and goosed the gas, trying to get the weight back onto all four wheels.

I felt a sickening thud from the right fender and the truck slid sideways. I over-corrected and skated on the damp road completely around, finally coming to rest pointed back the way I had come. My heart was hammering in my chest in time with the thump of the windshield wipers.

The animal was a black lump motionless in the beams of my headlights.

Grabbing the flashlight out of the center console, I got out of the truck. I approached slowly, not anxious to tangle with an injured bear. The rain washed soot from my face and clumps of mud from my jeans which landed around my feet with soggy splats.

As I got closer the shape resolved itself into legs and a tail and a great head the size of a basketball with a long muzzle and floppy ears. It was a dog, some kind of Mastiff or Newfoundland.

It didn't look like it was breathing.

Should I move it? It probably weighed two hundred pounds and I wasn't even sure that I could. If I managed to get it into my truck, where was the nearest emergency vet hospital? With so many roads flooded and closed would I be able to find my way there?

I was startled by an enormous cracking sound that filled the air as a Douglas Fir came down. The tree landed diagonally across the bed of my truck in an explosion of bark and branches that scattered tufts of pine needles on the road like heaps of discarded clothing.

I ran back to the truck and fought my way to the driver's door. The frame was bent, but with a little work I got it open. I pulled the cell phone from the charger on the dashboard and looked at the screen, not even remotely surprised to find that I was in one of the town's many dead zones. With two cell towers recently down and out, it was more like the town had small islands of coverage in an ocean of nothing.

Through the cracked windshield in the beam of the one remaining headlight I saw the poor inert figure of the dog lying on the road in the rain.

What the hell was I supposed to do now?

Forty-Two

He came out of the back room, his coveralls smeared with fluids, wiping his hands on a towel. He regarded me sadly.

"Well?" I prompted.

"Back's broken," he said gently, "Damned near severed through."

I swallowed, "Is there anything you can do?"

He looked away from me, up towards the ceiling as if seeking divine inspiration, then looked back. "Maybe," he stopped, cleared his throat, and tried again, "Maybe it would be better if you just let her go."

When he said it aloud it became real for me, and I got a hollow feeling in the pit of my stomach. "Is she in any pain?" I asked.

From her seat on one side of the waiting room Valerie sighed, exasperated. This was no doubt accompanied by a patented eye roll, but as she was seated behind me I couldn't see it. "Jesus, Jack, it's just a truck. You can buy another one."

The enormous black dog on the floor at her feet groaned contentedly and rolled onto its side as she scratched it between the ears.

"It won't be the same," I said unhappily.

The mechanic gave me a nod; he knew just how I felt.

Still, I had to be strong, and not dwell on what could never be. I shook his hand, "Thanks for trying. Sell whatever parts you can and scrap the rest. The insurance company will be in touch with you." I thought but didn't add that it would be nice if he put a nightlight in the garage when he left for the day, that she didn't like the dark, but he would probably think I was nuts. Or maybe he would do it. Like the commercials said, New England is truck country.

Valerie moved from scratching between the dog's ears to rubbing his chest and belly. "I think we should name him Lurch."

"Really? Not Truck Killer?"

She ignored my comment. "Too bad Tonk would never accept him. Lurch is such a big cuddly bear."

"Tonk does like being an only child."

Lurch sighed and relaxed bonelessly, his jowls puddling on the floor. He probably thought he had died and gone to doggie heaven, which he very nearly had. I had bounced that dog off my fender at forty miles an hour and he had no injuries that we could find. How he had managed that feat was likely another mystery I would never solve.

I turned back to the mechanic. "Could I clean out the glove compartment and grab my Ipod?"

"Sure," he hooked a thumb over his shoulder, "she's in the rear bay."

Valerie snorted. "We'll leave you two alone to say goodbye. Come on, boy." She got up and thumped Lurch on the side. He sprang to his feet and followed her outside obediently.

The mechanic led me into the garage area where I got my first look at the truck in good light. It was a mess. The frame where the bed met the cab was bowed downwards. The drive shaft lay on the floor in two pieces. The left rear tire was blown and had been bent outwards at the axle bracket from the weight of the tree.

The driver's door opened, grudgingly with a high-pitched squeal from the hinges. I noticed that the cab had been knocked all out of true, the windshield crazed with a spider's web of cracks. I grabbed the Ipod from its charging cradle and a few papers from the glove compartment. There was an ice scraper and umbrella behind the seat. And I guessed that was about it.

I had to shoulder the door closed and couldn't get it to catch, so I left it partway open, the dome light glowing forlornly. I leaned my forearm on the truck bed wall and regarded my broken girl sadly. We had been through a lot together, she and I.

As I turned away from my truck for the last time I noticed a familiar shape across the bay. I walked to it slowly with the mechanic following behind me. When I got there I placed my hand on the black-lacquered aerodynamic curve of the fender.

"This is Garrison West's Porsche?"

"Yeah."

"What is it still doing here? I thought it would have been repaired weeks ago."

"No, I'm just getting started on it now."

I looked at him, "I didn't realize you were that busy."

He hitched a thumb in a belt loop. "It's not that. A couple of years ago I got him a water pump for his BMW and he waited a year to pay for it. I almost took him to court. I told him that I wouldn't touch the Porsche unless he paid the estimate in advance."

"And he just did?"

He nodded, "Two days ago in cash."

"Huh," I said, wondering where Garrison had found a sudden income.

The truck key snapped off my ring with a sound like the breaking of a dry twig and I tossed it to him. "Thanks again," I said on my way to the door.

I felt myself accelerating, my heart rate increasing. The answer was right there. I blew by Valerie where she was waiting under the overhang with Lurch.

"What's the rush?" She asked, trotting to catch up.

"Garrison's got money."

"So? We knew that. From his parent's insurance."

From the nine eleven fund. He also made something
from the snowboard endorsements."

I shook my head, frustrated that she didn't understand, not
realizing that my mind was already three steps ahead, and that I
was explaining myself poorly. "No. First he couldn't pay to
have the Porsche fixed, and then he did."

"What? What does that mean? Where are you going?"

"We've got to get to the library before it closes."

"The library?"

I tried to slow my brain down and explain it to her more
clearly as we loaded Lurch into the back of Valerie's car, an
electric blue Toyota Rav4. He was such a big dog that it was
actually a tight fit, and after we closed the door he pressed his
face against the glass leaving a big, wet nose print. When we got
in the car he stuck his head between the front seats and stared out
the windshield.

Valerie drove with me navigating.

"You think Garrison is spending the million dollars from
Ambrose's bearer bonds?" She asked.

"That or he managed to sell the diamond. Take the next
left. The road is flooded out at Deer Run near Elm." I directed.
"Either way, he knows where Lauren is."

With Lurch's huge head between us I felt like I was having
a conversation with him.

"Why the library," Lurch asked using Valerie's voice.

"The Dunboro paper prints lists of properties with
delinquent taxes. It's all public records. I want to see if

Garrison's house in on that list."

"What would that prove?"

"He may have plenty of money but just be screwing with the mechanic – stay near the middle of the road through here, both edges have deeper water than you think – or maybe he was debating if he wanted to fix the car at all. He has another dozen to choose from at home. But if he's not paying his taxes, that means something."

Lurch nodded like it all made perfect sense to him, which was encouraging.

At the library we left him in the car and ensconced ourselves in a quiet corner with a stack of town newspapers from the last five years. It took hardly any time at all to see that Garrison was underwater and sinking fast.

Four years ago Garrison's parents were alive and the taxes had been all paid up, but over the past three Garrison had fallen farther and farther behind. New Hampshire has no income tax, and state coffers rely on heavy property taxes to fill them. Garrison, on a big piece of land with a major view and a large house, had racked up more than a hundred grand in back taxes and penalties.

"So that's it," Valerie said, folding up the paper she had been reading and placing it back on the stack, then neatly squaring it.

"Maybe," I said, doubt eroding my previously certain logic.

"Maybe? You said it yourself. He's not paying his taxes. Garrison is up to his eyeballs in debt. He killed her for the money."

"I don't know," I reconsidered. "All we really know is that he doesn't pay his taxes and that he waited a couple of weeks before paying the mechanic. He could have plenty of money and just not like paying taxes. Or he could be absolutely bankrupt, and he doesn't have Ambrose's money, and he somehow managed to scrape up a few grand to get his car fixed."

Valerie was silent, tapping her foot, as she considered my new interpretation of the events.

"It doesn't matter if Garrison is in debt," I pointed out. "It doesn't even matter if he pays his taxes. All that matters is if he has Ambrose's bearer bonds and the rings or not. We find the rings or the bonds, we find Lauren."

"How do we do that?"

"I hate to keep saying this, but I don't know."

We left the library and on the way home dropped Lurch off with Bobby. Since the dog had no collar or tags, Bobby told us that he would get him to the animal control officer as soon as he had the chance. That was what his mouth told us at any rate, but the look in his eyes told me that it was love at first sight. I suspected Lurch would never see the inside of the humane society kennels.

At home Tonk got one whiff of Lurch from us and acted as though we had committed some heinous crime, possibly involving murder or brussel sprouts. His cold shoulder routine lasted up until we got dinner into his bowl, at which time all was forgiven.

If only our world was as simple as his.

Forty-Three

I was a frazzled bundle of nerves, feeling as if there was extra current crackling along my neural pathways and I absolutely could not sit still. I was pacing off a short loop around Dr. Layton's waiting room – around the couch, past the end table, by the pair of single chairs, down the long wall past the windows – I took a quick peek at Valerie's car as I went by to make sure it hadn't burst into flames since my last trip – and then I was back by the couch again. On one of my laps I noticed a small coffee setup on a table in the corner – Krups machine, cups, sugar packets, powdered creamer, little red plastic stirring sticks. Yeah, caffeine, that was what I needed.

I would have been driving the other patients crazy with my pacing except that the only other person in the room with me was Valerie.

She was seated on the couch with a magazine on her knee. She hadn't turned a page in six laps.

Under tension she turns into a statue and I become the Tasmanian Devil.

I was sure that would have been a source of some amusement to us if we were not so stressed.

I had come dangerously close to wearing a track into the carpeting when his assistant guided us into his office.

Dr. Layton was more or less dressed as before: white hemorrhoid cream lab coat with the legs of brown slacks and dark shoes visible beneath. He shook my hand, got us seated, and went around to his side of the desk and sat down.

"Your test results have come back," he said, his hands pressed flat on a manila folder on his desktop, which presumably contained said results.

What followed felt like a cruel pause, a moment he was using purposely to build suspense as if he was waiting for a drum roll. Surely that perception was a result of my frenzied brain and heart. In reality the delay was no longer than the time it took for him to open the folder and find the page that he was looking for.

"Mr. Fallon," he focused on me, "your sperm count is average with motility on the low side of the normal range."

I let out a breath that I wasn't aware I had been holding. Cracks about my manhood aside, I was perfectly OK being on the low side of normal.

"Mrs. Fallon," he began, and the logical part of my brain jumped way ahead of him. The process of elimination was pretty simple, right? If the problem wasn't me, it was her.

"You have benign fibroid cysts in your uterus."

"Cysts?" Valerie asked.

He held his hands out in a calming gesture, "Benign cysts. They're not cancerous. Fibroid cysts almost never are."

"But she can't get pregnant?" I asked.

He frowned. "Some women with fibroid cysts can get pregnant and carry a child to term, but the cysts make both events unlikely. Ovulation can be impaired, though your ovulation appears to be cycling normally. Implantation of the egg is more difficult, and the pregnancy can be impacted by a number of complications."

"So that's a no," Valerie said.

"By all means, you can keep trying. There's no harm in that, right?" He smiled, realized his attempt at injecting some levity had failed, and continued, "But realistically, with fibroid legions as widespread as yours, yes, that's a no. I'm sorry."

Valerie was once again still, but this was different from her stillness in the waiting room. Her eyes had a dull sheen, as some part of herself, some critical part, died.

There was of course the option of adopting, but now was not the time for that discussion. We had both wanted a child that was ours, and it would take time for the rawness of that impossibility to sink in.

I felt lost. Valerie was going to have to find some way to come to terms with this. All I could do try to convince her that my love for her had not lessened or changed; try to express to her that the lack of a biological child in our relationship did not alter the fundamental equation of our marriage.

That was going to be hard to do because, as much as I hated to admit it, I thought that on some level that it did.

Forty-Four

In a way I had been lying to Valerie, and had she not been so distracted with the results of the fertility tests surely she would have realized it by now. The fact that Garrison was deep in debt didn't prove anything – that much was true – but if he had suddenly paid off his taxes he must have done so with Ambrose's money. Why else would he go years without paying his taxes and then abruptly pay them? All I had needed was in the public records and I confirmed everything with a single trip to the town hall. Garrison's account was fully paid up.

Therein lay a problem.

With the payoff of his tax bill the state already knew about Garrison's fortuitous windfall and was likely preparing to ask questions of their own. The town or IRS might get involved as well. Heck, maybe Ambrose would find out about it and descend with his own set of lawyers and accountants, trying to recover what he could of his million bucks and the ring.

In the ensuing circus Lorrraine would be lost.

I didn't want to see Garrison spend a few years rattling around in bankruptcy court. I didn't want him going to prison for theft or tax evasion or whatever else might come of all of that. I wanted him to tell me what had happened to Lorraine.

And the only way I could see to get that to happen, I told myself as I drove Valerie's RAV4 into the clearing at the top of the hill, was to confront him with what I knew and get him to confess.

I realized that approach had landed me in a coma the last time I had tried it, but I wasn't expecting Garrison to attack me as Patricia's killer had, and if he did he weighed about ninety-seven pounds, and his house wasn't on fire. I knew; I had checked the roofline carefully for smoke as I parked among the ten or so other cars that were already there and approached the front door.

I could see Garrison through the living room windows standing in front of the gigantic television, swaying to some music video, a crowd of other people were lounging on the couches and standing around talking. The volume on the TV was turned up so high that I could actually see the windows deflecting with the thump of the bass. The music was almost uncomfortably loud, and I was still outside.

I didn't bother to try the doorbell as I was certain that no one would hear it, but the front door was unlocked so I went in. No one gave any indication that they even noticed me as I stepped down into the room.

What I had thought was a music video was actually the

video game *Guitar Hero*. Garrison held a miniature guitar made of shiny black plastic, which had little buttons instead of strings. Color coded notes to *Slow Ride* by Foghat streamed down the screen. Each note exploded in a starburst of light has he hit it, the audience cheering for him. Letters a foot high told him that he was OUTSTANDING before disappearing in a shower of fireworks.

I waited, figuring that his curiosity would cause him to turn off the game, but he remained absorbed.

"Garrison, could I talk to you for a moment?" I shouted.

"I'm kind of busy." He shouted back.

"Curing cancer, I can see that."

"How's that?" He gave me a quick head check without missing a note.

"I'd like to talk to you about Lauren." I said forcefully.

He said nothing.

Garrison was really pissing me off. If I was right, he had been playing me since the first time I had walked through his door. I was beyond the end of my patience, and decided to pull out my sharpest knife and go for the heart.

"I know you killed Lauren." I shouted at what felt like the top of my lungs.

I didn't know what response I had been expecting from him – denial, feigned misunderstanding, anger – but I had to give him credit. He didn't stiffen. He didn't flinch. His response was a complete and perfect zero.

Other conversations went on around us undisturbed.

Perhaps they hadn't even heard me.

I forged ahead. "It was the safe that really started me thinking." I began, "I had been in that closet two minutes earlier and I couldn't find it, but you did. What would make you look on the top shelf behind all those sweaters for that pull ring, especially after I had told you that the safe was heavy and would be near the floor? You looked up there because you already knew where the safe was and how to open the panel. You kept coming back out to the house without complaint, and you left that key on the ring, hoping that either the sheriff or I would find it and the safe. And when we didn't you *discovered* it yourself."

He crossed the guitar bridge without missing a note. The virtual audience was on its feet cheering. Some of the people in the room started to clap along with the beat.

"She didn't put in that big safe to hold four driver's licenses, and she would have had the New Hampshire one on her the night I saw her in the Porsche. You took that license from her when you killed her. You put it in the safe along with the other licenses to try and lead me away from you, and you took out the bearer bonds and the rings she kept there. You cashed out the bonds and used the money to get the Porsche repaired and pay off your taxes."

Whatever rock-and-roll reality he inhabited, I wasn't a part of it.

"One more thing: your BMW was wet the day I first came up here to tell you about the Porsche. It was wet because you had been out looking for her."

I felt a growing urgency, like this was my one chance to break him and I was blowing it. I found myself talking faster and even louder, my throat becoming raw. "Was Lauren here when I was? Was she locked up in a room or tied up somewhere, or was she dead already?" There was a fine sheen of sweat on my forehead and my breathing was a little labored.

He hit some combination of buttons on the guitar and the word PAUSED covered the middle of the screen. The sudden silence was jarring, unnerving; everyone in the room was staring at the two of us.

He shook his head slowly. "Dude, I have no idea what you are talking about." He resumed the game, the notes flowing in a steady stream, his rhythm unbroken.

I stood there feeling like an idiot. Had I really thought this was going to work?

I considered tossing in some threat about not giving up, about my plan to keep digging until I proved it, but he would probably ignore me. Heck, he might not even hear me. The buzz of other conversations restarted, the clapping, the cheering.

Instead I left him to his adoring audience, walked out of the house, got into Valerie's car, and drove away with my ears ringing.

Forty-Five

"I've got good news and I've got bad news." John said.

This brought a collective groan from the group of
assembled firefighters who were familiar with the perverse sense
of humor of their Chief. The good news was probably bad; the
bad news was likely worse.

We were standing in the lower equipment bay in the space
that would normally have held the Forestry unit, which was off
somewhere pumping out a basement. We had pumped so many
basements that I had lost count. As I looked around the bay I
realized that I couldn't figure out who was with Forestry. Maybe
it was the Chief's eldest son; he was almost of legal driving age.

"But first," he continued, "I'd like to take this opportunity
to introduce two new members of the fire department. Most of
you have already met Tank."

Tank stepped out of the line and did a little shadow boxing, clasped his hands above his head like a prizefighter to a smattering of applause, and then rejoined the group.

"Also joining us is someone else many of you know, Rachael Woods."

Know was something of an exaggeration and an understatement at the same time. I had caught the murderer of Rachael's sister last year, almost getting killed in the process. While I was in the hospital she had visited and expressed an interest in leaving college and becoming a firefighter, which I had taken as a form of misplaced hero worship at the time. I figured it was a phase she would pass out of. I guess I had been wrong.

She came out of the upstairs meeting room in full gear, her red hair bobbing in a ponytail behind her. The gear was brand spanking new, without a crease or a smudge of dirt anywhere on it, and would mark her as a rookie at fire scenes for months to come.

Her arrival was greeted with some catcalls I'm not proud to say. In many ways fire departments are the last bastion of politically incorrect behavior.

She noticed me in the group and came to my side.

"Welcome to the fire department," I said to her.

"Thank you. How have you been?"

"I'm good."

"How do I look?" She did a little twirl for me.

I had forgotten how little she was, probably around five feet even, and she swam in the gear. Even size 'small' only meant so small in the fire service.

"If you're done socializing," John said to the room, but intended for us, "now the good news." He pressed the button on the wall panel and the bay door rattled opened. The rain was coming down at a slant and it spattered off of the ground onto his work boots and dotted the concrete garage floor. Outside was a massive dump truck with six rear tires on two heavy axles. It was low on its springs, likely carrying a full load, with the bed cover rolled over whatever was inside. "The state has generously provided us with twelve tons of sand and canvas bags to reinforce Baxter's Dam."

"Wonderful, do it yourself sand bags," I muttered, which earned a tired laugh from several fire fighters nearby.

"Yes, Jack," the Chief continued, "the bad news is that the National Guard can't spare anyone. We'll have to fill and stack them ourselves. But we can do it. We can save the dam, right Jack?"

I shrugged. It was probably not the vote of confidence he had been looking for, but in fact I no longer knew. I had rerun the numbers last night and the dam had blown past all the safety margins two inches of rain ago. I had no idea what was holding that dam together and wouldn't have been the least bit surprised if someone had run in at that very second to report that it had failed.

I waited. No one did.

"When do we start, Chief?" Bruce Jonet called from the back of the group.

"ASAP."

Forty-Six

We were working at sandbagging in four-man teams. Two guys were back at the firehouse filling sandbags while two others took a truckload of them up to the dam and stacked them. It might have been more efficient to fill the sandbags at the dam, but with the rain coming down everything – the bags, the shovels, the sand – would have been sopping wet, and the bags were hard enough to fill and handle dry.

Tank and I were unloading and stacking, and he was putting me to shame, moving three sandbags for every one that I managed. I tried to fool myself by pretending that I was the brains of the outfit, stacking and shifting them to produce the maximum structural benefit. In reality stacking sandbags hardly requires a PhD, and Tank was doing a far better job than I was simply by moving more of them.

When our shirts were soaked through, pasted flat against our bodies, we stripped them off. I was showing a slightly above average physique for a guy approaching middle age. Tank was like a work of art, a Rodan sculpture of planes and ridges, bulges of muscles with sharply defined boundaries. Were it not for the rain I suspect women from town would have been out here with lawn chairs. We might have been able to sell tickets, make a fundraiser out of it, and would have had to call out Bobby for crowd control.

There had been another inch and a half of rain in the past twenty-four hours, which put every single model that I was running up into the red. A fisherman taking a leak on the lakeside of the dam could have been enough to bring disaster. I was sure the sandbags were adding something, but I hadn't managed to add that math to the models yet. It was probably not as much as most people would think – sandbags are not as structural as brick or stone because they are neither rigid shapes nor are they fixed in place with any mortar – but I was hoping it would be enough.

There was nothing going on with Garrison, unless he had been overcome with remorse and killed himself up in the house on the hill. I thought about going up there and rattling his cage again, but from my last trip I felt that his cage was pretty unrattleable. Maybe when the rain stopped, if the rain stopped, and hikers got out into the woods Lorraine's body would turn up and that would shake something loose. I didn't know of anything else that I could do in the meantime, though an anonymous tip to the IRS was starting to sound tempting.

"Jack, you OK?"

I looked over at Tank who had two sandbags slug over each shoulder, something like two hundred pounds of sand, canvas, and rainwater, and he was carrying them like they were no big deal. In my ruminations I had apparently come to a stop at the edge of the lake.

"Fine, Tank. I was just thinking."

He unloaded the sandbags on top of the others where they landed with heavy thumps. He joined me at the water's edge. "You think it's going to hold?"

"I don't know."

I turned back towards the truck to get another sandbag, just one for me thanks, and noticed that the truck was empty. "We're out?"

"Yeah, there were only the four of them left. Grab another load?"

"Can you take care of it? I'm going to count out the ones we have here, maybe try to make an estimate of how many we still need."

"Sure. Back in a flash." He slung his wet shirt over his shoulders but didn't bother buttoning it. He climbed up into the truck and drove slowly down the access road and away.

I scaled the line of sandbags and stepped onto the uneven top of the dam. From that position I could count them easily, rows and columns. Using an average estimated weight per sandbag I added the additional loading factors to the dam and compared that to the lateral forces from the water in the lake. The math got pretty involved, but I've always been good at moving large numbers around in my head.

I looked down the face of the dam at the level of the water lapping just a couple of inches below the top, but almost immediately I was inside my head, staring at a big mental blackboard full of equations, oblivious to the rain falling on my head, the lapping of the water, everything in the world around me.

Forty-Seven

Garrison tackled me from the side, hitting me high on the right shoulder, and the two of use tumbled off of the dam into the water. He had caught me halfway through an exhale, and I had little air to work with as I struggled to get my feet under me. Garrison seemed like he was all arms and legs, a human octopus entangling me from behind.

I drove back with my elbow. Hampered by his arms and the drag of the water there wasn't much behind it, and the blow struck something bony and unyielding, probably his ribs. I quickly struck with the elbow again as a slightly different angle, this time rewarded with a softer target and a blast of bubbles past my head.

I peeled Garrison off my back and stood up. The water was only about three feet deep. I managed to clear my eyes and turn towards him when he came at me again, wrapping his arms around my waist. His head came up and clocked me a pretty good one to my chin and then we fell back into the water.

I had more than half a lungful of air this time and I outweighed him by eighty pounds. The shot to my jaw hurt some, but hadn't done any real damage.

I used the strength of my legs to roll him, like wrestling with an alligator, and forced him away from me until his hold broke. My hands against his shoulders, I pushed him into the muck on the bottom of the lake. I was on my knees, my head above water, holding him down.

It was only a matter of waiting him out now.

He tried a quick series of short jabs to my stomach, but he had no room to work with and, though I'm not a sit-up king, there was enough muscle there to keep him from getting any penetration.

Just as his struggles were starting to slack off I was hit with a power failure. My arms no longer had enough strength to hold him down; they didn't even have enough strength to hold me up. Garrison scrambled out from under me.

Before I could stagger to a full standing position he climbed on top of me, his knees jammed into my back, his hands grasping the back of my shirt. I hit the bottom hard, losing most of my air and getting a bunch of grit in my eyes.

I bucked feebly, but nothing changed. His head was above water now while mine was below. He could stay on my back all day.

My arms and legs felt cast from lead, and I was out of air. My lungs burned with their need, and I was right on the brink of taking a deep breath of water and mud and decayed leaves.

And then I would be done.

Forty-Eight

I felt it first as a subtle shift of Garrison's weight. He fell
off to one side, his fists clutched and twisted deep into the fabric
of my jacket.

The world turned on its side, gravity pulling from a new
and unfamiliar direction.

Disoriented, dizzy, and with my eyes filled with silt it took
me critical seconds to understand what had happened. With that
understanding came an image in my mind's eye, probably
something from an old Hollywood movie about World War II
submarines, of grease-streaked men in sweat-stained work
clothes looking up from sonar screens and depth gauges at a
warning panel flashing a single word -"BREACH."

The sudden current dragged Garrison away from me but he
maintained his grip on my collar and I was hauled to the surface.
I broke into the air sputtering. The rain washed the grit from my

eyes even as it streamed from my hair and spattered off of the lake into my face, making it difficult to determine which way was up.

We rolled, a tangle of arms and legs, as we passed through the break in the dam, a deep V-shaped hole that widened, the rush of water pulling lose more stones and ancient mortar. I managed to fling out one hand blindly and snag the flap of a sandbag, but it fell off of the stack, pulling me down into the muddy churn at the base of the dam before I released it. The water bounced me along the bottom, tumbling me against the layer of sandbags which was vastly preferable to jagged rocks beneath, and then spit me out so that I actually became airborne for a moment before crashing back into the torrent.

I clipped a small tree with my shoulder, and then was hit in the head by the very same tree as it fell. It was just a glancing blow, but I tasted blood in my mouth and it pushed me under just as I was inhaling. I got a lung full of water, and barely managed to get my head up before I vomited, one quick clench of my stomach that left me even weaker than before.

Somehow I ended up looking upstream at a miniature tsunami bearing down on me. I recalled my calculations that showed ten to fifteen million gallons of water would flow from even a moderate dam breach.

So that's what fifteen million gallons looks like.

I was furthermore fairly certain that the whole thing was going to let go. What did that mean? Twenty million gallons? Thirty?

I slammed against an enormous flat tree with what felt like enough force to bruise my entire back. Garrison piled into me, driving what little air I had from my lungs, and then began to slide away in the current.

"I can't swim!" he cried as he lost his grip on my jacket.

"Then why did you fucking try and drown me," I growled, but managed to grab him by his collar before the water swept downstream.

It was then that I realized that what I was against was not a tree, but a house – twelve Baxter Bridge Road, and the first of eight houses that I was sure would be destroyed today.

I recalled a training class on water rescues I had taken just after I had joined the fire department. The instructor had quoted statistics which said that lots of people drowned in storm surges, but the majority were killed by the debris. When this house behind us collapsed it would turn into a churning mass of jagged boards and splintered furniture, bricks and appliances, twisted metal and glass. It seemed solid now, almost like a sanctuary, but I knew that we had to get away from it.

Even as I had that thought I felt the house shift sickeningly, the edge of the foundation wall jutting out against the back of my knees.

I started to scrabble sideways along the wall against the force of the water one-handed and with both feet, the other hand holding onto Garrison. The siding was old and weathered, and slivers of wood jammed under my fingernails like a form of exotic torture. I managed to reach the corner and get into the main current just as the house broke free of its foundation. It tilted up on one edge and paused, looming monstrously above us before tipping slowly onto its side. Remarkably intact, it followed us downstream as I stroked and kicked like mad to stay ahead of it.

We cruised by number ten, a house set on a small hill far

from the river that I had thought would be spared from damage if the dam burst. A large oak tree, felled by the first rush of water, lay diagonally across the property, further diverting the water out and away from the house. It was nice to see I had been right about something.

Number eight passed in a blur as we gained speed, the water around us thick with mud and branches. I caught a glimpse of a mailbox and, inexplicably, a suitcase.

The next house we came to, number six, was one of the oldest houses in Dunboro. The owners had been adamant that the house had survived up until now and would come through this flood as well. It was only after Bobby had threatened them with a court order that they had finally agreed to stay somewhere else until the danger had passed.

It was a colonial, small and square-ish, painted dark green with white trim. The foundation was made of fitted granite blocks probably quarried out of Milford. It was situated towards the rear of its property away from the river, but the land was flat and the water rushed across it and smashed against the house in a muddy plume. The majority passed around the near side of the house. The far side was, relatively speaking, just a trickle – six or eight feet of fast moving rapids funneled between the house and the nearby roadway.

I swam in that direction, hoping that where the rush of water was narrower I could get Garrison and me up onto the road. It was hard going, holding onto Garrison, snagged on all sides by debris, and colliding unpredictably with submerged rocks. I felt as though I was being endlessly beaten with a meat tenderizer.

We reached the wall of the house, barely, and I began dragging us along its length. More Chinese clapboard splinter torture. Then I looked back over my shoulder to see number twelve bearing down on us, roof first, the chimney pointed at us like a medieval jousting lance.

I froze. We were trapped. Halfway down the wall we couldn't possibly make it to either corner before the two houses collided and obliterated us both. It would take tremendous luck just for the authorities to find enough pieces to make a burial worthwhile.

I pushed back the way we had come, towards the center of the flood, hoping that the current would snatch a victory from the rapidly closing jaws of our defeat. The house coming at us was all that I could see, a span of shingles extending left and right and up to the sky.

We began to rise as the volume of water between the houses was compressed. It formed a wave that lifted us even with the line of windows on the second floor. From this angle I looked straight down into the black maw of the chimney. The wave crested, turned us over, and washed us sideways, clear of the houses moments before they met with a crash that sounded like the end of the world. The air was filled with shrapnel of wood and flying shingles and bricks from the chimney raining down all around. I considered us incredibly lucky that nothing of real substance landed on us.

Number twelve caromed off of number six, shearing away one wall, exposing wires and floor joists and insulation. Torn wiring started a flash fire in number six. With the destruction of its roof and foundation, twelve lost its structure and folded in on itself, walls and floors separating into pieces that the current snatched at hungrily.

Half of the first floor of number four was underwater. As we tumbled past, choking and gasping, I saw the back door blow off its hinges from the internal pressure and a refrigerator shoot out into the yard as through fired from a cannon.

The water around us was a mass of sludge and debris, large and small. I saw a sofa go by, saturated and half-submerged. There was a car, the roof just visible above the water's surface, nine-tenths of it underwater like and iceberg. My left leg snagged on something which jerked me back violently with an unpleasant tearing sensation in my ankle, causing pieces of lumber caught in the current to pummel me before I managed to shake my foot loose.

Garrison had stopped flailing his arms some time ago and now hung limply in my grasp. I did all I could to keep his head above water. I was concentrating on Garrison and so missed number two, a gambrel constructed in the seventies that sat on a small hummock that would likely save it this day.

Ahead I saw the horizontal line of Main Street and the arc of the six-foot section of concrete culvert that passed underneath the roadway. Normally meant for a much smaller runoff, the water funneled through that opening at a terrible rate, the pipe nearly filled to the top, the overflow undermining the roadbed on both sides. I remembered giving this piece of Main Street a fifty-fifty chance of survival if the dam failed. Looking at it at that moment I thought it had a snowball's chance in hell.

I didn't know if I wanted to go through the pipe, if we would survive the passage, and deal with whatever we might find on the other side, or if I should aim for the embankment and try and climb up it and get clear before the road washed away.

In the end the current decided for me, sweeping us helplessly towards the opening. I pulled Garrison close and kept my left arm out like a rudder, hoping to hit the culvert more or less on center. My outstretched arm smashed into the concrete lip, breaking with a wet snap that I heard more than felt. Then we were both into the inky darkness, my hand flapping at the end of my broken wrist, trailing along the rough concrete surface in the narrow air gap at the top of the pipe.

At the far end my face burst through the surface and I managed to choke down a breath of air along with a mouthful of muddy water. I turned to check on Garrison and the jagged end of a two-by-four shot between us like a spear. It caught me in the forehead, carving a groove in the skin that spilled blood into my eyes. I rolled over, lost up from down, took in a lungful of water, and rapped my broken wrist against something passing by in the water. The sudden bolt of pain obliterated the world, my vision going white, then red, then dimming to darkness, the sounds of the flood and destruction becoming distant.

I floated dazed on my side. Garrison was completely underwater beside me, but I was unable to help him. I couldn't help myself. All I could see in every direction was dark shadows and churning water, with nothing to grab onto and nowhere to go.

I was finished, at the bottom of my gas tank, done.

Forty-Nine

One moment I was barely treading water and Garrison was likely drowning beside me, and the next we were tumbling across mud and rocks tangled together. We came to a stop, my head rapping sharply against a stone the size of a basketball.

I managed to struggle into a sitting position and looked back in confusion at the culvert, which was trickling out the last few feet of water like a huge faucet being shut off. Something big, like a section of wall, must have blocked the pipe. As I watched a spray of water shot up high into the air from the other side of the roadbed. The car I had seen earlier, or at least one that was the same color, launched skyward and smashed down on its roof not more than ten feet away from us. The road surface broke at both ends and the entire structure – roadbed, culvert, and road – slid several feet in our direction from the force of the water behind it. The sudden loss of solid reference point made me lose my precarious balance and I slumped onto my side.

"Garrison," I tried to say, but only managed to induce a choking fit. I got up slowly, ending up hopping on my one good leg. Blood from my forehead pattered onto the rocks. When the coughing passed and I could speak I tried again, "Garrison, get up. The road's not going to hold."

Garrison groaned so at least he wasn't dead, but he wasn't moving either.

I tried to haul him to his feet and succeeded only in pulling myself to my knees. I decided to stay on my knees and tried dragging him. It was getting me nowhere. My left hand and foot were useless, my right foot slipping on mud-slick rocks, and somewhere along the ride I had lost that shoe and sock.

A section of roof, likely from number twelve, flipped into the air like a playing card and slammed down next to the car. The road slid forward again, and water started running around the northern end, taking clumps of soil and asphalt with it, steadily shifting and widening the gap.

The walls of the drainage canal we were in were nothing special – six feet or so of jumbled stones and scrub grass that on any other day I would have vaulted up in two or three bounds with Garrison on my shoulder if necessary. In my present condition the climb compared unfavorably to El Capitan in Yosemite.

I wiped blood from my eyes and began considering the section of roof, wondering if it would float, thinking that maybe we could use it as a raft. If my cell phone was still working I could call Valerie and have her pick us up in Massachusetts. Or Connecticut. Or the Gulf of Mexico. Several inches of water covered the bottom of the canal while I considered my dwindling options.

I knew that I couldn't take any more pounding. Garrison and I had to get out of this goddamned drainage ditch. I hung my head and closed my eyes and took some deep breaths, trying to muster what strength I had left as the water deepened around me.

A strong hand grabbed hold of my collar and jerked me upright. Tank was there, the forestry truck parked at the edge of the canal with its headlights pointed at us. He draped Garrison over his shoulder and wrapped his other arm around my waist.

"Go! Go! Go!" He shouted in my ear.

As if I needed any encouragement.

We hustled for the truck as the road disintegrated behind us. I was looking over my shoulder right at it. One second there was a road, and then the next it collapsed in upon itself leaving nothing but a churning froth of debris.

We plowed a path through muddy water that was knee deep, then thigh deep.

When we reached the side of the ditch Tank threw Garrison up to the top like a rag doll, then scrambled up himself, pulling me, hopping, behind him. He leaned me up against the truck passenger door and ran around to the driver's side. As I reached out to grasp the handle, the truck fell, the wall of the drainage canal torn away by the water and the two front wheels hanging over the edge.

I backed away, dragging Garrison with me. Tank put it into reverse and mashed the accelerator to the floor. The back wheels spun, unable to find enough purchase to get the front of the truck back onto solid ground. He slammed it back into park and jumped out, joining me in pulling Garrison farther away. When Tank took Garrison's weight I stumbled to the ground by a large pine tree. Tank seated Garrison at the base of the same tree and then leaned against it himself, his chest blowing bellows like a draft horse.

I expected the water to rip the land out from under the truck almost immediately and drop it into the wash, but it was actually something of an anticlimax.

At some point Garrison opened his eyes and the three of us watched as the flood gnawed steadily away at the slope, dipping the nose of the truck further down onto its frame. From that position it rolled slowly forward until it slid almost peacefully into the water. The weight of the engine dragged the front end down, but the tail remained up, the taillights shining at us as the current swept it away. Just before it cleared the next bend in the river, some short in the electrical system caused the right taillight to blink, and that blinking light was the last thing we saw. Next stop: The Atlantic Ocean.

Garrison pulled himself up the tree and tried to make a run for it, but I stopped him. It wasn't hard. I just grabbed hold of the untucked tail of his shirt and held on, and he fell back against the tree and slid back down to his sitting position.

"Forget it, Garrison," I croaked, then cleared my throat marginally and continued, "I know you killed Lauren and even if I can't prove that, you just tried to kill me. It's over. "

Tank looked from me to Garrison and back. He thought he had just rescued me while I was trying to rescue someone else. Now he didn't know what was going on. "What-" he began, but I waved him off.

Garrison drew his knees up to his chest, his thin arms

wrapped around them, his long wet hair obscuring his face.

I took his chin in my hand and lifted and turned his head to face me, but like a sheepdog I had no idea if he could see me though all the hair. "Did you see her going into the safe at some point?" I asked him.

He didn't answer me, but I didn't need him to.

"You must have, and you needed that money. The thing is that she probably would have given it to you. She didn't even want that money. She certainly wasn't spending it, living in that small rental house with little furniture and no car. She was happy here, and I think she loved you, and you killed her."

He wrenched his chin away from me and dipped his head, and then he started to cry. Great, wracking sobs, high and somehow childlike, that shook his whole body.

Tank turned away in embarrassment.

Fifty

When the dust settles, all you are left with is dust.

I think that's a lyric from a country western song, or maybe I had read it in a book somewhere. Whatever its origin, it encapsulated my feelings nicely as I stood at Lorraine's funeral which was held at dusk just outside of her mother's trailer in west Texas.

I watched as Arlette fed pungent herbs and flowers into a small fire built over Lorraine's ashes, a ceremony with a Native American feel, more spiritual than religious. Digg stood nearby her with his head bowed and his rough, blunt-fingered hands hanging down by his sides.

On the flight over, while Valerie was sleeping and I struggled to find a comfortable position – because a really nice airplane seat will only take you so far when you should be at home lying in bed blitzed on Percocet – Alex had come over and tapped me on the shoulder, beckoning me to follow him. I carefully climbed over Valerie and hobbled up the aisle on a single crutch to join him in the front row.

He watched me with concern as I lowered myself into the seat next to him. It was a tricky maneuver with casts on my left ankle and wrist. I somehow screwed it up and fell the last few inches. I grimaced and held my breath expecting a lightning bolt of pain to strike from somewhere. When it didn't come I let the breath out in a whoosh.

"Are you OK?"

"Nothing that won't heal." I said. I didn't see it as a good time to mention my new, stylish limp that I was likely to have for months if not forever. "Thank you for coming to get us."

"It was nothing," he replied. "It was on my way."

I wondered at the geography of his world, where New Hampshire lay somewhere between California and Texas.

"It wasn't nothing," I insisted. "To us it was a big deal. Thank you."

It was too, because, to put it succinctly, I was a mess, and in absolutely no condition to wedge myself into a coach airline seat. There were also enough screws and pins in my wrist to keep me from getting through the metal detectors at airport security. The wound in my forehead had been nearly down to the bone and had taken twenty-seven stitches to close. The injury to my ankle was perhaps the worst of it; a torn Achilles tendon and some nerve damage that was going to keep me on crutches and off the fire department for a minimum of sixteen weeks, which should make Fiske happy.

All the people who owned stock in companies that sold

bandages likely saw a nice little bump because of me.

"You're welcome," he smiled shyly, then he frowned. "Can I ask you a question?"

"Of course."

"The police called to tell me that they recovered my grandmother's ring from a pawn shop."

"Lorraine pawned it?"

He shook his head quickly, "Garrison did."

That was news to me. Of course, it was all a police matter now, an investigation that spanned at least three states, so it wasn't exactly surprising that I wasn't being kept in the loop. I had heard on CNN that the Star of Kashmir had been recovered from Garrison's house, so apparently he had been unable to pawn it. I guess Ambrose was right about that after all. It would be returned to him after the trial, I was hoping postage due.

"She kept the ring," I said aloud, but mostly to myself, just to see what it tasted like. I leaned my crutch against the aircraft bulkhead next to the window and turned back to Alex. "What do you think that means?"

He chuckled mirthlessly, "I was going to ask you that question."

I looked out the window at the lights of some unidentified city in Middle America below: Wichita Kansas or Toledo Ohio or Springfield Missouri.

It would have made a slick Hollywood plotline, a neat little bundle, if Lorraine had simply stolen from every man she met, picked up stakes, and moved on, but her story was more complicated than that. Initially driven to a false identity to escape her debts, it somehow became her solution to every problem. When the going got tough she would contact her friends and pick a new name. It was not only possible but likely that there were still more identities in her past about which I knew nothing.

A psychiatrist could probably have explained to me the forces that guided her life. Growing up in relative poverty, without a father, Lorraine was drawn towards men and wealth, and her looks and magnetism helped her get them both. But somehow the quiet of the west Texas badlands remained resonating within her, and the very money that attracted her created a frenzied lifestyle that forced her away. Then again, what do I know? My PhD is in physics, not psychology.

Why she had kept the rings and the bearer bonds, I didn't know. Perhaps fleeing the destruction of nine eleven she had not even realized she had them until she was well away, and then there was no way to return them without revealing herself and uncovering the fact she hadn't died. Or maybe her reasons were more practical, thinking there might come the day when she would need the money.

Regardless, all of this probably wasn't what Alex needed to hear.

"I think it meant that she still cared for you," I told Alex.

He smiled a smile that was at once happy and sad, full of warm memories and loss. "Thank you."

At the funeral I stumbled as my crutches sank into the sandy soil and it took me a moment to get the one on my left untangled from the cast. Valerie caught my bicep and held me up until I got my feet back under me. I looked over at her, expecting to see her face pinched with concern, but she wasn't looking in my direction at all. Her gaze was settled far in the distance, at infinity perhaps, but I knew that her focus was deep inside herself, at her very core.

I didn't know how she was dealing with her infertility. That part was closed off to me. What that boded for our marriage I also didn't know, but it was probably not good. On the other hand she seemed to have discovered another part of herself, her inner Sherlock if you will. I wondered if it would fill the void within her or if, like me, it would only highlight that void, emphasize the feeling that something in my life was missing.

I was coming to the realization that catching killers was essentially unsatisfying, and I wasn't just thinking that because it had nearly gotten me killed, twice. My hope for finding Lorraine alive, as naive and unrealistic as it may have been, came to an end when a tearful Garrison led Bobby to her body which he had dumped together with a bag of quick lime into a shallow ditch on his property. He hadn't even bothered to cover her over.

Lorraine's mother stood up from the fire, brushing grit from her knees. Digg, behind her, had his head down and his hands folded in front of him. Alex Nidal stood off to one side alone, his eyes closed, swaying slightly as though unsteady or poorly rooted to the earth. A sere wind blew through the mesquite bushes and rocked him, but he remained upright.

Closure, whatever that meant, didn't look all that hot from where I was standing.

The dead remained dead and try as I might, risking everything that I had, I wasn't going to change that.

Afterword

As in my previous novel I have drawn from my experiences as a volunteer firefighter to create many of the scenes in this story. Though by and large not based on any specific fire calls, many of the activities of the Dunboro Fire Department are like those undertaken by my own department during the Mother's Day flooding of 2006. During that flood the Brookline Fire Department did rescue a horse named Chance from the mud essentially as described. The remnants of mud in my boots stained my socks for more than a year afterwards, and no, I don't know if the horse ultimately survived or not.

I got the idea for this story from the following line:

"All I had to do was get out of town. Now he's going to find me and kill me for sure."

I actually had a woman tell me that.

I wasn't a firefighter at the time. I was living in Houston, Texas, this would have been about 1993, and driving with my then girlfriend, now wife, when the region was struck by one of those thunderstorms that make you wonder if there is a God and what we might have done to piss him off. Real opening of the heavens stuff. Because so much of the city is paved, when the rain really falls it essentially has nowhere to go, and flash flooding is a common occurrence. Trying to locate a way home, finding road after road underwater and impassable, I meandered around the neighborhoods near Rice University looking for dry ground.

I approached an intersection, noticing as I did so that the stop sign at the corner was mostly underwater, only the top half of the letters visible above the level of the water. Do you know how tall a stop sign is? Me neither, but I figured seven or eight feet, far taller than the car I was driving. I stopped well shy of the water and tried to consult my internal map seeking alternate routes.

At that time a car pulled up behind us and honked its horn.

My girlfriend, stressed from creeping around in the rain for a couple of hours, laughed in an angry way, "Where do they expect us to go?"

The car honked again, and then pulled around us, accelerated towards the intersection, and hit the water. It threw up an enormous wave and sank.

I got out of my car and waded over. It was a big car, a Caddy I seem to recall, and the woman behind the wheel was crying. She said what she said, got out of the car, and ran off into the rain.

I never found out what happened to her.

For those who wish, you may contact me at psoletsky@gmail.com.

Now turn the page for a special preview of *Dirty Little Secrets*, the third Jack Fallon mystery.

One

Funerals. Damn but I've been going to a lot of these recently.

I stood with the other Dunboro firefighters, twenty-seven of us in three rows of nine facing the open grave. The white-enameled, flag-draped coffin was suspended above it on heavy canvas straps. We stood at attention; spiffy in our class A uniforms with brass buttons gleaming, as the strains of *Amazing Grace* from the bagpipe corps floated through the air. My dress blues were fresh from the cleaners, the seams sharp and crisp. The department insignia and my rank medallions were polished and perfectly aligned on my collars. My name tag, *Jack Fallon, Firefighter*, was exactly square to the line of the breast shirt pocket. We all took great pride in our appearance, and in full regalia the department made quite a sight.

The rest of the mourners sat on the other side of the grave on folding chairs. They were civilians here, apart from us.

We were burying Ellis Banks, one of our own, a retired Chief no less. Dunboro is a small town in New Hampshire and we have a small fire department. Each death, even of an elderly and long retired member, is an emotional blow.

The widow and her two sons sat under a tent between the two groups at the head of the grave, physically and psychologically belonging to neither.

The town cemetery had an unreal quality about it, the white picket fence too perfect, the grass mown recently and almost too evenly emerald green. The graves lay, not in orderly rows, but in circles and whorls, clustered together by ancient clans and old blood. The physicist half of my brain began to play connect-the-dots, the positions of the markers forming segments which joined and spread creating fractals, molecules, and strands of DNA.

Perhaps the heat was getting to me.

The air was a suffocating blanket of humidity and we were tormented by swarms of mosquitoes. Both were due to an exceptionally rainy spring, one that had burst a dam in our sleepy little town, destroying seven houses and a section of roadway in downtown. Brookline to our south had had even more damage, and Townsend, Massachusetts south of that had been declared a disaster area. I had my own personal reminders of the flood, I thought as I leaned uncomfortably on my cane. I had been caught behind the dam when it blew and was lucky I wasn't dead. My injuries, as bad as they were, could and probably should have been much worse.

Beyond the fact that I sometimes used a cane and often walked with a limp, outwardly my face was the worst of it. What had started as a short line of stitches up near my hairline had become infected. To drain the accumulated pus the cut had been elongated. It now meandered like a strip of N-gauge model railroad track across my forehead and down my right cheek. The antibiotics were still having a hard time getting a handle on it, and the wound felt hot, swollen, and angry.

Amazing Grace ended and I and the other firefighters saluted, twenty-seven white-gloved hands rising as one. I felt the material of my glove snag on the flyaway end of the line of stitches on my forehead. The flag that had been draped over the coffin was folded by an honor guard with precision and presented by John Pederson, the chief of the Dunboro Fire Department. The widow, an ancient and gnarled woman, her hair a frizzy white puff that showed a lot of scalp like a sparse cotton swab, accepted it. She reached out with one quaking hand to take the flag, maneuvering her arm around the oxygen tube clipped to her nose in the way of someone long used to living with it. Her other hand clutched heavily at the handle of a walker with wide tires and a heavy aluminum frame, a cross between an ordinary walker and an SUV, suitable for cemetery off-roading. John returned to the line and snapped back to attention, a thing he was really good at as an ex-marine.

The winch whirred, the arresting gears clicked, and the canvas straps creaked as the coffin was lowered into the patiently waiting earth. The Marshall of the corps shouted "Dis-missed!" broken into two words like a drill instructor would say it. We dropped our salutes and drifted off in small groups, listlessly murmuring bits and pieces of stilted conversation that were quickly smothered by the heat and humidity.

My wife, Valerie, came over from where she had been sitting among the other mourners. She placed her hand lightly on my cheek, what would normally be an intimate touch reduced to a clinical inquiry. Her hand felt cool compared to the heat of the infection. "Does it hurt much?" she asked absently, without really making eye contact.

I shrugged. "Probably not as much as it looks like it

should."

When I had caught a glimpse of myself in the bathroom mirror that morning I thought if it hurt nearly as badly as it looked, I would probably be lying in a bed somewhere screaming all the time or blitzed to the moon on Vicodin or Percocet. Personal experience at the supermarket last week had shown me I had a face that quite literally frightened children.

She had paid little or no attention to my response, lowering her hand from my cheek and turning away. I sighed inwardly, probably outwardly too, the distance growing between us already too great to fathom.

I spotted my friend Jonas Gault standing alone in one corner of the cemetery. With the death of Ellis Banks, Jonas was the oldest surviving retired chief of the fire department, perhaps the oldest surviving member of any rank.

I tried to entwine my fingers with Valerie's but she deftly avoided my grasp and we walked separately across the grass past gravestones, some sharp and clean, infused with that new tombstone smell, and some hundreds of years old, reduced by time and acid rain to unreadable shapeless humps of rock.

"Nice funeral ceremony, Jack" Jonas said to me as I approached, "we do a very good job, very respectful."

"We've had a lot of practice," I said somewhat sadly, recalling the funeral last year for Russell Burtran, this funeral for Ellis Banks, and between them the funeral of Althelia Temple, who had been one of the first women to serve in the Dunboro Fire Department.

"Yeah, there is that," he replied and then fell awkwardly silent.

"You OK, Jonas?" I asked him.

He frowned as he shrugged off his class A jacket and hung it from the tips of two fingers over one shoulder. His dress shirt hung loosely on his age-withered frame as though it was intended for a much larger man, which in a way it was. "Jack," he said with a tired exhale, "growing older is a subtle thing. It seems like just yesterday that I was a young, or at least middle aged, man. Ellis was Chief, I was a new First Lieutenant, and Russell Burtran and Roger Fiske and John Pederson were as green as new wood. In here," he tapped his temple with his free hand, "I'm still that man."

Valerie stepped forward and gave him a gentle hug. "It must be very hard."

"Growing old? Easy as falling off a log. But it is hard sometimes reconciling those thoughts in my head while standing here at Ellis' funeral." He was silent for a moment after he said that, probably thinking that at eighty-four he was very far from those memories indeed.

I realized that he was standing at the grave of his wife, Elizabeth, when he put his hand lovingly on her headstone. His expression changed, his eyes becoming frightened, haunted. "I've, uh," he began uncomfortably, his eyes looking at everywhere but the two of us, "got a favor to ask of you."

I was concerned for my friend and couldn't imagine what had him so unbalanced. "Shoot." I said.

"It would really be better if I showed you."

"Showed us what?" Valerie asked.

He didn't answer immediately, instead rubbing a hand across the back of his neck. "That's going to take some explaining and a fair amount of time."

"Whatever time you need," Valerie answered for both of

us.

"It's also a little bit of a walk, if you're up to it," he said eyeing my cane.

I gave him a small nod, "As long as we go slowly."

His eyes did a sweep of Valerie, assessing her funeral attire, her modest black skirt, black fitted jacket over a white silk blouse, and sensibly-heeled black shoes, "And I think you'll need to change. Meet me at the Bartlett trail cutoff when you're ready, say," he checked his watch, "an hour?"

"Sure," I replied, "But seriously, why all the mystery?"

He frowned, his gaze wandering over the thinning crowd of mourners, and then he looked back at us. He lowered his voice, though there was no one nearby to hear us. "What would you say if I told you I think Ellis was murdered?"

Ghastly as the thought was, I had to choke back a laugh. "I'd say you have a very impatient killer on your hands. Ellis was ninety-two and riddled with bone cancer. The killer might have literally taken him minutes before his time."

"He was murdered," he insisted while nodding, more to himself than us, as if proving some internal point, "and so was Althelia Temple. And the killer has murdered two other people besides them."

"What?" Valerie said loudly, emphasizing and dragging the word out, an elongated explosion of disbelief.

"Meet me at the Bartlett trailhead," was his only reply.

I hesitated, debating telling him that I had no interest in getting involved in whatever mystery he was thinking about, that perhaps I had already bled enough getting tangled up with murderers, but before I could put those thoughts into words Valerie chimed in, "We'll be there."

"Thank you," he said. "Now, if you'll excuse me, I'd like to catch Laura before her kids take her home."

He nodded to me and tipped his hat to Valerie, a pleasantly old-timey gesture, and walked over to the widow who had been transferred to a wheelchair, the flag on her lap. I watched as Jonas lifted one of her hands from the flag and took it in both of his own, kneeling down to speak softly to her.

Her sons stood behind her with slack expressions on their faces. I recalled that both were mentally impaired, the elder borderline functional, the younger able to follow simple instructions and nothing more. Staring into the grave of her husband, no doubt wondering who will care for them after she is gone, the tragedy of her remaining life was wrenching

"What on earth could he be talking about?" Valerie said softly.

"I have no idea," I replied, squinting in the haze and heat of the bright summer sun as I watched Jonas release the widow's hand and get slowly, painfully to his feet.

He walked out of the graveyard, his head hanging and his shoulders hunched as though he were carrying an enormous weight.

CPSIA information can be obtained at www.ICGtesting.com
Printed in the USA
BVOW06s1834160316

440614BV00015B/212/P